A Good Year for Roses

ALSO BY
SUE CHAMBLIN FREDERICK

The Juan Castillo Spy Series

The Unwilling Spy

Madame Delafloté, Impeccable Spy

The Ivy Log Series

Grandma Takes A Lover

The Boardinghouse—Return To Ivy Log

EverSweet

The Madison County Series

The Front Porch Sisters

Visit the author at:

www.suechamblinfrederick.com

A Good Year for Roses

A Novel

Sue Chamblin Frederick

ISBN: 978-0-9852104-8-9

This book is a work of fiction. Events are a product of the author's imagination. Names and places are gleaned from the local folklore of Pinetta, Florida, Boston, Georgia, and Thomasville, Georgia.

Print Formatting: By Your Side Self-Publishing
www.ByYourSideSelfPub.com

Brenda Cochrane, Proofer Extraordinaire

WORD JEWELS PUBLISHING

ACKNOWLEDGMENTS

In Madison County, Florida, the Gibson's relish their history as though it were gold. Dale and Carol worked tirelessly to ensure Cherry Lake and Pinetta teemed with rich memories of its colorful residents and gladly shared their warm stories.

For the love of her town's history, accolades go to Ann S. McCrickard, Boston, Georgia's premier matriarch, for her love of clay roads, roses, farms with red barns and the sweet southern air she breathes. You won't find a sweeter southern belle anywhere.

A town like Thomasville, Georgia, rejoices when one of its citizens lauds its history with such love. Peggy Barhite (Earp) provided such wonderful information on Thomasville that the novel was kept alive and well with her vibrant recollections of the *City of Roses.*

Prologue

She'd get on that damn train. Catch the Atlantic Coast Line coach at 3:59 p.m. and travel east to Waycross, then northeast to Savannah. At Savannah, she'd say goodbye to Georgia as she boarded the *East Coast Champion* and arrived at New York's Grand Central Station at 11:45 a.m.

The Thomas H. Fox Literary Agency had proclaimed her the fresh, new voice of the South, her novel, *The Watermelon Queen of Madison County,* slated for release on November 1. She'd never heard of the Hudson Theatre, the same theatre where Elvis had performed the previous July, where the renowned literary agent had made elaborate arrangements that would surely propel her to stardom.

The efficient Mr. Fox had also made a reservation at The Premier Hotel, just off Times Square, on 44th Street, where she'd stay at least a week promoting her novel. It was true Mr. Fox was enamored by her southern charm. Said he'd like to see her novel adapted to a Broadway play. *The sky's the limit*, the energetic man had said.

And why shouldn't she go to New York? Leave Madison County. No family left, except Uncle Lester. Her sister Jewell's grave still fresh. Sam Washington busy putting Stanley Barnwell in prison for attempted murder.

Essie Donnelly had been up since daylight and packed two fancy dresses, some of her mama's jewelry and Jewell's cashmere sweater. At the top of the stairs, suitcase beside her, she closed her eyes, her breath coming quickly, her heart pounding into the word *no.* She shoved the suitcase down the stairs and watched it tumble end over end.

Oh, hell. No way I'm going to New York City. Come on, Jewell, let's go find your baby.

Part One

The Journey

CHAPTER ONE

Not every woman is born a queen. Perhaps fated, instead, to be a princess who wears satin slippers on her dainty feet or a jewel-encrusted comb in her hair. Some women are born as common girls, girls who load watermelons every summer of their lives; common girls who work in fields where temperatures are so hot that even the mule pulling the wagon balks when shade eludes his back.

Essie Donnelly was neither a queen nor a princess. From birth, she worked on her daddy's 300-acre farm in Pinetta, Florida, near Grassy Pond and the dark waters of the Withlachoochee River running nearby.

On a breezy Saturday morning in June, when Essie was sixteen years old, she escaped the hot fields for a few hours when she was crowned *Watermelon Queen of Madison County*. The crowd had lined Base Street and cheered as she sat atop a large float, along with her court, and a spray of yellow roses in her arms, a rhinestone tiara nestled in her auburn curls. Only hours later, she was back in the suffocating fields, the memories of the crepe-paper lined float filled with watermelons and beauty queens becoming hazy, and then fading away into her life as a farm girl with nowhere to go.

Following the death of her sister in July of 1956, there were melancholy moments that took her to other places, places where she flew high above the tobacco-filled fields of Madison County and tiptoed across giant hump-backed clouds, always looking for Jewell. From the clouds, she saw her sister dancing across Cherry Lake.

"Jewell," she called out, her words falling to earth like rose petals. She laughed as she waited for her sister to look up. "Here, Jewell. It's me—Essie. Above you. I'm flying."

In the dream, Essie saw herself sweeping down to earth and standing by the edge of Cherry Lake. Just as she stepped into the water, where a light glowed in the mist over the lake, Essie opened her eyes. Jewell wasn't there, not in the shadows, not in the light hovering over the dark water; still, she wanted to wade into the water, near the yellow candle-like flame she'd seen in her dream and touch her sister.

"That you, Miss Essie?" A small black shadow worked its way around the wild cherry trees and stopped a short distance away, at the water's edge. "It's the middle of the night. Not sleeping good?"

Essie recognized the high, squeaky voice of Edgar "Shorty" King. The glow of his cigarette bounced in the night like a firefly as he walked toward her, closer, where she could smell cigarette smoke on his skin. "It's me, Shorty. No worries. Just restless."

"I understand, Miss Essie. I get that way sometimes, too. That's why I'm out here night fishing." He cleared his throat and spat into the lake. "Want a warm swig of my grape buck?" He reached into his pocket and pulled out a jar and held it toward her.

Looking down at the five-foot-tall man, Essie shook her head. "Don't care for it." She backed out of the lake, the soft sound of moving water following her. "I'm going to ride around awhile. See you later."

Essie hurried across the yard of her daddy's fish camp and slipped into her 1948 Pontiac. The engine roared and she was off like a rocket. A harrowing spin-out at Highway 253 to 53, a sharp left turn onto 150, burning rubber all the way to 145. Then, an unleashing of hot breath as Essie pushed the Pontiac until it shimmied a hard left onto Highway 145 in Pinetta, the wind howling in her ears.

On the Bellville road, she barreled past Lon Terry's general store, then caught a glimpse of Grassy Pond as the Pontiac's engine screamed down the wet dirt road, the mud grabbing the tires like ghosts in the night, whipping Essie back and forth in her seat. She braked at Bellville and whipped the car around, heading west.

Essie eased off the accelerator and pulled off 145 and caught Captain Buie road back to Cherry Lake, curving around Rootman Road to her daddy's fish camp. The Pontiac slowed and slapped the mud from its tires, its engine almost panting. She eased the rumbling car down the lane to the shack of a house and parked under a 200-hundred-year-old oak tree, its low limbs touching the ground like giant fingers.

East, on the other side of the lake, lightning streaked across the sky and chased the thunder that followed. Essie's eyes roamed the lakeshore and the fish house and saw the outline of Sam Washington's body leaning against a porch post. Even in the dark, she knew he was angry.

He called to her. "How come you're doing this, Essie?" His words were harsh, fire-like as he hurled them across the yard. "You're gonna kill yourself tearing through Madison County like you're some kinda racecar driver." He stepped off the porch. "Everybody around here thinks you've lost your mind."

Essie slammed the door on the Pontiac. "Can't do anything 'bout that, can I? People think what they want to think." She moved a slow step at a time toward Sam and the tiny fish house. She saw an unlit cigar between two fingers and watched him strike a match and touch the end.

"I'm beginning to think they're right. Nothing you do anymore makes sense. Living out here at Cherry Lake like a hermit. Breaking your book contract."

The glow of the cigar tip warmed Sam's face when he pulled in smoke and released it into the night air. Essie saw his blue eyes, clear and honest. Eyes she knew would plunge her into deep guilt. There was no way she could answer his beseeching questions. *Why had she been at her daddy's fish house since November, only months after Jewell's death? Why didn't she catch that train to New York to promote her book? Why was she flying across the backroads of Madison County in the middle of the night, night after night?*

Essie found the edge of the porch and sat down on the old boards, her feet dangling as if they wanted to run somewhere. Cigar smoke drifted along the porch and invited her to remember all the times she had sat in the porch swing at her daddy's farm and watched Sam smoke his cigars.

"The farm makes me sad." Her voice seemed child-like, far-away.

Sam sat down beside her on the porch edge. "I know, Essie. But you have your life to live."

"The farm's not the same without Jewell."

Sam took a deep breath and shook his head. "Of course, it's not. I know you miss her, Essie. But what about you? What about you and me?"

Essie nodded slowly. "I think about us a lot, Sam. I don't want to hurt you."

"But I *am* hurting, Essie."

Essie left the porch edge and shuffled through the fallen leaves to the lake. Sam followed. "Come on back to the farm. DooRay needs you there. And so do I." He placed his arms around her and squeezed gently.

Essie laughed softly. "Soon."

"We belong together, Essie." Sam tossed his cigar into the lake and rested his chin on top of Essie's head, then kissed her hair. "The two of us—you and me?" He laughed, a rumble in his chest. "And DooRay and Murphy and Killer."

Long minutes passed. Essie felt the warmth of Sam's body next to hers, felt his love for her. "I reckon when I find Jewell's baby."

Sam swung his arms from around Essie and stepped back. "Find Jewell's baby? Essie, that baby's seventeen or eighteen years old now. You don't know if it's a boy or a girl. There's not one single clue as to where that child is."

Essie nodded. "I'm at least gonna try. I'll talk with Miss Bootsey again. Maybe go to Atlanta."

"Atlanta?" Sam yanked another cigar from his shirt pocket and paced along the lake's edge, mumbling to himself. When he turned and neared Essie, he pointed his finger at her. Like bullets, his words spewed toward her. "Essie Donnelly, you're never going to find Jewell's baby." He ran his hand through his hair, while behind him fireflies flicked on and off in the tall lake grass. Only a few feet away, Sam's body seemed to slump. The cool night air felt ominous as it moved across him, his words a mere whisper. "Let me understand you, Essie. You're leaving *us* to go find Jewell's baby?"

The wind picked up, pushed by the March rain headed their way. A few large drops splashed around them; and, at the same moment, thousands of frogs began their loud cacophony of unmelodious croaks. Essie, her face shadowed and her hair blowing around her shoulders, lifted her arms, and with upturned hands said, "Sam, the baby is all I have of Jewell."

CHAPTER TWO

Essie Donnelly's presence in her daddy's Cherry Lake fish house triggered a rumble of gossip all along the lake, stories abounding at Larry Roffe's Standard Oil station, where H. A. Browning ran the station late on Saturday nights.

The small station was on the corner of Highway 53 and 150, a ride-by and wave place that landmarked the Cherry Lake area with its many personalities, individuals who proclaimed it *their corner,* and who fervently believed it was their conversations on that corner that sorted out the problems of the day: the drought, pine beetles, udder fever, President Eisenhower's golf game and, most of all, current gossip concerning the citizens of Madison County.

Shorty King and his brother Claude's imagination ran rampant, most likely a swallow or two of something stronger than RC Cola in them that fueled their creative minds. They congregated around the three gas pumps outside the station, the night air filled with the sounds of crickets and the call of night birds skimming across the lake. Candle bugs swarmed around the one single light hanging from the apex of the building, their dance chaotic around the bright light.

"Shorty," hardly taller than a small child, but acting like he was eight feet tall, was a fireball. "Why, I'll bet you that Donnelly woman is hiding from somethin'. Maybe she's done taken all her dead daddy's money and buried it somewhere 'round Cherry Lake. She ain't been at that big ole farm since last November."

His brother Claude passed a snort to Manley Reeves. "Why you reckon she buried it at Cherry Lake?"

Manley, a big fellow, quiet, with a harelip scar, merely shrugged. "Can't say as I know."

"Simple!" Shorty clapped his hands together. "She's afraid that one-armed black fella who lives on the farm 'd find it." He hesitated and shook his head. "Naw, I don't reckon that's it. DooRay Aikens is an honest man."

Claude rubbed his chin. "I'm thinkin' she might have a lover shacked up in there with her. Ain't seen nobody, but that don't mean she's alone."

Shorty turned around when he saw a pick-up pull in and park, then heard whistling coming from around the side of the station. "Howdy, Benton."

Benton Sale, a prosperous dairy farmer whose family settled in Cherry Lake in the 1800's, waved a hello. Benton considered himself an authority on Holstein cows, boasting about their milk production and his prize cow, Geraldine, who won *Largest Milk Producer* by the Florida Dairy Association in 1954. Benton took Geraldine's picture and had it pasted on a billboard along U. S. 90 in Madison County, a big red ribbon around her neck. Sometimes he'd ride out U. S. 90 and park underneath the billboard, playing country music on his radio, and staring at Geraldine's picture.

"Hey, fellas. What's going on?" Benton pulled a crippled wooden chair from the side of the station and sat down near the gas pumps.

Shorty stepped closer into the group of men. "We's wondering what in the world Essie Donnelly's doing livin' in her daddy's old fish house. Why she's got millions of dollars—she could live anywhere she wanted to."

Benton shook his head. "No, no. Don't you folks ever think about anything but money? Essie's healing. Jewell's death done tore her up real bad."

The men became quiet. Even Shorty had nothing to say. At that moment, Essie's Pontiac flew past, windows down, her auburn hair catching the wind.

"Reckon she's tearing up the roads again." Shorty took a few steps toward the road and watched the tail lights of Essie's car disappear down 150, the rear-end fishtailing as she floorboarded the gas pedal.

He shuffled back to the late-night group. "Well, folks, talking about money, me and my brother Claude have sketched out a map of possibilities to make money." The little man pushed himself to his fullest height, self-importance washing over him. "We've been thinking it prudent to add to the food supply in Madison County and, most importantly, to Cherry Lake," he said in his shrill voice.

Benton Sale's brow furrowed. "The only thing that can add to our food supply here in Cherry Lake is for you and Claude to stop helpin' yourselves to every garden on the lake."

"Now, that ain't true," said Claude. "We work for our food."

"That's right," yelled Shorty. "Ain't never got nothing for free. And that's a fact." Shorty, red faced, puffed out a hot breath. "Now, if you'll shut your mouth and let me continue with this brilliant enterprise, you'll soon see how you all will benefit from mine and Claude's progressive thinking."

Shorty became business-like, a hard thing to do for a man who had never earned a dime in his life. "You need to listen up here. 'Cause tomorrow, the Southern Railroad is shipping us five thousand little biddy tadpoles."

The men's faces riveted toward Shorty. "Tadpoles?" they said in unison.

"Yes, sir. After much study, Claude and me have decided frog legs will feed this here community for a long time to come. There's lots of nutrients in frog legs, you know."

"Five thousand tadpoles!" Manley, his hair-lipped mouth quivering, slapped his head. "Where are you going to raise five thousand tadpoles?"

Shorty grinned and nodded his head. "You're a smart fellow, Manley. We 'uns have thought this through for sure. We contacted the Georgia State Fish Hatchery up at Lake Altoona and they's shipping our tadpoles on the 3:30 train coming in to Pinetta from Valdosta.

"While you boys been fiddling 'round with unimportant things, me and Claude went over to the mill and got us some scrap lumber and built us a frog corral at the south end of the lake."

"A frog corral? You're gonna raise five thousand frogs in Cherry Lake?" Benton shook his head.

"'ats right," said Shorty. "We're gonna release these tiny black amphibians into our frog corral soon as that train gets here."

Claude stepped next to his brother. "Yep. They'll be fat bullfrogs 'fore you know it, and we'll all be eatin' fried frog legs." Claude swept his hat off his head and slapped his knee. “Yehaw!” He danced a jig in a big wide circle. “Then, we’s takin’ all that money to the bank.”

Benton Sale was speechless. “Let me know as soon as that train arrives so I can get my laugh for the year.”

“Tomorrow afternoon, my friend.” Shorty walked off, a strut in his walk. He was going to be a rich man.

Chapter Three

"You awake, DooRay?" Essie poked her head inside the dark tack room. She heard a soft bleat from Murphy as the goat ambled toward her.

"Yes, 'em. I's wide awake. Heard your car comin' down the Bellville road five minutes ago." DooRay sat up. "You don't sleep no mo', Miss Essie. Every night I lie here and listen to that ole Pontiac go up and down the road. Your daddy was alive, he'd skin you for sure."

Essie pulled a bucket from a nail on the wall and placed it at the tack room door, half in and half out, the heavy night dew cool on her back. She sat and leaned toward DooRay, elbows on her knees. "I don't think I'm ever going to sleep again, DooRay." Her words were soft, resigned, filled with a sadness that had wilted her spirit.

"Oh, yes, you is, Miss Essie. Everything's gone be alright. All you needs is a little time." DooRay saw her silhouette in the doorway, her shoulders quiver, and knew she was crying. He heard a small gulp. He watched as Murphy nudged Essie, his goat tail flicking nervously. "You know what I say, Miss Essie. I say we go in the house and fry us up some bacon and eggs. Let's make a big ole pot of grits and a pan of biscuits. Ole DooRay's only got one arm, but he can sure make some biscuits."

The sound of lowing cattle drifted from the south pasture, lonely in the night, as though lost and searching. Wispy clouds covered a half moon that had centered itself above the barn as if indecisive about which way to go, east or west.

Essie thought for a moment she heard the Withlacoochee rushing by, but it was the wind, a wind that made March cool and doubtful that it carried the warmth of spring.

"You'd make some biscuits for me?"

"As sure as fleas on a dog, Miss Essie. Come on, now." DooRay left his bed, Murphy right behind him. "No, you old goat. You don't git no biscuits. They's jus' for me and Miss Essie."

Outside, atop the pump house, Killer, the Donnelly farm's resident rooster, squawked and flapped his wings. His head swiveled around in confusion. He saw no sunrise on the horizon and tucked his head back under his wing, his feathers ruffling.

No words between them, Essie and DooRay walked across the yard and up the back steps into the dark house. The wooden floor of the back porch creaked loudly, almost a greeting *'where's everybody been?'*

The house was eerily quiet. No sounds of footsteps on the stairs, no creak of the chain on the porch swing, no slamming of the screened door. At that moment, Essie turned on the light and the past swept across the kitchen as if from an old movie. She saw her mama's pie pans lined up on the counter, the glass tea pitcher with its curving handle. The coffee pot seemed regal. Tall with its barrel-like bottom and glass percolator top, it seemed to sit on the gas burner in anxious anticipation.

Behind her, DooRay shuffled to the refrigerator. "Miss Essie, got some real good fresh eggs here. Them hens been laying real good."

Essie, her dark eyes hooded, sat at the kitchen table, where she folded her hands and tried not to look at Jewell's chair. Jewell's place at the table.

DooRay pulled out a biscuit bowl and began singing quietly. *I got a home in glory land that outshines the sun….*

"DooRay," Essie began. "I've decided I'm going to go looking for Jewell's baby." She hesitated. "I… I know it's not a baby anymore but…."

DooRay stilled, his one hand floured, snow white against his black skin. "That right?"

Essie glanced up to see the black man's face. "I was wondering if you'd look after the place. Most likely, I'll be leaving Madison County for a while. I'll pay you—you know, like you were the farm's caretaker."

DooRay's eyes left Essie. He pulled the biscuit bowl closer and scooped cold lard into the flour. His one hand moved quickly inside the wooden bowl. "DooRay don't need no pay." His words were soft. "I jus' want you to be happy again, Miss Essie."

Happy again? A broken heart does not mend easily, if ever. Had her heart been put back together after Autrey Browning's desertion so many years ago? Had her heart recovered after she discovered Autrey, her first love, was the father of Jewell's baby? And Jewell's death? Hearts are fragile, not meant to be tossed into heartache, not immune to pain and neglect.

Essie left the table and ran cold water in the coffee pot. "I'll get my things together from the fish camp and come back to the farm for a few days before I leave." She turned around and found DooRay's large round eyes watching her. She saw his eyes glisten with tears. "I'll be back, DooRay. Don't you worry. I'll be back."

CHAPTER FOUR

At 3:30 the next afternoon, the Southern Railway train moved slowly down the tracks in Pinetta, heading south, its steel wheels grinding loudly as they slowed to a stop across from the cucumber house. A crowd had begun gathering about 3:00 all along the platform. Clarence Buchanan, the station manager, hollered and waved his arms. "You folks get back from that train until it comes to a complete stop. A complete stop, I say!" Clarence stomped down the platform, pushing back Shorty and Claude. "I told you boys to stand back until these boxcars are unloaded!"

"Oh, heck, Clarence. This here train done stopped. Ain't gone hurt nobody." Shorty, his small body hardly seen among the crowd, puffed himself up. "I'm here to get my tadpoles."

Claude, nearby, yelled. "They's 5,000 of them critters."

The news of the 5,000 tadpoles had spread quickly. The faces of the bystanders were wide-eyed, their anxiousness evident as they craned their necks and watched the doors of the box cars. All the Bass boys were there: Jerry, Charles and Ronnie. Danny McDonald stood on tiptoe and kept his eye out for the infamous tadpoles. Larry Surles pushed his way across the train station platform, excitement brimming in his young face.

"Stand back!" Clarence hollered again. "Shorty, before you can get your tadpoles, we got to unload Alvin Henderson's chickens. He's got eight-hundred pullets waitin' to be unloaded. They's in need of water real bad. So you just hold your horses a while."

Several strong men pulled back the doors on the boxcar, exposing crates of young chickens, their heads darting in and out the sides of the crates. One man jumped into the boxcar and handed a crate down to another man. Each crate was placed on the platform, where buckets of water were poured into a small trough at the edge of the crate. The pullets drank thirstily, a soft cawing emanating from within the crates.

Nearby Nels Falk, Nicky Strickland and Wayne Cantrell skirted around the crowd. They'd skipped school just to see what five thousand tadpoles looked like.

"Get away from there, you boys!" yelled Clarence. "Go on home, or I'll call your mama."

A few feet away, more boxcars clanked open and pallets of plastic bags filled with water and hundreds of tadpoles were strewn out on the platform. Shorty and Claude pushed themselves through the throng of onlookers. "Hot diggity! There's our tadpoles. Look at those little fellers swim!!" yelled Shorty.

"I can't believe it!" hollered Claude. "Five thousand of 'em!"

Benton Sale eased up and peered into the plastic bags. "And that's what's gonna feed the people of Cherry Lake?"

"Why sure! It'll take about six months for them frogs to grow big ole fat legs on 'em and then they'll be in the fryin' pan. Tender and juicy. Like eating chicken, only tastier."

"Now, let me get this straight," said Benton. "You're goin' to put them tadpoles in a frog corral in Cherry Lake until they's grown big?"

"'hat's right, Benton." Shorty hitched up his pants. "Nothing to it! Just gots to feed them every day." He wrinkled his brow. "Got to make sure that corral fence is high 'nuf so they don't jump over."

Behind the crowd, where the chickens drank water in their crates, Nels, Nicky and Wayne saddled up to the crates and loosened the latches on all of them. In mere minutes, eight hundred chickens scattered across the depot platform, flapping their wings, screeching and squawking. Their feathers filled the air as they ran back and forth in fright, leaping into the crowd. Many landed on the plastic bags full of tadpoles, their feet tearing the plastic, releasing buckets of water and hundreds of tadpoles. The hungry chickens, hundreds of them, pounced on the tadpoles and gulped them down as they flopped on the platform.

A rush of chickens trampled the plastic bags, tearing them open one by one, until the platform gushed in water, chickens and tadpoles. "Somebody call the fire department!" Clarence jumped from the platform onto the tracks, several chickens following him.

The diesel engine of the locomotive roared to life, the engineer waving his hands from his engine window. "Got to go! Got a schedule to keep. Git them damn chickens off the tracks!"

From the street, Sheriff Simmie Moore came running. Usually a calm man, his face flushed red as he ran into the middle of the pandemonium. Chickens covered the tracks, the train depot platform and even the tops of the boxcars. Everyone in Pinetta chased chickens. Benton Sale stood speechless, his mouth moving but no sound coming out.

"Is it that Falk boy again?" the sheriff called, anger bouncing across the tracks.

From the train engine, a whistle blew. Long and loud, it brought everyone to a stand still. Simmie Moore had climbed on top of the engine and waved his hat. "We've got to get these chickens rounded up! This train's got to leave!" Without another word, Simmie jumped from the train and started grabbing chickens. "Somebody open those crates and let's get the chickens back in them."

Without another word, everyone grabbed as many chickens as they could. Some were shooed through the door of the depot and held inside, while others were captured against the wooden fence. Simmie, his shirt wet with sweat, saw Nels, Nicky and Wayne cowering inside a boxcar, laughing and slapping their knees. "Hey, you boys! Get over here!"

The three boys sobered quickly; Sheriff Simmie Moore was a no nonsense man. "You talkin' to us?" yelled Nels. He glanced at Nicky and Wayne, who shrugged their shoulders.

"You darn right I'm talking to all of you!" Simmie looked around the platform and pointed at the crates. "How'd those crates get opened?"

Clarence Buchanan shook his head. "I checked them latches and they was locked real good. Somebody had to open them." He glared at the boys. "You boys! I told you to stay away from those crates."

Simmie placed his hands on his hips and waited. Nels, Nicky and Wayne climbed down from the boxcar and shuffled over to the sheriff, their faces long, unsmiling. "Aren't you supposed to be in school."

Nels gave the sheriff a half grin. "Well, we only left a few minutes early. We wanted to see those tadpoles."

The sheriff stepped closer to the boys. "You boys catch everyone of these chickens and then I want you to come talk to me."

"Yes, sir!" they said in unison and ran off.

The train's steel wheels inched forward, the horn tooted three times. The engineer waved his hat at Sheriff Moore and took his train south to Madison. As the last boxcar passed the train station, the switchman swung out one lone chicken from the caboose. It sailed through the air and caught Melvin Ragen square in the head, knocking him to the ground.

The last orderly act of the day was Simmie Moore, one hand on his hip, his other hand pointing his finger at Nels, Nicky and Wayne. The three boys sunk low and shuffled to Simmie's police car.

CHAPTER FIVE

After a four-mile walk around Cherry Lake early that morning, Essie's head had cleared somewhat. She'd go see Bootsey Birthright one more time. She dreaded the visit, but if the old woman had just one tidbit of information about Jewell's baby, that would be more than Essie had.

She cranked up the Pontiac and slowed at the curve toward the highway and eased behind Emogene and Ronnie Bass, who were crossing the road with fishing poles across their shoulders. "Hey, kids. How's your mama doing?"

Emogene, a pretty sixteen-year-old, smiled at Essie. "She's fine, Miss Essie. She's out in the collard patch this morning."

"Tell her I said hey. You doing okay, Ronnie?"

Ronnie Bass, a lanky boy, had brown hair like his sister. Their daddy was dark headed, a man who had loaded his wife in a wagon and drove from Cairo, Georgia, to Cherry Lake years ago, the mule seeming to show them the way. "Doing okay. Hoping to catch some fish for dinner. Mama said if we didn't catch fish, she was frying up chicken gizzards."

Essie laughed. "Chicken gizzards aren't so bad."

"I don't care for them at all. They're too tough to chew." Ronnie grinned at Emogene. "She likes them."

"Good luck with your fishing. Tell mom and dad I said 'hello.' Essie pulled away and sped toward the gas station.

Hanky Dank, a young black boy, stood at the gas pump putting gas in Shorty's truck. Shorty was slumped back in the truck seat, eyes closed. Hanky Dank was in the employ of Shorty, who paid the boy $3 a week, most of which he spent on crackers and cheese at lunch time.

"Hey, Hanky Dank. You okay?" Essie smiled at the skinny young boy. "I'll buy you a cold drink if you want."

"That's mighty fine, Miss Essie. I sure do like them RC colas." He grinned wide, a smile aimed at her. "I like them Little Debbie cakes, too."

Essie laughed. "Meet me inside."

Inside, brothers Virgil and Harold McHargue drank Nehis next to the counter, behind which H. A. Browning counted change into the cash register.

"The way I see it, Virgil, is mama never did whip you as much as she whipped me." Harold raised his eyebrows, wrinkling his forehead. "And I just don't understand that."

Virgil slapped his brother on the back. "Harold, it's pretty clear to me that you misbehaved more than I did."

"Not true." Harold gulped his Nehi orange. "Come on. Fish are bitin'."

The two men passed Essie as they left the store. "Hey, Essie. Shorty told me you were gonna sell that Pontiac." Virgil, a half smile on his face, held the door for Essie.

"Why, Virgil, there's no way I'd part with that car."

"That's what I heard. Just one of those rumors, I guess. You know how small Madison County is."

Hanky Dank slipped in behind Essie. "Go to the drink box, Hanky, and get you a cola," said Essie.

Virgil and Harold left the store, their back pockets full of crackers and sardines. They were going fishing.

Willie O'Neal pulled up in his truck, the motor loud, valves clacking. "Where you boys going?" Willie was a legend around Cherry Lake and Pinetta, an intelligent man whose welding skills were renowned.

Harold hollered out the truck window. "Going fishing. Wanna go?"

"Got an extra pole?"

"Sure do. Git in the truck."

"Let me grab a drink." He hesitated, pulling his cap off. "Gussie don't need to know about this." He shot a quick glance at the brothers and went into the store.

"Well, I'll be danged. It's Miss Essie. I been meaning to talk to you." Willie swept off his hat and smoothed his hair.

Essie smiled at the tall man. Willie had married Gussie Norris, who gave birth to their son Jimmy, a quiet, but mischievous boy who delighted in teaming up with his Uncle Johnny, who was only six months older, to wreak havoc on Saturday nights all around Cherry Lake and Pinetta.

For some reason, the boys found it most rewarding in their Saturday night fun to ride by Wanda Brown's house in their old International truck and fire shots in the air in front of her house. "Hey, Wanda," they had yelled. "Think you can catch us?"

Wanda was a fearless woman. It only took her five long strides to jump in her truck and peel out onto 150 and chase down the Norris boys. And she always caught them.

Willie and Essie had known each other their entire lives and, as Willie twirled his hat in his hands, he looked as though he was searching for words.

"Essie, I been meaning to tell you I followed you down 145 the other day and noticed your car's a needin' some new shocks. That rear end was bouncing all over the place. And that's not all. I also heard your brakes squeal when you slowed at Pinetta. Reckon you ought to have a little work done on your car? Jack Woodard over at the garage in Pinetta would do a good job. Kinda dangerous riding around at such high speeds... Oh, I didn't mean to..."

"That's all right, Willie. I know I drive too fast. I'll stop by and have Jack take a look. It's kind of you to be concerned."

"Yes, mam. Don't want nothing to happen to you." Willie found the drink box, pulled out a 7-Up and then grabbed a can of Spam and a box of soda crackers. Hanky Dank lingered nearby.

"Mr. Willie, I sure do like me some Spam."

Willie grinned. "Hanky Dank, I don't believe there's anything you don't like." He winked at H. A. Browning. "Give the boy a can of Spam and crackers."

Essie paid for her Dr. Pepper as well as Hanky Dank's RC Cola, Little Debbie cake and a Babe Ruth he had snuck into his pile. She noticed the Spam and soda crackers Willie had bought him.

Outside, a bright red Ford Fairlane convertible pulled into the station, easing along side the gas pumps. A blond, pony-tailed Bonnie

Lou Hinson jumped out of her car, her tight dungarees rolled to mid-calf; white bobby socks with penny loafers covered the young woman's feet. She wore a man's white shirt outside her bluejeans. She pranced inside the store, her forever smile lingering on Essie. "Well, hey, Essie. Been a while since I've seen you." Bonnie Lou looked Essie up and down. "Going fishing?"

Essie held her tongue. The sassy Bonnie Lou thought she was Madison County's most fashionable woman, her days filled with fashion magazines and shopping in Tallahassee. Only twenty-three, she had skipped college and raced her Ford Fairlane all across the county. Sheriff Simmie Moore had given her at least four speeding tickets. With her pretentious personality, along with large blue eyes, Bonnie Lou felt rules were not for her. Her good looks were captivating, but Simmie, as well as his deputy Son Stokely, gave her the tickets anyway.

Bonnie Lou had dated the mayor's son for a few months, then moved on to a star football player for the Florida Seminoles. She lived a flippant life, her cheeky habits supported by her family's money.

"Got a minute, Essie?" Bonnie Lou didn't wait for Essie's reply. "I heard you and Sam were no longer a couple. I believe I'll ask him to that country music show over in Live Oak. I hear Ferlin Husky'll be there. I've got his new record *Gone.*" The prissy woman, the top button of her shirt unbuttoned and showing cleavage, grinned at Essie. "Why, Sam Washington is the most handsome man in Madison County."

"Who says Sam and I are no longer a couple?" Essie stepped closer to the door of the store.

"Oh, it's all around town. Nobody in Madison County thought Sam would marry you." There was a slight smile forming on Bonnie Lou's lips.

Essie studied the bright pink lipstick on Bonnie Lou's full lips. She wore tiny pink earrings and a poodle pin on her shirt collar. "Bonnie Lou," Essie said evenly, "your social calendar does not have to be approved by me. You date whomever you'd like."

"Why, Essie, do I hear a little jealousy in your voice?" Bonnie Lou flipped her ponytail and swatted the air. "I'm sure Sam would like to date a younger woman—"

Essie brushed past Bonnie Lou, then called over her shoulder. "Bonnie Lou, get rid of the ponytail and bobby socks. You're not seventeen anymore!"

Essie left the store and drove down 145 to Pinetta, past Lon Terry's general store and turned left at Ran Terry's road. She noticed the Pontiac shimmied easily, even at slow speeds. The brakes squealed just as Willie had said. She'd see Jack Woodard at the Pinetta garage in the morning.

The Mt. Horeb Cemetery lay quiet. The sunlight filtered through the leaves and limbs of the wide oaks and painted yellow paths across the soft gray tombstones. Jewell's grave lay on the west side of the cemetery, in the second row behind the old church. It was known as the Donnelly section, with tall, ornate headstones that recorded births and deaths as well as loving tributes to the dead. *Rest in Peace. Gone But Never Forgotten. Rest Well Until I See You Again.*

A gust of wind blew last winter's leaves across the grass around the church. They looked like small crabs running home to their mama. Moss hanging from the oaks swung like sheets on a clothesline and pulled on the limbs as if trying to escape.

Essie parked at the edge of the church. She had stopped at the farm and cut boughs of early blooming azaleas and, much to her surprise, found one of her mama's rose bushes blooming, a white called *Maiden's Blush. Jewell will love these.*

Essie touched Jewell's tombstone, ran her fingers across the soft gray stone. *Jewell Agnes Donnelly An Angel on Earth, Born August 4, 1921 Died July 15, 1956.* She placed the flowers in a milky white vase that had been filled with flowers every other day since Jewell's funeral.

Hello, Jewell. I brought you some of mama's flowers.

Essie brushed dried leaves away from the tombstone and sat on soft green grass, fresh from warm spring sunshine. *Jewell, I'm going to look for your baby. Then, I'm going to come back here and tell you all about what's been going on with your baby for the last eighteen years.*

CHAPTER SIX

Bootsey Birthright's house was small, cottage-like, with three offset gables and gingerbread trim. A chimney ran up the east side of the house, ivy clinging to the red brick all the way to the top. On the front porch, two white rockers with flowered cushions sat side by side, their backs tall and waiting for company.

On each side of the brick steps, large round ceramic pots the color of holly berries were stuffed with daffodils, their yellow heads welcoming spring. The pot on the right housed a garden troll, his tall red hat poking up through the flowers, his eye in a wink on his ceramic face.

Essie opened the screened door and stepped inside the porch. She was nervous. Miss Bootsey was well known for her disdain for drop-in company. Essie had tried calling for days, but had no success in reaching the former girls school administrator.

"Miss Bootsey," she called, as she knocked softly on the door. She waited a few moments, then knocked again. Then, in a rush of harsh words, Miss Bootsey yelled through the door. "Who in the hell is on my porch?"

Essie licked her lips. "It's… it's me, Miss Bootsey. Essie Donnelly. Edith Donnelly's daughter."

"Essie Donnelly? I don't know any Essie Donnelly."

Miss Bootsey seemed to growl her words. Had Essie not known her, she would have thought Miss Bootsey weighed 300 pounds. "Yes, you do, Miss Bootsey. Your friend Edith's daughter."

"Edith's dead."

"Yes. Yes, I know. Remember me, Essie... and Jewell? The Donnelly sisters?"

Long moments passed. A wren pecked along the screen of the porch, while across the yard a big yellow cat stalked a lizard on a woodpile.

Finally, the door creaked open and a pair of bright blue eyes peered up at Essie. "You're not the pretty sister," she said.

Essie felt slow heat rise up her neck and onto her cheeks. "Miss Bootsey, may I come inside and visit a while?"

The white-haired woman seemed disheveled, unfocused. "What do you want?"

"I... I want to talk about Jewell's baby. The baby she had while with you in Atlanta."

Miss Bootsey blinked several times; her tiny body rocked slightly back and forth. "Oh, yes. The baby." She opened the door wider. "Come in." She looked down at Essie's shoes. "Your shoes clean?"

"Yes, mam," said Essie. The room, too warm and smelling of Vick's salve, was cluttered. A cup of tea sat on a small table in front of a Queen Anne chair. A knitted shawl was draped on the arm, its purple color clashing with the orange floral fabric of the chair.

"Sit over there on that loveseat. Don't touch the arms if your hands are dirty." Essie sat primly. After all, Miss Bootsey ran an all-girls school where etiquette was paramount to a young lady's success in life. "How's Edith?"

"Edith? Oh, mama?" Miss Bootsey's eyes were closed. She raised her voice. "Mama passed away, Miss Bootsey."

Bootsey Birthright's eyes popped open. "And Hubert?"

"He's gone, too."

"Well, it's just you and Jewell." She sighed. "Guess it'll be me next. No matter. I got a dress all picked out to be buried in."

Essie leaned closer. "Miss Bootsey, Jewell died last July."

The fragile body stiffened, the jaw became rigid, Bootsey's eyes burning their blue light straight at Essie. "Jewell's gone?"

Essie nodded. "That's why I'm here, Miss Bootsey." The buttons on Miss Bootsey's dress were placed incorrectly. She had skipped the second button, leaving a wide gap in the dress front. Her hose rippled up and down her calves. The pristine woman, renowned for her impeccable dress, had become old.

The blue eyes seemed to sharpen as she leaned forward. "Why are you here?"

Essie swallowed hard and tried to find saliva in her dry mouth. "The baby. I want you to tell me more about the baby."

Bootsey grimaced as if eating a sour pickle, an expression that offered nothing but contempt for Essie's inquiry. "There's nothing more I can tell you about the baby. Jewell gave birth; they took the baby away. End of story."

A coldness swept the room. Essie stumbled in her speech. "Took her where? But, surely, you—"

"Please don't." The woman's face was unyielding. "Why, there are girls all over this world giving birth to unwanted babies and Jewell—"

"Jewell wanted that baby! I know she did. It was taken away from her." Essie trembled. She felt her heart flutter, a nervous jerk in her body.

"Well, that's what your mama wanted. She said she wanted nothing to do with that baby."

Essie's eyes became narrow slits, a heat coming from them. "What about Jewell? I know Jewell wanted that baby."

"Oh, pooh." Miss Bootsey flitted her fingers in the air. "What did Jewell know? She was seventeen years old. Midwife came to the school, delivered the baby and left. Happens all the time to these promiscuous girls who think they can have sex and not suffer the consequences."

The heat in the room was unbearable, suffocating. Nausea rose to Essie's throat. "Do you remember the name of the adoption agency?"

The old woman jerked back. "Adoption agency. There was no adoption agency. Edith wanted me to just give that baby away and I did."

Gave the baby away. That's what her mother wanted and that's what her best friend did. Here. Have a baby. Want it? Take it. It's yours.

Essie stood from the love seat. The muscles in her neck squeezed and her words came out in a feeble plea. "So, you know nothing about who took the baby?"

Miss Bootsey looked away. The lace handkerchief she held in her hand was dingy and yellowed. She pressed it to her chest. "Not a damn thing."

Chapter Seven

On the front porch of the two-story farmhouse her father had built, the remnants of Jewell's life remained where she had left them before her death the previous summer. The soft coolness of March swept down the porch and ruffled the pages of the black Bible that lay untouched on the table beside her empty chair. Without her sister, Essie's life had been nothing but unending torment, a squeezing of the heart that made her painfully aware that her life would never be the same.

She heard DooRay before she saw him, his rich baritone voice slipping through the new leaves of trees heralding the arrival of spring, while the Withlacoochee gurgled and swirled with fresh rains. *Bringing in the sheaves, bringing in the sheaves. We shall come rejoicing, bringing in the sheaves.*

"You catch any fish, DooRay?" Essie hollered from the front porch and watched as the one-armed black man sashayed down the farm lane, his bare feet shuffling through the leftover leaves from winter.

"That I did, Miss Essie. Big fat bass. You got that grease hot?"

A few yards behind DooRay, silhouetted by the rising sun, a woman, thin and long-legged, took hesitant steps, even turning her body sideways, as if retreating toward the Bellville road.

"Who's that you got with you, DooRay?" Essie squinted into the morning sun and stepped from the porch out into the yard.

Laughter rumbled from the tall man's chest. "Oh, I got me a woman, Miss Essie." He slowed his walk and gestured behind him.

"A woman? Why, DooRay, what woman is that?" Essie began

walking down the lane, all the while watching as the bare feet of the woman found their way toward the Donnelly house. "You go off fishing, DooRay, and come back with a woman?"

Again, deep laughter. "Yes, 'em. That be right." DooRay stopped only a few feet away, the woman easing up behind him, half-hidden, her eyes wide. Following DooRay and the woman, a mule left the Bellville road and plodded down the farm lane, no hurry at all. It was a molly. A short thick neck and thin limbs, she placed her small narrow hooves one in front of the other and stopped beneath a nearby tree. Her intelligent eyes surveyed her surroundings and decided this was a good place to be.

Essie smiled and reached out her hand to the young woman. "Well, come on out from behind DooRay, missy. Let me get a good look at you."

The girl/woman peered from behind DooRay, a half smile flickering along her pouty lips. Her head was wrapped in a bandana, red with yellow figures of chickens running across it. Her skin was as smooth and black as new asphalt. When she opened her mouth and grinned, her teeth sat like snowflakes lined up in a row.

Essie took a step closer. "Now look at you. You're so pretty. Where did DooRay find you?" Essie wiggled her fingers at the girl. "And what's your name."

Essie saw she was barely a woman, mostly a young girl. Thin and dressed in a drab dress that had been washed more times than a kitchen pot. "Come," said Essie, reaching out and beckoning again with her fingers.

The girl eased from behind DooRay and reached out her hand. "My name is Minnie."

"Minnie? Who's your mama?" Essie studied the girl.

"My mama's dead. We's from Boston."

"Boston?"

DooRay shifted the cane pole from his shoulder to the ground. "That's Boston, Georgia, Miss Essie."

Essie looked from DooRay to Minnie. Then, back to DooRay. "You had to go to Boston to get you a woman, DooRay?" She frowned. "You talk with Murphy and Killer 'bout this?"

DooRay shook his head. "Nah, Miss Essie. I's found Minnie at Mr. Ran's pond. In my very own fishing spot. I 'bout chased her off

’til I saw all those fish she done caught.”

Essie’s eyes found the string of fish slung across DooRay’s shoulder. “You didn’t catch those fish?”

Laughter came again. “No, mam. Minnie done outfished me, for sure.”

Essie smiled while her eyes studied Minnie. “Where are your shoes? Chilly today.”

Minnie’s dark eyes fell to her feet. “Don’t have no shoes. ’cept for Sunday.”

“Only Sunday shoes?”

“Yes ’em. They’s too small but I can wear them for a spell.”

Essie nodded while she counted the fish on DooRay’s stringer. “DooRay, you go clean those fish and Minnie and I will meet you on the back porch. We’ll get the grease good and hot.”

DooRay grinned. “I knew you couldn’t resist these fish, Miss Essie. You fixin’ grits, too?”

“And cornmeal flaps with lots of butter.” Essie took Minnie’s hand. “Let’s go find you some shoes.”

Essie and Minnie followed the lane to the house, climbed the porch steps and walked through the front door and into the parlor, where Essie’s mama’s prized ceramics glistened on the tables, along with family photographs in frilly frames. The house was warm, the smell of fresh firewood lingering in the air.

Beside Essie, Minnie hesitated. “I ain’t never been in no white woman’s house ’fore.” The black woman’s eyes widened as they roamed the room, then suddenly stopping on a large framed photograph. “Oh, my. That’s my friend there in that picture.”

Essie followed Minnie’s gaze. A portrait of Jewell looked out at them, her green eyes smiling, her hair swept back into a wave tied with a yellow ribbon. “Your friend?”

“Yes, em. My friend in Thomasville.” The girl grinned and nodded her head vigorously. “She be at a plantation where I worked.”

Essie shook her head. “No, that’s my sister Jewell. She died last summer.”

Minnie wrinkled her brow. “Oh, no, mam. That cain’t be. That’s my friend over at the plantation and she sure ’nuf is alive.”

CHAPTER EIGHT

Minnie Pryor rode her uncle's mule two miles down the Bellville road, past Lon Terry's general store, to a stand of pines, where she turned left onto a narrow lane that took her two miles to a small wood frame house whose faded boards made it almost indistinguishable in the piney woods.

Her uncle, Hezekiah Pryor, sat on the slat of a front porch while chickens scratched in the dirt of a yard that was bordered by azalea bushes in full bloom.

"Girl, you gone a mighty long time. Best you got some fish." Hez left his chair and walked out into the yard, taking the mule's reins.

Minnie slid off Sally and reached around to her back. "Look what I got." She held up the carefully wrapped filleted fish, the newspaper wet and tied with twine. "These here are from Mr. Ran's pond, for sure." Her dark eyes danced as she opened one corner of the package. "Look here, Uncle Hez. Prettiest bass ever was caught."

Hez Pryor, the youngest brother of Minnie's father, cackled. "Well, Minnie, you done made your uncle proud. And your Aunt Myrtle, too. I say we go in the house and get these fish fried up."

The birth had not been an easy one. Myrtle Pryor's first child had struggled for two days to leave her weary body and enter the world. A midwife finally pulled the five-pound, six-ounce baby out, not a breech baby, just wide shouldered. A boy. Hez Pryor rejoiced all night long.

Minnie's Uncle Hez and Aunt Myrtle had traveled to Boston,

Georgia, at the end of January and persuaded Minnie's daddy to let her return with them to Pinetta to help her aunt. It was a good decision. Minnie cooked, cleaned and doted on her favorite aunt. After the birth, she assured her aunt "Everything gone be alright, Aunt Myrtle. I take care of you and that baby just fine now."

"Aunt Myrtle," Minnie squealed as she came through the door. "We's havin' a fish fry!"

A nursing baby in her arms, Myrtle squirmed out of her chair. A big woman, but not as tall as her husband, she waddled to the kitchen. "Oh, my. Get some of that corn meal. We'll get some hushpuppies in that hot grease." Myrtle pointed to Hez. "Hez, get a big ole onion and let's chop it up real good. Got to have onion in my hushpuppies."

A busy few minutes filled the small kitchen, chopping, scraping and stirring. Soon an aroma of fresh frying fish filled the small house, the warmth of a woman-filled kitchen delighting Hez Pryor. He sat at the kitchen table and held his new son. "Who cleaned those fish for you, Minnie?"

Minnie dropped hush puppies into the hot grease and watched as they turned the color of dark caramel. "Oh, a new friend. I was fishing just fine, and this one-armed skinny man told me to leave his fishing spot right away."

Minnie grinned. "Ain't no way I gone leave my lucky spot. Those fish was a bitin' every time I threw out my hook. They was as hungry as I was."

"Was that DooRay Aikens who cleaned your fish?" Hez moved the baby to his shoulder and patted his back, his big black hands gentle and loving.

"Yes, sir, it sure was. He done clean all the fish and gave me most all of them. We fried some up at Miss Essie's—"

"Miss Essie's? Essie Donnelly? That white woman on the big farm. I knowed her daddy. Worked for him five summers. A real fine man."

"That be true, Uncle Hez. Miss Essie let me sit down at her table and eat fried fish wit her. She's a nice woman, all right."

Hez, Myrtle and Minnie sat at the small table, blessed the food and devoured four bass, seven fat bream and a dozen or so hushpuppies. "Oh, lawd. I cain't eat another bite." Hez leaned back in his chair and pulled out a letter from his back pocket.

"Got a letter from your daddy today, Minnie. He says he wants you to come home. Said you been gone too long. Ain't nobody cleaning the house or washing their dirty clothes."

Myrtle shook her head. "That's a house full of men. Ain't nothing gone git done."

"Now, that's not true, Myrtle." Hez pulled the last hushpuppy from the platter. "What do those boys know. Their mama's been dead eight years. Ollie's got an eight-year-old and a twelve-year-old. What you expect that man to do?"

Minnie sat quietly, her hands in her lap. Across the room, the baby stirred in its crib and a sound like a kitten came from the blanket that covered him.

"Ollie's in that field every day getting those fields plowed. Then, he'll have to plant them. It's all he can do to get supper on the table." Hez crossed his arms and looked at Minnie. "You got anything to say, Minnie?"

Minnie looked up at her uncle. Her sad eyes roamed the room before she spoke. "I don't want to go home. Since mama died, ain't no happiness nowhere in that house."

The screen door flapped open and shut as a wind kicked up through the pines. The chickens scattered across the yard and ran under the house. Hez left the table and shut the door. "Too chilly to leave this door open. Don't want my baby gettin' sick." He looked at Myrtle and smiled. "Want some more tea, baby?"

Myrtle shook her head. "No. How we gone git this girl back home to Boston? That ole truck of yours cain't go five miles."

"I don't have any idea, Myrtle. Ollie wants his daughter back home, but he's gone have to come get her."

Minnie pushed around hushpuppy crumbs on her plate. "Oh, I got me a ride back to Boston."

Hez leaned toward Minnie. "What'd you say?"

Minnie's eyes widened. "That white woman, Miss Essie, she says she'll take me to Boston whenever I want to go back home." Minnie's fingers fiddled with the tablecloth hem. "She says she wants me to help her find her sister's baby."

CHAPTER NINE

Cherry Lake lay serene in the afternoon sun. Wild cherry trees wound around the lake as though a knitting needle had entwined them in and out of the lake's edge, their white blooms like jewels as spring tucked itself among the blossoms.

Inside Hubert Donnelly's small fish house, Essie folded linens and placed a few pots and pans in a box, along with cans of beans and tomatoes. Mason jars held potatoes, pears, peaches and pickled okra. She was going home.

At dusk, she walked around the lake, where fish plopped on top of the water and where a raccoon skittered along the shoreline in front of her. His delicate paws left tracks that were fine and dainty. Essie watched him until he entered the tall lake grass and disappeared. The eastern star sat on the horizon as pure and bright as quartz crystal, perhaps sending a message just for her. Essie gazed at the star for a long moment, until her eyes watered and shrouded her vision.

At the curve of the lake, she passed the 4-H camp. Visions of her youth came to the surface, a memory of her embarrassment at thirteen when wearing a bathing suit that revealed she had the beginning of bosoms.

She passed Robert's Store and continued around the lake and to the path that led to her daddy's fish house. She smelled cigar smoke almost instantly and saw Sam Washington in the waning light of day.

Essie knew he was watching her. She slowed her walk and contemplated her feelings for him, a man who had loved her since he was a boy. A man who had described in minute detail her yellow prom dress as she rode the float in Pinetta's homecoming parade so long ago. She knew she loved him. What she didn't know was how to go forward with her life. A life without Jewell. Had she failed Jewell? How had she not known Jewell had had a baby. Was she so self-absorbed at fourteen that she didn't notice the family tragedy that simmered beneath the surface of their lives.

Her life was floundering, and she knew it. Her only thoughts were of finding Jewell's baby, of putting their family together again, even if it was only her and the unknown child. Until she accomplished that, her life stood still.

Sam stepped off the porch and waited for her. His face was expressionless, no smile, no greeting. Her breath caught as the realization of his strength overwhelmed her. He had always been there for her, waiting on the sidelines. Always waiting. They had never made love, though she knew his desires were deep. For that matter, her desires were as fervent as his. Her restraint had been self-imposed, a reluctance that kept her from unleashing and freeing herself from the fear of self-discovery. She had always lived in Jewell's shadow. She was the hard woman who fell far short of her beautiful sister.

"How was your walk?" Sam, tall and lean, crossed his arms and waited for her. She finally saw the hint of a smile at the corners of his lips. His blue eyes were riveting, pulling her closer. She smiled back.

"Lovely. I saw a fat raccoon waddle along the shore. Frogs hopping everywhere. Is it going to rain?"

Sam looked at the sky. In the west, where the sun had disappeared on the horizon, the sky was clear. Above, the remainder of wispy clouds raced east. He returned his gaze to Essie. "No. No rain."

Essie moved closer. "I've packed everything here. Guess I'll go back to the farm for a day or two." She stepped onto the porch. "I'll be leaving… soon." Her voice caught.

In one fluid movement, Sam stepped onto the porch and pulled Essie into his arms. "Don't go, Essie." His words were muffled as he buried his face in her hair.

"Sam," she whispered. "I'll be back." She kissed his neck and felt the warmth of his arms around her. "Please know I'll be back."

Sam lifted her chin and kissed her. "I love you, Essie." He turned and left her standing on the porch, his kiss lingering. She would remember the kiss forever. It was a goodbye kiss, a sad parting that haunted Essie and left her sleepless in the many nights that followed.

Cherry Lake faded in Essie's rearview mirror, a slow ride down the dirt road to highway 150, past the Standard Oil station and east toward Pinetta. Sam was wrong. Rain gathered in the distance, a scattering of lightning across the dark sky.

The Bellville road carried her back to the farm, where there had once been the bustle of farm life. Her daddy, the son of a sharecropper, cultivated almost three-hundred acres of crops that put money in the Madison bank and bought him the finest John Deere tractors made. His wife Edith, the faux queen of the plantation, raised their two daughters in hopes they would marry blue-bloods from Charleston or Atlanta. She spent Hubert's money on china and crystal and had the finest Sunday hats that members of the Pine Grove Baptist had ever seen.

Edith Donnelly sang in the choir, listened to the sermon and rushed home to receive Sunday afternoon visitors, who clamored for her famous buttered rum pound cake as if it were gold. Edith had traipsed up and down the Donnelly's long front porch, her glorious hat still on her head, and served peach flavored iced tea from a crystal pitcher she had bought in Atlanta. Edith Donnelly was a pretentious woman; her daughters were not formed in her image.

Raindrops battered the windshield of the old Pontiac while wind buffeted the car. The beginning of a mid-March cold spell spread across Madison County, temperatures falling, and the once vibrant, delicate blooms of the azaleas became limp with cold.

That night, in the upstairs bedroom of the farmhouse, Essie drifted into sleep and then the dream that sent her searching for Jewell. Across the hills of Madison County, down the winding Withlacoochee and to the edge of Cherry Lake, where the lights flickered in the middle of the lake. *I'm coming, Jewell. I'm coming.*

Chapter Ten

Killer's crow was louder than the whistle of the Southern Railway train from Valdosta to Madison. The sound carried from the top of the wellhouse and across the farmyard to Essie's upstairs bedroom. In the inky dark of early morning, how did Killer know the sun would rise in another four minutes?

Nearby, Murphy, Madison County's most beautiful one-eared goat, ran out of the barn, his tail flipping wildly. He pranced over to the wellhouse and waited while Killer flew down to his back. Together, the two raced into the tack room and ran around a sleeping DooRay.

DooRay threw an empty Mason jar at Murphy. "What is going on here? Can't a man sleep?"

Murphy stomped out of the tack room, his hooves loud. His bleating began slowly, then ended in a crescendo of shrill bleats that most likely awakened the dead at the Mt. Horeb cemetery.

DooRay, dressed but sleepy-eyed, stood at the tack room door, a puff of frosty air escaping as he huffed at his goat and rooster. "If this ain't somethin'. You two is ruining my morning." He scratched his head and walked to the chicken yard, where a few dozen chickens clamored against the fence, waiting for their breakfast. DooRay scattered corn along the fence line, picked up an egg bucket and entered the pen. "Let's see how many eggs you done laid for me yesterday." He rummaged the nests and filled the bucket. Fourteen eggs. "A nice breakfas' coming up."

The smell of coffee wafted through the early morning mist and he knew Essie was awake. DooRay walked across the farmyard and stepped onto the back porch, wiped his shoes on a braided rag rug and knocked on the kitchen door. "It's the egg man," he laughed. "Got some fresh eggs for the lady of the house."

Smiling, Essie opened the door. "Good morning, DooRay. My, look at all those eggs."

"Yes, 'em. These eggs is right out of the nests. You want DooRay to make biscuits this mornin'?"

"I'd love that, DooRay. Let's have a good breakfast before I leave." Several logs burned in the dining room fireplace, sending the fragrance of oak into the house. The chill of late March had surprised them, seeping into the old house and reminding them of their recent winter.

DooRay stilled, his eyes downcast. "You really gonna leave, Miss Essie?"

Essie turned on the gas stove and struck a match. "DooRay, I told you I was leaving for a while. But, I'll be back. I'm picking up Minnie at Hezekiah Pryor's house in a little while."

"Yes, 'em. You done told me that. Then what?" DooRay sat down at the kitchen table, his desire for hot biscuits dwindling.

Essie placed an iron skillet on the stove burner and laid several pieces of thick-cut bacon inside the pan. "I'm taking Minnie back to her home in Boston, where she'll do a little work for her family. Then, we'll travel to Thomasville. Minnie's not sure exactly where she met… met… my niece." Essie felt her heart flutter. *A niece. She had a niece she'd never met.*

DooRay sank into his chair. "That's a mighty long way from home, Miss Essie." His head turned slowly from side to side, a weary non acceptance of Essie's belief that she could, indeed, find Jewell's child. When he looked up at her, his eyes were filled with tears. "DooRay jus' don't feel good 'bout you leavin' this here farm."

He stood from the table, pulling the chair across the wood floor. "I has jus' one mo' question for you, Miss Essie." The black man, a man who had received a Medal of Honor for his World War II service, as well as a Purple Heart, pulled himself up to his full six foot, two inches, mostly skin and bones. "If 'n you find Jewell's baby, you gone take it away from its new mama?"

CHAPTER ELEVEN

Essie left the sprawling farmhouse her daddy had built at the turn of the century. The house was grand, with a magnificent front porch, a porch that had become the heartbeat of the two-story house, where three gables soared into the skies of Madison County, where she and Jewell had been born. She slowed the Pontiac at the end of the farm lane and looked back over her shoulder, her eyes scanning the second floor where Jewell's bedroom window faced south. She squinted her eyes and pretended she saw Jewell waving to her. The Pontiac lurched forward, and her journey began.

She turned right at the Bellville road and left her memories of the farm. She left thoughts of her mother and father entertaining after church on Sundays, their mother and her friends talking of recipes, their canning of green beans and finally the accomplishments of their children, all fading in her mind's eye, the echoes of those times lingering in the nearby Mt. Horeb cemetery where their grandmothers and grandfathers, mother and father had been buried long ago.

Essie glanced back at the house through the trees. She caught a glimpse of DooRay standing in absolute stillness in the middle of the farm lane, watching her, his one arm still and unmoving. Murphy and Killer lingered nearby, both knowing something had changed. Essie felt a sudden catch in her throat, a tightening. She couldn't breathe and rolled down the car window where the air, crisp and cool, blew life into her face. At once, the truth was in front of her: she was leaving Madison County and wasn't sure if and when she'd ever return.

Chapter Twelve

Hezekiah Pryor, a proud man who attended the Mt. Zion AME Church on the edge of the woods not far from where he lived, sat on his front porch in the early morning cold. In another chair next to him, Minnie waited for Essie, her small cloth bag by her side. She wore a brown hat, brushed to perfection and nestled in her stiff black hair. Her somber expression shaded her pretty face, her dark eyes lowered and almost closed. Her lips, unsmiling, set in a grim line. She was going home to Boston, a place she didn't want to be.

"You tell your daddy how much we appreciate him letting you come and help Myrtle out with the baby." Hezekiah sipped his hot coffee and watched the road.

"I will." Minnie's hands clasped together in her lap. If only her mama hadn't died and left her in the care of two younger brothers and her daddy, on a farm out in the middle of a hundred acres. On a sharecropped farm all her life, she felt her life could be so much more.

"Now, Minnie, your Uncle Hez gone be truthful with you. Ain't no way your daddy's gone let you go off with a white woman for God knows how long, all over Georgia looking for kin of that woman."

Minnie's eyes widened. "Uncle Hez, I's twenty-four years old. I ain't no child. I worked plantations work all over Thomasville for the last five years. Got my own money. Daddy cain't say nothing 'bout what I do."

Hezekiah Pryor nodded. "Minnie, you didn't mention your daddy put a roof over your head, fed you food from crops he planted and farmed. That gives him some say so in what you do, doesn't it?"

Minnie's body slumped in her chair, a soft breath released. After a few moments, a tear rolled down her young cheek. "Uncle Hez, I don't have me a life at that there farm. They's nothing there for me. I wants to leave and go other places. Miss Donnelly done give me an opportunity to do just that."

Minnie stood, picked up her small bag and walked to the edge of the porch. Her body went into a defiant stance, her shoulders rigid, her chin lifted high.

At that moment, a car turned onto the lane that led to their tiny unpainted house. Three dogs came from out under the house and barked until Hezekiah shouted at them. In a nearby pen, Sally the mule raised her head and emitted a long, loud bray.

Essie parked near azalea bushes whose blooms were limp. The late cold spell had crushed tender plants, dispelling the idea that it was spring. There was no sun warming the yard, only cold shade that caused a shiver up Essie's spine. She pulled her coat lapels together and walked the short path to the front porch.

"Hello," she called, smiling at Minnie. Her gaze travelled to Hezekiah Pryor. "Well, my goodness. Is that you, Hezekiah?" Essie hurried up the steps. "Been a long time. How's Myrtle?"

Hezekiah stood from his chair and nodded at Essie. "We're doing just fine, Miss Essie. We's sorry to hear about Jewell."

Essie faltered for a moment, missed a step and almost stumbled. "Thank you, Hezekiah." Her voice remained steady. "I hear you have a new baby."

Hezekiah grinned. "That be the truth. A fine boy. Myrtle done real good." He turned to Minnie. "My niece here been helping out for a few months. Been mighty proud of her—wish she could stay a while longer."

Minnie said nothing as she huddled behind her valise. Her eyes watched the chickens scratching in the yard. Finally, in a small voice, she said. "Best we get going, Miss Essie. Might be fine if we get to the farm by dark. What you say?"

"Yes, let's get on the road. Daylight's getting away from us, for sure." Essie stepped off the porch. "Take care, Hezekiah. I'll get Minnie to her daddy's safely."

Hezekiah walked off the porch and stood at the bottom of the steps. "Miss Essie, if'n it's all right, I'd like to pass on some words that might be helpful to you." The tall black man paused and sucked in his breath, looked across the yard at Sally the mule and cleared his throat.

"Minnie's daddy's my older brother, and I been knowing him a mighty long time. He's not exactly a friendly man. Don't be scared of him—he's gruff, all right. Just let it go when he starts rantin' and ravin' 'bout things." Hezekiah glanced quickly at Minnie. "I don't expect he's goin' to let Minnie go huntin' no kin with you."

Essie stared a long time at Hezekiah. "Minnie's no child, Hezekiah. She's a full-grown woman and she has a mind of her own. I reckon she can do what she wants to do, with or without her daddy's approval." Essie heard her own words and felt the hardness form around them. She was a hard woman, for sure, and it looked like Minnie Pryor was working toward the same thing if she had anything to say about it.

CHAPTER THIRTEEN

The Pontiac traveled south on 145 and turned right on 150 and then picked up 53. Neither women spoke until they crossed the Georgia line on Highway 333 toward Boston.

Essie felt the car shimmy as she increased speed on the narrow two-lane highway. She had not taken the car to Jack Woodard's garage for repairs; procrastination on her part or perhaps an urgency to leave Madison County. She'd find a garage in Boston.

Crossing the state line had imparted in Essie an untethering of emotion that had wrapped itself around her and, after the sudden death of Jewell, squeezed her mind into blatant disarray. She felt her determined spirit, fired by an unquenchable faith, could lead her to Jewell's daughter. All she had to do was forget the farm, Sam and the house that held all the memories of her thirty-three years.

"You know what I'm thinking, Minnie?" Essie glanced at the profile of the lovely black woman. Her little brown hat seemed delicately pristine on the mound of rigid black hair.

Minnie turned to Essie, eyes wide. "No, Miss Essie. I has no idea what a white woman thinks."

"White woman?" Essie laughed. "Don't separate us, Minnie. We're two friends going on a trip together."

Minnie smiled wide, the row of white teeth shining bright. "Yes, mam. I's happy DooRay done grabbed me and took me home with him."

"You don't have to say 'mam' to me, Minnie. Do you know what the word subservient means?"

Minnie wrinkled her face. "I surely do not."

Essie thought for a moment. "Subservient simply means obedient and submissive to others. I don't consider you a meek person, Minnie. You've got a good mind. I don't know if I can teach you anything, but I hope I can inspire you to appreciate who you are." Essie slowed the car and pulled off the road. "I am your friend, Minnie.

"Thank you, Miss Essie." Minnie took a deep breath. "I wish everybody feel that way."

"Well, we can't worry about those who do not appreciate the wonderful person you are." Essie opened the car door.

"Why did you stop here?"

"Oh, I hear a noise. This old car is ten years old and I have a feeling it's about to misbehave." Essie left the car and pulled up the hood. A little steam was coming from the radiator. "Looks like we better get to a garage when we get to Boston. Heater's not working either."

Inside the car, Essie blew on her hands. "Only 42 degrees today for a high. That wind makes it feel like it's freezing. Let's stop up the road and get some hot coffee."

"Yes, 'em. This car sure is cold. I thought spring was here for sure."

"'fraid not. This front came out of Canada from what I hear. Going to get even colder tonight."

They traveled a few more miles and saw a small roadside store. The gas station had no pumps, but old trucks sat around it, a hunting dog in one of them. He barked at Essie when she pulled the Pontiac into the front of the small, wooden store. His forepaws were on the rim of the truck bed, his red tongue lolling to one side. A *Southern Pride* chewing tobacco sign hung lopsided near the front door. A larger sign, missing letters, spelled *E X AC O.* Next to what should have been *Texaco*, a hand-painted sign read *Whites Only*, an ominous message indeed.

"Oh, Miss Essie. We cain't go in there. No coloreds." Minnie squirmed in her seat, wringing her hands. When Essie looked at her, Minnie's eyes were bulging.

"Minnie, I'm not leaving you in the cold car. Come inside with me and let's get some hot coffee and a pack of peanut butter crackers. We won't be in there but a few minutes." Essie tugged on Minnie's coat sleeve. "Come on. Nothing's going to happen to you."

Reluctantly, Minnie opened her car door and snuggled up behind Essie. They walked through the front door, right underneath the sign that said, "Whites Only" and immediately felt the warmth of a pot bellied stove in the middle of the store, filled with crackling wood. Wood smoke permeated the room, beckoning them to enjoy the warmth.

Most everyone in the store was huddled around the hot stove, where a stack of wood leaned on a pole next to the stove. Every head turned, and every eye rested on the coal black skin of Minnie.

Essie, her hog-calling voice in full working order, called to the man behind the cash register. "Got some hot coffee for us?"

The big man, a pair of faded blue overalls covering his big belly, and a long-sleeved blue flannel shirt covering his massive frame, lifted his chin and replied to Essie. "Nope. No coffee today."

Essie's eyes traveled to the large coffee urn that sat on the counter in front of the towering man. She had smelled the coffee as soon as she had passed through the door. "What's in that big urn?"

The man grinned. "Why, that's coffee… but it ain't for you." He jerked his head toward Minnie. "Or that nigger."

Essie heard snickering coming from a circle of five men who held coffee cups, a lingering sneer on each face. Behind her, Minnie cowered into the smallest ball she could make.

To her right, where laughter had erupted, Essie glared at the men. "Something funny?" She took a step closer. "Give us some room at the stove while that fella over there brings us some coffee." She glanced at Minnie. "Come on over to the stove, Minnie. Let's get warm while we wait for our coffee."

At the cash register, the barrel-chested man, whose beard was dirty and filled with cracker crumbs, pulled a shotgun from underneath the counter. He raised it casually and placed it in front of him, but did not point it at Essie and Minnie.

Essie gave the shotgun a cool, long look. "Don't believe you'd try to intimidate someone who's a bullseye champion and has a loaded .38 in her coat pocket, hammer cocked, would you?" Essie's finger warmed the trigger. She had pulled the hammer back as she snuggled her hand in the large coat pocket.

Most of the men at the stove quieted. One called out, "It's a bluff. She ain't never shot a gun in her life."

At that moment, the gun fired through Essie's coat pocket and struck the urn. Coffee spewed out in a river to the wooden floor. "My first shot was for the coffee pot; the next one will be for your fat belly." The odor of cordite filled the small room as Essie held the fat man's eyes with her own.

"While that coffee's pouring out, you fill two big cups. Sugar and cream in both of them." Essie's peripheral vision caught the statue-still men to her right. It was clear they believed she was a champion shooter, for sure.

The big man slugged over to the urn and filled two cups. "You gone pay for puttin' a bullet hole in this urn."

A bullet left Essie's gun again and struck the large ceramic coffee cup in the man's right hand, sending fragments six feet in every direction. "I lied to you. I said the second bullet would be for your fat belly. My countin' got mixed up. It's the third bullet that will be tearing into your gut."

Essie saw the sweat on the man's face. He had paled, and his hand shook as he filled another cup. "You best get your coffee and go," he said, a hoarseness in his quivering voice.

Essie smiled, her hand still in her coat pocket, her finger on the warm trigger. "That's all we wanted in the first place." Essie hesitated. "After you finish pouring that coffee, I want you to take down that *Whites Only* sign."

The man began to protest. Essie moved the gun forward in her coat pocket and the man's eyes saw the shape of the barrel poking in his direction. "You ain't gone get away with this. You done broke the law."

"Throw in some peanut butter crackers. I'll leave two dollars on the counter." Essie walked slowly to the counter, Minnie a leech on her side.

"Get your coffee, Minnie. We've got a long drive ahead of us."

Essie stood at the door and called over her shoulder, "Mister, follow me outside and knock that sign down, would you?"

Indeed, the man slithered outside. "Grab that two by four over there and pry that piece of wood away," Essie commanded. The man did as he was told and in only seconds the sign lay on the ground.

"We'll be leaving now," she said, poking the barrel of the gun farther into her coat pocket. The man hurried inside, only to hear the screech of tires as the Pontiac sped away.

Chapter Fourteen

There she was again: the hard woman of Madison County who belied her feminine facade and extolled a propensity for strength in all situations. Her only weakness was Sam Washington, but she'd allow herself that one indulgence.

Her daddy had put a gun in her hand at seven years old. They shot targets every time Edith went to Madison to lunch with her friend, oblivious to the crack shot her daughter had become. From the beginning, it humored her daddy; Hubert rejoiced that his daughter was as tough as he was. No boys in the family—but he had a daughter who could measure up to any male in the county when it came to precision shooting.

Jumping in the car, Minnie wailed and rocked in the seat beside Essie. "Oh, Miss Essie," she cried. "We done let the devil out of its cage. Sure 'nuf, we have." The shaking black girl glanced behind her. "Ain't nobody comin' after us yet. Can you make this here car go faster?" She trembled as she ducked her head and covered her face.

Essie kept the car steady as she rounded a curve and gave the Pontiac gas. They passed newly turned fields, readying for spring crops. Cows grazed peacefully while egrets flitted around them looking for insects.

The scream that left Minnie's throat filled the Pontiac, shrill and full of terror. "Oh, Miss Essie. They's comin'." Minnie whipped her head around and looked out the back window of the car. The truck that was parked at the old store was full of the five men who had huddled around the wood stove and was only a half mile behind them. "Oh, lawdy, Miss Essie. We is dead women!" She moaned and fell against the car window.

Essie glanced into the rearview mirror and watched as the truck came closer. She could see the face of the driver, grim and dead set on catching the Pontiac. In the bed of the truck, four or five bodies hung along the sides, their fists in the air, the wind blowing their clothing and faces. Essie could see their mouths moving and knew for certain they slung threatening words into the wind.

The truck was gaining. The Pontiac's speedometer read sixty miles an hour as Essie pushed the accelerator as far as it would go. The car shot forward, its tail wavering side to side. The sound of the motor squealed like a Florida panther as it sought more gasoline. The big car seemed to lift itself above the asphalt as its tires whizzed at seventy-five miles an hour.

Minnie wrung her hands and swayed back and forth. "We gone die. I jus' know it. Yes, mam. We gone to see Jesus." She threw her face into her hands. "Here I come, Lord. Here I come."

Essie reached into her coat pocket and felt for the .38 and pulled it out. "Here, Minnie. Take this gun and put more bullets in it." She reached back inside her pocket and pulled out a handful of bullets.

Minnie whimpered. "I ain't never touched a gun, Miss Essie." Her eyes, wide with fright, stared at the gun.

"Do it, Minnie! Now!" Essie flicked opened the cylinder with one hand. "Shove them in there, just like the others."

The old truck, unbelievably matching the Pontiac's speed, eased up near its bumper and stayed there. Essie watched from her rearview mirror and then suddenly swerved to her left and braked hard, the truck barrelling past her on the right. "Give me the gun, Minnie," she said, as she kept on the truck's tail. The men huddled in the truck bed, peeking over the rim of the tailgate.

Essie eased the car to the right, just enough room to swing her left hand with the .38 out the window. Just like target practice, she popped two rounds into the left rear tire of the truck and braked hard. In front of the Pontiac, brake lights flaring, the truck swerved into the ditch and came to a stop. Essie gunned the Pontiac and they flew by the truck of cursing men.

Her heart beating fast, Essie calmed her breathing and guided the Pontiac toward Boston. "Minnie, there's one thing for sure and I want you to remember this." Essie reached over and patted Minnie's shoulder. "You are just as fine as anybody walking this earth. There's no one who can tell you you can't have a hot cup of coffee." Essie glanced at Minnie. "No one."

Minnie's face was wet with tears when she looked at Essie. "Oh, Miss Essie. You don't know nothing, I tell you. I's black, black as midnight and no white man is going to give me a cup of hot coffee."

Essie slapped the steering wheel and let out a squeal. Her laughter came in a melodious chorus that filled the inside of the cold car. "Oh, yes, they will, Minnie. As long as I've got this .38 in my pocket, with the hammer cocked, they'll do exactly what I say."

Minnie was quiet for a long while. When she spoke, her words were soft, searching. "Miss Essie, you cain't always fix things with a gun."

Essie said nothing as the car sped across southern Georgia and into Brooks County. Farmland stretched on each side of the highway, broken only by stands of pines. The dirt was plowed and tilled, soon to be planted with corn, tobacco, peanuts and cotton.

Minnie drank her coffee and opened a pack of Lance peanut butter crackers. "Uncle Hez was right about daddy, you know. He ain't gone let me go off with a white woman."

Essie nodded. "I know. I can't do anything about that. Only you can."

"He can be mean sometime," she said wistfully. "I think he's still angry 'bout mama dying. Leaving him with three youngun's and all."

"How'd she die?"

"Died while having my brother Orland."

"How old were you?"

"Sixteen."

"You have another brother?"

Minnie nodded. "Yes, Orland is eight and Pitch is twelve."

"So, you've been their mother for the last eight years." A squirrel dashed across the road, followed by a mockingbird in pursuit. Essie tapped her brakes and gripped the steering wheel.

Essie heard Minnie sigh. The girl stared out the car window, field after field flying past. "Yes. A mother at sixteen. Cared for Orland from his first breath. Pitch was only four. He didn't know what happened to his mama."

"How'd your daddy handle it?"

"Oh, daddy went crazy. Went way out in the field and stayed for days. At night, I heard him hollering and cussing. He's still angry. He loved my mama."

Essie glanced at the young woman beside her. "You're an important part of your family, Minnie." Essie slowed as she approached a tractor pulling a disc harrow. The farmer waved her by. They crossed Clark Creek and entered an area of maples and sycamores, all with the fresh green leaves of spring. A vast stand of pecan trees towered in the distance. A flock of crows scooped down into a pasture where cows grazed.

"I know. Guess I'll be their mama til they be grown."

"They need you, Minnie. I'm surprised your daddy let you go to Hezekiah and Myrtle's for a few months."

"Oh, those boys do just fine. They's some church women who comes and checks on them. Makes sure they go to Sunday school and is reading their Bible. Daddy just wants me there to do the cooking and cleaning. Wash them dirty clothes."

"Your daddy go to church?"

"Not since mama died."

Essie fell into a deep quiet, the road a monotonous asphalt, a road as sad as a Christmas tree without presents underneath it. How could she take Minnie away from her family while they searched for Jewell's daughter?

"Miss Essie, after we find your niece, do I have to go back home?"

"That's up to you, Minnie."

Minnie stared at the highway ahead. "If we find her, you 'pose your niece gone leave her new mama and go home with you?"

My niece. How do we know it's Jewell's daughter? Resemblances are common. Dark hair, green eyes. Minnie's fleeting friendship with a girl during the summer a few years past. Was this a whim? Was there really a girl out there who was Jewell's daughter?

Chapter Fifteen

Highway 33 was known as the Barwick Road to the folks who lived in and around Boston, Georgia. It took travelers to Moultrie, where the Southern Railway train loaded spring and summer vegetables from the fields throughout Brooks County and carried them north to large cities that survived on crops grown in the southern states. The farmland was owned by Georgia crackers whose ancestors had farmed in faraway places like Ireland and Scotland—farms worked by muscled laborers whose roots were scattered across the vast plains of Africa.

"Miss Essie, you need to slow down a bit. Coming up here on the right is Hodges road and we needs to turn right."

"So, we don't go into Boston?" asked Essie.

Minnie shook her head. "We's sixteen miles from Boston. All we's gone do is turn right on Hodges road, then the Okapilco Church road and go on over to Tallokas road. Just a little way down Tallokas is where my daddy and brothers is."

Essie slowed and looked for a road sign. "I don't see a road sign."

"Ain't no road sign. Ever'body knows where Hodges road is at."

"This it?" Essie braked slightly.

"Yes, em. Turn here." Minnie sat forward in the seat. She smoothed her hat and brushed the front of her coat; the coat Essie had given her. Jewell's coat. Navy blue wool with gold buttons. Her fingers fiddled with the cloth bag she held in her lap, rubbing the fabric anxiously.

The road was narrow, unpaved, and prone to holes from heavy rain. The old Pontiac's shocks were worn out and she bounced and swayed like a rodeo horse. Essie slowed to a mere crawl, the engine idling slowly as they found the Okapilco Church road, which was also unpaved and rutted. At the Tallokas road, they turned south, this time on a road that connected Quitman, Georgia, to Moultrie, Georgia.

Three-quarters of a mile down Tallokas road, a lone house sat back off the road. It was a small, box-like house that seemed tilted somehow, as if it had shifted on its foundation blocks. Essie stopped the car at the end of the lane. Had she made a poor decision bringing Minnie back home? The gray cold of the day wrapped itself around the house and gave no impression of warmth as she eased forward slowly.

The yard around the house was all dirt, swept clean of leaves and grass. A rooster squawked and ran back and forth, chasing a tabby cat. On the porch, a tall thin man looked out at them. Beside him were two small boys, as ragged and thin as their father. None of them smiled. They merely watched in silence as Essie pulled under an oak tree, the Pontiac tired and weary as she turned off the motor.

Ollie Pryor did not move, his unfriendliness almost palatable, sliding from the porch across the yard and into what was once a pleasant afternoon for two women traveling in southern Georgia. His unsmiling eyes never left Essie, giving her a haughty scrutiny that promised an unpleasant meeting between the two.

"Mr. Pryor, good afternoon," Essie called from outside the car.

Minnie slipped out on the passenger side, timid, her small cloth bag clutched tightly to her chest. "Hey, daddy. Orland. Pitch. Ya'll doing okay?"

Ollie's hand went to the taller boy's shoulder, a firm grasp. The younger boy leaned closer to his brother. "Minnie," said her father in a deep, low voice of authority. "Supper needs cookin'."

Minnie stepped forward a few steps. "Yes, I'm coming." She turned and gestured to Essie. "This here is my friend from Pinetta. She knows Uncle Hez and Aunt Myrtle."

The apprising eyes of Ollie Pryor remained aloof. "She cain't stay here." The thin man with the cropped gray hair stepped from the porch into the yard. "We got no beds here."

Essie smiled. "I understand." She saw the younger boy smile timidly. "I brought some quilts to make a pallet if that's all right." She began walking across the yard, eyeing the long, sharp spurs on the yard rooster. "Just need a little space." She looked at the barn a few yards behind the house. "Might sleep in the barn if that's all right."

"That's right, daddy. She gots quilts and can make a bed in my room. It's gone be real cold tonight." Minnie looked hopeful, her eyes bright and pleading.

"Don't have nothin' to feed company," he said, slipping his hands in his pocket.

"I brought food," said Essie with a half-smile. "I moved out of my daddy's fish house and brought lots of canned goods. Cornmeal, potatoes, lots of eggs. Even a slab of thick-sliced bacon."

The black man's face softened. Essie saw a glimmer in his eyes that wasn't there before. Her words were not spoken in her hog-calling voice, but gentle and soothing. "I make the best cornbread in Madison County. Even brought some cracklings," she said. "Why, between Minnie and me, we can cook up a feast."

The younger boy jumped from the porch and ran to Minnie. She put her arms around him and squeezed. "I done missed you somethin' awful." She looked up at Pitch. "Come here, Pitch. Don't be so shy."

Pitch hesitated, then slowly stepped onto the first step. He was crippled, his left foot turned inward, forming a club foot that was smaller than his right foot.

Essie slipped her hand into her coat pocket and pulled out two packs of peanut butter crackers. She said nothing as she held out her hand and offered the crackers to the boys. She smiled and felt herself wanting to touch their sweet faces and tell them how happy she was to meet them.

Ollie Pryor moved aside as Minnie and Essie stepped up on the porch. "We get up early around here," he said. Around the edges of his chin, a gray stubble of beard hardly moved as his worked his jaw into a vice around his teeth. He left the porch and walked to the barn, the rooster following. Each step was defiant; his shoulders stiff and unyielding. No white woman was going to sleep in his house more than a few hours. He'd see to that. She'd be on her way come daylight, with or without those canned beans and tomatoes.

Minnie watched her father and the rooster amble across the dirt yard. "Lawdy, Miss Essie. If you didn't mention that slab of bacon, you'd be sleeping somewhere else tonight."

Chapter Sixteen

Within the house, a cold heaviness crept across the bare floors and colorless walls, a house without a heartbeat, dying of unhappiness. Across the room, the fireplace sat dark and empty, its opening like a black cave, needing light. A single small table with four chairs was arranged to the side of the kitchen. Against the north wall, an old floral couch seemed out of place; too happy to be in the dismal room. There was no electricity and soon the end of the day would bring darkness as late shadows filled the room.

"Let's light this lantern, Minnie." Essie found a box of kitchen matches on the fireplace mantel and touched the flame to the lantern's wick. "Nice," she said. "Where's your stack of firewood? We need to get a fire going soon."

"On the back porch, I reckon." The younger boy, Orland, ran through the kitchen to the back door. Limping behind him, Pitch eagerly followed, his small foot curving inward, while his body swayed sideways with each step.

The two boys cleaned out the cold ashes and laid out the wood, a piece of fat pine underneath. Pitch struck a match to the liter and, in moments, orange flames sputtered to life, while the smell of wood smoke filled the house.

Essie slipped on her coat. "Let's go out to the car. We'll unload it before the temperatures drop. I can feel that cold coming."

In the farmyard, outside the barn, a solemn Ollie Pryor sat on the rusted deck of a mower and watched as boxes of food were carried into the house. He struck his pocket knife to a corn cob and began whittling. He looked across the plowed fields all around him, endless rows of newly planted crops.

A wind kicked up from the west and, in the waning light, he saw a dirt devil form in the field across Tallokas road. He watched it spin south and skip one way and then the other, almost a dance that lifted into the sky and then disappeared.

He studied the waxing moon for a long moment, just above the eastern horizon, then walked slowly to the house, his shoulders bent, his legs weary. The three-month absence of his daughter had been hard on him. She had taken her dead mother's place for eight years, had become a mother to her brothers. He knew it was time to let her go and find a life of her own, to marry. His wife's death had crippled him; his daughter's exodus would put him in the grave.

Ollie's heavy boots struck the wood of the steps and he clamored onto the porch. From inside, he heard laughter. Even better, he smelled frying bacon. He'd never had a white woman in his house before and no matter how good she cooked supper, she would be out of the house come daylight.

Essie watched the boys set the table, each of them eager to please. Pitch, though walking his seesaw walk, moved around the table setting out forks, occasionally glancing at Essie with an "am I doing it right" look.

Orland gathered five plates and placed them on the table. They were tin, tan with a green rim around the edge. Essie had never seen a tin plate before and thought of her mother's China. "You boys are doing a good job. Bet you're hungry."

"Oh, yes 'em. We had breakfas' early this morning."

A pot of rice and tomato gravy simmered on the wood burning cook stove, fat bacon stretched across an iron skillet, cornbread in a lard-smeared pan found its way inside the small oven, while two young boys sat wide-eyed at the kitchen table and watched two women create a magical hot supper. Minnie flitted around the stove and put the rice and tomato gravy in a big bowl.

Behind her, Essie pulled a platter from a cabinet and arranged the bacon and sliced cornbread on it. She stirred a pot of green beans, then added salt.

For dessert, Essie opened a can of sliced peaches and placed them in a small crock in the middle of the kitchen table. The aroma of hot food floated like a symphony inside the tiny house, touching noses and promising a full stomach by bedtime.

The front door swung open, and Ollie Pryor's silhouetted frame filled the doorway. Cold March air followed him, and the lantern's flame trembled, its light dancing across the faces at the table. Ollie's large, dark eyes swept the room: from the fireplace, to the wood stove, to the kitchen table where a bounty of hot food sat jewel-like, steaming in thick crockery bowls.

"Come sit down, Daddy. We're ready to say the blessing." Minnie pulled a wooden chair from the end of the table. "Here, Daddy. Sit here."

Ollie hesitated, his large hands hung by his side, and his dark eyes glistened. He stepped forward. "Got to wash my hands." He walked through the house to the back porch where a hand pump sat on a long wooden shelf across the back of the porch. The pump handle squeaked as it moved up and down, and cold well water spilled out into an enamel pan that had belonged to his mama. He scrubbed his farm hands slowly, deliberately, scraping underneath his nails with his pocket knife. He dried them carefully and shivered as the wind whipped around the corner of the porch and brushed his skin with cold.

Back inside the house, the man of the house sat in his chair. "Whose turn is it to say the blessing?" He looked at no one, his eyes downcast, his hands folded. Weary lines creased his forehead.

Pitch raised his hand, his boney fingers flickering his excitement. "It be my turn, Daddy." He bowed his head, one eye open and ogling the plate of cornbread. He licked his lips and remembered the prayer of thanks his mama had taught him so long ago. "God is great, God is good, and we thank Him for this food." He paused, the only sound coming from his open-mouthed breathing. "And we thank God for the pretty white woman and the food she brought. Amen."

A stillness followed Pitch's innocent words, words filled with truth and gratitude. A white woman. Food. Generosity. "Cornbread, please," said Pitch, grinning at Minnie. "We got any jelly?"

Minnie nodded, her heart-shaped face shining. "'course, we do.

Orland, would you please jump up and get that jar of corn cobb jelly off the shelf?" Orland, like a taunt rubber band, darted to the shelf, grabbed the jar and was back in his seat like a flash of lightning.

"What about your schoolin'?" Ollie broke his cornbread into small pieces and dropped them into the green bean juice. He glanced sideways at Orland and Pitch. "Miss Tully ain't sent no notes home."

"Miss Tully gave us spelling words is all." Pitch leaned back in his chair. "Miss Tully said both me and Orland gone go to the next grade."

Ollie grunted. "Your teacher said that last year. Only she kept you back."

Pitch lowered his eyes. "Miss Tully said I got to read better, practice my letters."

"I ain't seen you doing any of that." Ollie stood from the table and walked to the fireplace. He shuffled the logs, sending orange sparks spiraling up the chimney, and said over his shoulder. "Minnie been gone so long, you ain't had no help."

Minnie squirmed in her chair. Her father deemed her the matriarch of the family; she wanted freedom. "Daddy, I ain't no teacher."

Ollie returned to the table. "That's true. But, you're their sister. You got a responsibility to your family, you see." His words were measured, final. He snapped a piece of bacon in half, the sound like the far-away snap of a bullwhip. He lifted his eyes to Minnie, then his gaze slowly traveled to Essie. "Soon as Miss Donnelly leave in the mornin', we all be a family again."

Essie felt the hard woman inside her simmer, felt the heat touch her face, and then adrenaline course through her chest. Minnie was tied to the farm—just like she had been. Essie had been the watermelon queen all her life and had been planted on three-hundred acres of fields as though she were a plant, a vine, a corn stalk. From one year to the next, her life was surrounded by endless fields, monotonous like her life and the realization that it was what was expected of her.

Just like Minnie, she had been trapped. And now, across the table, in the small wooden house with no electricity or running water, Minnie was tethered to responsibilities that suffocated her and left her without hope. Minnie sat motionless, unable to speak.

"Mr. Pryor, Minnie and I wanted to travel to Thomasville for a few days—"

"Won't be no traveling for Minnie." Ollie's jaw tightened, his teeth clamped together, a burning fire in his eyes.

Minnie jumped from the table. "I got to wash these dishes, you hear. You boys get washed up and ready for bed." The tin plates clanked loudly as they were gathered from around the table. Without looking at her father, her words came softly. "I be going for few days, Daddy. I be back."

Ollie Pryor stiffened his back, rigid, his body unmoving while words passed through his lips, quietly, but heard by everyone in the small room. "Looks like a leather strap gone be needed 'round here."

A hard Essie Donnelly lifted her eyebrows and stared at Minnie's father. "Won't be a leather strap used while I'm in this house." When Ollie looked up at her, Essie merely smiled, all the hardness inside and waiting. "I'll leave in the morning with Minnie. Like she said, we'll be back in a few days. She's a grown woman, free-thinking, free-acting. I'm thinking your daughter needs to breathe a little, broaden her horizons. She'll be back; just like she said."

Ollie slammed his fist on the kitchen table, the noise shattering the room and the people inside. "You ain't in charge of my family. You can leave now!"

Essie nodded, her breathing slow. She watched the dying fire, thought of home, of Jewell and her baby. Years lost when Jewell almost drowned; years lost when the baby was given away. She knew she wanted to save Minnie, restart Minnie's heart. "I can leave now, but Minnie's coming with me." The young woman from Pinetta stood from the table. "I understand your needs, Mr. Pryor. A family lives here—you, Minnie and the boys. But families help each other. Minnie has spent the past eight years taking care of this house, raising these boys."

Essie turned and looked at Minnie. Minnie would help her find Jewell's child; but Minnie would also find herself. "Minnie, in the end, it's your decision. But, I'm leaving at daylight; I'm hoping you'll come with me."

Before Minnie could answer, Ollie jumped from his chair and stomped outside, slamming the door behind him. He walked quickly through the farmyard under a sky glimmering with stars. But, it was though he saw the stars from a deep well, unable to see the top of the mountain that could be his life.

"I cain't go," said Minnie. The young black woman could not see what lay in the distance: she could only see what was clearly at hand.

Chapter Seventeen

The quilts had been made by her grandmother long before she had been born. Scraps of fabric, all colors and designs, held together by coarse thread and the perseverance of weary fingers, lay folded underneath Essie in Minnie's small bedroom. She lay in a ball, her knees pulled up to her chest, socks on her feet. Still, cold air seeped into her tiny nest under four quilts, where her thoughts, as always, were of Jewell.

Minnie lay a few feet away in her narrow bed, her body a lump under covers piled high on top of her. "Miss Essie, my nose is so cold, I cain't feel it."

Essie laughed, certain frosted air floated from her mouth into the inky dark. The room had no ceiling, no walls, no floor; it was merely a black hole of cold that carried within it a deep loneliness that settled in her bones. "You'll warm up soon."

Far off, a barred owl trilled: *Who cooks for you, who cooks for you all?* Nearby, an owl answered, his call soft and melodic.

"Minnie, tell me about… your friend. The girl."

"Oh, lawdy me. She was the prettiest thing I ever did see."

"Just like Jewell's picture?" Essie sat up on her elbows.

"Spittin' image, I'd say. Her eyes were green, her hair was shiny black. And that smile. Why, her face was like a big bright star. Yes, 'em. My friend done be a movie star, I'd say."

"How come you can't remember her name?"

"Oh, Miss Essie. I's in and out of so many plantations last summer. Saw so many people. They's had parties 'bout every day. I peeled so many taters for tater salad, I dreamed 'bout them."

Essie closed her eyes, traded one darkness for another. "What did you talk about when you were with her?"

"Well, one day's I workin' at the big sink in the vegetable area. Shucking corn, getting the silks off and them little green worms hidin' under the silks." Essie heard Minnie shuffle toward the edge of the bed, closer, as she whispered. "I put those little green worms in my pocket to feed the chickens when I git eggs."

"Goodness, Minnie. I never heard of such a thing."

"I know. I jus' like to feed things." She paused and turned over on her back. "This girl come bustin' through the door with an armload of more corn and I says 'no room for no more corn.' That girl, she smile real big. 'This here corn is for you to take home with you' she says to me. I say, 'Missy, I got corn stacked up on the back porch a mile high. I got corn in the barn, in the corn crib. I got corn piled six feet high in the corn wagon. I eat corn til my skin gone turn from black to yella."

Minnie laughed, her throat rough. "That pretty girl done looked at me so sweet. And she says real innocent like 'do you know you can make moonshine out of corn'. Right there in that kitchen, I double over laughing so hard. Like I got time to make moonshine. Like I gone drink moonshine."

Essie scooted closer. She could touch Minnie's bed if she reached out. "What was her voice like?"

"Oh, her voice was like an angel's. So smooth. Sweet as honey." Minnie's words became hesitant, waiting, as if calling back the memories of last summer. "Then, you know what she say to me?"

"No," Essie whispered, the sound of wonder filling her quilt cocoon. "Tell me."

"She say 'can I be your friend.' And I look at that sweet face and say, 'I be your friend forever.'"

Chapter Eighteen

It was the dream again. Jewell in the middle of Cherry Lake. Jewell and Autrey Browning making love. A baby. Jewell's funeral. Searching for Jewell's baby.

A racing heart pounded in Essie's chest. Confused, she pushed the heavy quilts away and sat up. A few feet away she heard moaning. "Minnie! Wake up! What's wrong?" From her bed on the floor, Essie crawled through the dark to Minnie's bed. "Minnie? Wake up!" She shook her shoulder and instantly felt her feverish skin. Hot and dry, like a desert, Minnie's body lay still.

From the bedroom, Essie felt her way into the living room and the lantern in the middle of the kitchen table, where she struck a match and carried the light back to where Minnie lay. Minnie's eyes were closed, sounds like a crying baby coming from somewhere deep inside the thin body. "Minnie! It's me. Essie." She smoothed back Minnie's hair and ran her hand along her cheek. "Oh, my God, Minnie. You're burning up."

From behind her, Ollie Pryor called out. "What's happening in there? What's wrong with Minnie?"

Without turning around, Essie answered, gulping for breath. "This girl's got a high fever. So high she's delirious and won't open her eyes. I can't wake her."

Ollie crossed the room to Minnie's bedside and touched her forehead. "Oh, my. I ain't got nothing to help this girl." He slumped to the floor. "I don't know what to do."

"A doctor. Is there a doctor somewhere in town?"

Ollie buried his face in his hands, his words muffled. "Doctor? They's no doctor for black peoples."

"Mr. Pryor, this girl is not going to die if I can help it. I'm going into Boston and find her a doctor." Essie grabbed her coat. "You stay here with her. Get some cool rags and keep them on her face."

"You're wastin' your time. Ain't no doctor gonc come all the way out here."

"We'll see about that. How far is town?"

"Sixteen miles."

"West? On what road?"

"Go down Tallakos to 84. Go west on 84." He paused, gruff words, resigned. "All you gone find is a town full of white people and they be sleepin'. Ain't nobody gone be black, and ain't nobody gone help you."

Essie slipped on her coat. For a fleeting moment, she thought of her daddy's .38. Minnie had chastised her. *You can't always fix your problems with a gun.* She knew that. But she was her daddy's *boy* and, without a doubt, she had always been a hard woman. "Keep changing out those rags. Got to keep her cool. I'll be back."

Outside, she ran to the Pontiac and slipped inside. *Minnie, don't die.* She started the engine and whipped the car around the yard and pulled out onto Tallokas road, where the tires found traction and sped toward Boston. The dark road was deserted, a black ribbon of asphalt that ran in a sweeping line to Highway 84, which ran west to Boston.

High fever? What could cause high fever? And so quickly? What about the boys? What if they were sick, too. She should have checked them before she left. No matter. She'd bring the doctor back to the farm, even if it had to be by gunpoint.

In exactly sixteen miles, Boston, quiet and sleeping, eased into Essie's vision. She drove slowly. The first light she saw, she would stop and knock on the door. *Where does the town's doctor live? My friend is very sick, and I must find a doctor immediately? What do you mean 'why am I in my pajamas and wearing no shoes?' No, I'm not crazy! Just tell me where the damn doctor lives!*

Essie turned down Main Street and back to 84. One light. That's all she needed. See saw a truck parked behind a grocery store, a food truck where a man carried a box through an open door. She flashed her lights and screeched to a halt near the doorway. "Mister! Mister!"

She sounded her horn and almost immediately the man poked his head out the doorway.

"Who are you?" The gray-headed man's face was thin, his ears large, sending his head into a blatant imbalance.

"Not from here," yelled Essie. "I'm looking for a doctor. Can you tell me where he is?"

"If you're talking about Dr. Lundy, he's fishing in the mountains. Won't be back for another week."

"A week? Well, what do you do if somebody gets real sick?" Essie felt herself weaken. *Minnie's going to die without a doctor.*

The man walked from the doorway over to Essie's car. He wore a white apron, pens in the large pocket. He looked at his watch. "Well, if I was you, I'd go knock on Dr. Lundy's door."

Essie found herself glaring at the man. "Why would I knock on his door, if he's gone fishing?" She heard the irritation in her voice.

"Well, it's this way. He's got a young whipper snapper filling in for him and he's sleeping over at the doctor's office. I reckon you can talk with him."

Essie put the car in reverse and the man stepped back from the car. "Where's the doctor's office?"

"Right down the street." The man swung his arm up and pointed. "That-a-way."

Essie squinted through the car window. "Okay, I'll head that way. What's your name?"

"My name is Warmack. You new in town?"

Essie eased the car forward, her foot anxiously tapping the gas pedal. "Just passing through."

The doctor's office was situated in an old gabled house, neat with white clapboards and black shutters. A sign hung near the street: Dr. L. L. Lundy, MD. Brick steps led to an unscreened porch where ferns in large clay pots lined the edges, their fronds lush and green, even in March. An unpaved parking area was sectioned off to the right of the house, and Essie whipped the car in diagonally, its bumper crushing an azalea bush. She found herself shaking. *Minnie must not die.*

The house was dark and she stood at the bottom of the steps for a moment, gathering her thoughts. *Be calm. Minnie needs you.* She intended to tap the door softly, but was shocked when she balled her fist and pounded the door with all her strength. She was Essie Donnelly and she was an unusually hard woman.

Almost immediately, the door opened and was swung back by a tall man, sleepy eyed, hair tousled and wearing a pair of green and yellow plaid boxer shorts. He seemed not to be embarrassed as he stepped forward, giving Essie a bird's eye view of his naked broad chest. "What are you doing bangin' on this door, lassie? Sleepin', I am." An accent. No one in the South talked this way.

"Oh, really? It's 3:00 a.m. and you're sleeping? What is wrong with you?"

The man became flustered. "Well, I… it happens to be my best sleepin' at 3:00 in the morning. And I'm after a good sleep, I say." He had awakened enough to find a hefty dose of sarcasm as he lifted his chin and gave Essie his best middle-of-the-night sneer.

Essie didn't hesitate. "What about your oath?" She realized she had become confrontational, a bit of spittle flew through the air as she spoke the word 'oath.'

"My oath? Excuse me, but I do not have to discuss anything with someone who has just about knocked my door down and interrupted my sleep." He reached out to grab the edge of the door, when Essie kicked it open farther.

"Wait until I tell Dr. Lundy what a toad you are! Get your butt out into my car—you've got a patient to save!"

The man in boxer shorts stared at Essie for a long moment. "Well," he said, rather flippantly, "why didn't you say so?" He seemed to awaken fully, his eyes taking in the woman who wore pajamas and no shoes. "Did you know you're not wearing shoes?" He glanced at an outdoor thermometer hanging at the corner of the house. "It's 33 degrees."

"I'm not here to discuss the weather nor my lack of shoes. Follow me." Essie bounded down the steps and across the small yard.

The doctor hollered after her. "You may not be bothered with your attire, but I certainly plan to dress before I go traipsing after a bullish woman in the middle of the night." He slammed the door, the force of impact sounding like a gunshot in the serene, star-filled Georgia night.

Essie opened the door to the Pontiac and started the engine. She revved the motor and found herself breathing heavily, almost gasping for breath. She was an impatient woman, given to what she called 'blood boils.' Most people would call it anger; yes, that was what it was, and she had suffered from the malady her entire life. Yet, she had never stopped to consider why.

She heard the front door of the house open, a loud whistling from the man who wore the plaid boxer shorts. He had dressed in slacks and a windbreaker. His long legs took him across the lawn and down the driveway to a one-car garage. She noticed he carried a black bag—his medical apparatus, of course. Despite the plaid boxer shorts, she admitted he was a bona fide Doctor of Medicine. She felt herself shudder. The hard woman decided on the spot, if the Doctor of Medicine didn't heal Minnie, she would consider using her .38.

Essie pulled out of the driveway and barreled to 84 and the sixteen miles to the farmhouse where Minnie hovered between life and death. She pushed the accelerator and watched as the speedometer needle touched 70. In her rearview mirror, she saw the headlights of the doctor's car only a car length away. *Well, I'll be damned—he's keeping up with me.* The next moment the thought occurred to her that without his help, Minnie might die. It would be difficult, but she would try to be more agreeable.

The Pontiac swerved to Tallakos road, Essie decreasing her speed to make the turn. Then, only a few miles down Tallakos road, she braked hard and skidded to a stop in the farmyard. She looked up in time to see the doctor brake and wanted to laugh as he missed the turn and slid down and then up the ditch. *And he is going to save Minnie?*

"It'd be nice if you'd tell me your name," she yelled from the front porch. She thought of him as Dr. Boxer Shorts as she watched him walk hurriedly toward her. He would certainly have to gain some credibility at this point, although the doctor's black bag was impressive.

"Dr. Robert Grey." Oddly, his demeanor had stiffened and right before her eyes, Essie saw a Doctor of Medicine immerge out of the plaid boxer shorts and into a mission of mercy.

"Essie Donnelly," she said curtly. "This way."

In one long step, Essie maneuvered the steps and pushed open the front door. Ollie Pryor sat at the kitchen table, his head resting on his folded arms. A nearby lantern flickered. "Mr. Pryor, I brought the doctor. How's Minnie?"

Ollie slowly lifted his head and opened his tired eyes. "I reckon she done stopped breathing a while ago."

"Oh, no, she hasn't!" Essie grabbed the lantern and raced into

Minnie's bedroom, the light falling on Minnie's bed, where everything was still, no movement, only a pile of quilts that covered a young woman who perhaps had breathed her last breath.

Behind her, a voice she did not recognize softly filled the room; soothing and confident, it took command. "I'll take it from here." Dr. Grey moved to Minnie's bedside and gently pushed her swollen eyelid up, followed by a bright light. The doctor's smooth hands pulled the quilts to the side and slipped a stethoscope onto Minnie's chest, his own eyes closed as he moved the apparatus around and listened with intensity.

Behind him, Essie whispered, "She's not dead. I'm telling you right now, she's not dead."

The doctor straightened up and removed the stethoscope from his ears. Without turning around, he replied. "Well, how interesting. The woman in pajamas and without shoes is also a Doctor of Medicine. She has declared this young woman alive and so be it." He turned and smiled at Essie. "The patient is, indeed, alive. But I don't know for how long."

"What do you mean for how long?" Essie, wide-eyed and questioning, stared at Robert Grey.

"Right now, her temperature is 105 and if it continues at this high reading, her body will convulse. She'll have seizures." He paused and gave Essie a steady look. "And she may die."

"No, she won't!" Essie shot out.

"There you go again, Miss Donnelly. Diagnosing the patient."

"Do something!"

Dr. Grey threw the quilts off the bed and pulled up Minnie's gown and saw what he was looking for. "A rash." He touched her skin, dry and dehydrated. Her mouth was also dry, and she breathed sporadically through swollen lips. "It's either a virus or a bacterial infection. Where has she been these past few days?"

"Down in Madison County, Florida. With her aunt and uncle."

"They live in the woods?"

"Yes, in the country."

The doctor turned Minnie onto her side and looked carefully at her skin. Essie leaned closer. "What are you looking for?"

"An insect bite."

"An insect bite causes a 105 fever?" Minnie's back was hot and dry, a rash running up her spine and to her armpits.

"I'm afraid so. Just don't know what kind of insect." He lifted Minnie's arms, pushed back her hair at her neck line. "Hold that lantern closer."

Essie lifted the lantern higher and swung it over the bed. Her eyes followed the doctor's hands. The hands probed and searched and finally moved down Minnie's legs. The rash covered only one leg, red on the black skin. "Here," said Dr. Grey. "Right here."

"What?" Essie's eyes traveled to the end of the beam of light and saw what the doctor saw; a swollen area of skin above her ankle, an angry red.

"She's in severe anaphylaxes."

"Explain," Essie commanded, her patience non-existent.

"A severe, life-threatening allergic reaction to an insect bite. It all adds up. Racing heartbeat, fever, swollen eyelids, swollen lips, rash."

"What are you going to do?" Essie crowded behind the doctor and caught the soft fragrance of aftershave. Not Old Spice, something sweeter. *Bay Rum. The doctor wore plaid boxers and used Bay Rum aftershave.*

Dr. Grey reached into his bag and pulled out a vial, along with a hypodermic syringe. "The first thing I'm going to do is give her an injection of antibiotic for her infection. Then, we're going to strip her and lay wet towels all along her torso and limbs." He sterilized a spot on her hip and, with precision, stabbed the end of the needle into her muscle. "The next thing we're going to do is bring down that fever." He stood up and turned to Essie. "And you, Miss Donnelly, will try to coax some fluid down Minnie. If we don't act fast, she will seizure." He slipped the thermometer under her armpit. "Still 105. Get busy."

"What time is it?" Essie's worried face turned toward the window where the night pressed against the glass. Minnie had been unconscious at least four hours.

"Four-thirty."

She turned away quickly and passed a sleeping Ollie in the living room. "Towels," she screamed. "I want towels!" Ollie Pryor lifted his head and pointed to a cabinet in the kitchen.

"In that cabinet. You gone bury Minnie now?" His voice quivered; his body seemed atrophied, unable to move from the chair he was in.

"No, she's alive. Come pump water for me." Essie pulled four towels from the cabinet and swung open the back door. She looked behind her and saw Ollie had not moved. "Git your ass over here. Grab this pump handle and start pumping." It was that hog-calling voice again—it was always there, hiding deep inside. But when she wanted it, it came out strong.

Ollie Pryor, with sloth like movements, left the table and walked out onto the back porch. "What you doing?"

Essie placed a towel under the flowing water. "Wetting these towels to put on Minnie. Got to get her fever down."

Ollie worked quietly, every now and then glancing at the white woman who had invaded his home. Perhaps he wondered if she had brought a curse with her. White people had been bad to him all his life; now a white person had brought fever into his house. But, she was leaving at daylight. So was that doctor. Two white peoples is too many, he thought.

Essie twisted the towels to remove most of the water, her hands red with cold. The water was as icy as the night air. She rushed into the house, and when she entered the bedroom, she saw where Dr. Grey had turned Minnie on her back. So frail, she lay still, a shallow breath escaping as though there was not enough air. "Open that window over there, Miss Donnelly."

Essie did as she was told. Then, she spread three towels across Minnie, one across her chest and one each on her legs. She lay the fourth towel on her forehead, wrapping it around to cover each cheek. "I'm sorry. I'm not so sure how to get fluids down an unconscious person." The smallness of her words came softly, humble, barely audible.

Robert Grey glanced up. "A teaspoon at a time. Very slowly. Just dribble it into her mouth. It's swollen but her throat is clear." He leaned back and stretched. "Leave these towels on about fifteen minutes." He looked at his watch. "Then, let's cool them off again with more cold water. They'll get warm quickly with that hot skin."

Essie hurried through the kitchen again, noticing Ollie Pryor was not at the table. On the porch, she pumped cold water until it filled a quart jar. Back inside, she found a small teaspoon and returned to Minnie's bedside.

"Should I prop up her head?"

"No. Just turn her head to the side and slip in a small amount of water. Some will dribble back out, but that's okay. Keep the inside of her mouth wet. That water's cold and that's good."

Essie followed the doctor's instructions carefully. She found herself talking to Minnie, whispering into her ear. "You're going to be fine, my friend. You just need a little help. And I'm here. Right beside you, Minnie. I'm not going anywhere."

At the end of the bed, Dr. Grey bent over and continued to gently clean the festered area of the bite. "This is an obvious insect bite. Whatever bit her carried a potent bacteria or venom. Could have been a spider. A tick." He looked up at Essie with dark, intelligent eyes. "If it was a tick, I'm thinking we would have found it attached to the skin. Besides that, a tick bite would not manifest so rapidly into her body." He leaned back. "You said she was fine yesterday?"

Essie nodded as her mind swept backward to Pinetta, the drive up 333, cooking dinner and going to bed.

"Since we didn't find a tick, I'd say we're looking at a spider bite—maybe a brown recluse. Look here."

The doctor lifted Minnie's leg. "See this area right here?" He waved his hand over the side of Minnie's foot. He touched it. "See how hard this area is? Infection. All around the actual bite." He pushed a pillow under Minnie's foot. "Let's elevate her foot since it's so swollen." He wiped the bite area with alcohol. "Hand me my bag, please."

The doctor's black bag was mysterious. Its contents unknown to others, yet the Doctor of Medicine was amazingly aware of what the bag contained. Essie lifted it and carried it across the room. Again, she smelled Bay Rum. And, for the first time, she actually looked at the man. And, without a second thought, she decided he was handsome. Dark, almost black eyes sat beneath dark eyebrows. His hair was short and straight and also black. He did not wear the current crew cut style, but more like Cary Grant's pompadour. She guessed his age to be around thirty-five. She also noticed the dark shadow of a beard, as if someone had found a piece of charcoal and smeared it along his jawline.

"Thank you." He rummaged only a moment and pulled out another syringe and vial.

"What's that?"

"An anti-inflammatory medication. I know she's in pain. This will help with the swelling." Expertly, he wiped her hip with alcohol and inserted the needle. "Let's take that temp again." Once more, he slipped the thermometer under her armpit and waited only a few moments. When he read it, he smiled. "Ah, very good. We're down to 101. Need to get those towels cooled off again."

Essie nodded and leaned over Minnie. "You're doing fine, Minnie," she said, as she lifted the towels away from her body. She left the room and walked quickly through the house to the back porch. When she opened the door, across the plowed field to the east, light from the rising sun had swept the edge of the horizon, an orange glow spreading across the morning sky. She stood a moment in the frosty air and thought of Jewell. *Are you there, Jewell?*

She rinsed the towels with the cold pump water and returned to Minnie's bedroom where she saw Dr. Grey lift the teaspoon and dribble water into Minnie's mouth. "Here you go," he said, coaxing, as if speaking to a child.

Minnie murmured something, an unintelligible word. Essie gently laid the cool towels across Minnie's limbs. "What did she say?"

"Not sure. But I think she'll be coming around soon. Her eyes are becoming brighter, her breathing more stable. Let's give her a little rest and I think she'll start to improve."

Essie spread the cold wet towels across Minnie's body. "What time is it?"

"6:30. Let's take another reading at 7:00." He glanced at Essie. "Any chance you could make us some coffee?"

Essie smiled. The doctor seemed tired. She'd awakened him at 3:00 a.m., raked him out into the cold night, led him on a ride across the countryside on a mercy mission to see a young black woman and then demanded he heal her. "Yes, of course."

They left Minnie's room and found the rest of the house cold. Dr. Grey knelt at the fireplace and placed a few logs along the hearth. "Got any small slivers of wood? Matches?"

"Might be some fat pine on the back porch. Matches are on the mantel." Essie searched the cabinets for cups. The coffee pot sat cold and waiting. "Bring some fat pine for this stove." There she was again, ordering him around, but at least it wasn't her hog calling voice. "Please," she added.

The two of them worked silently in the small rooms. The fires began to crackle, a comforting sound in the early morning. The coffee pot begin to spurt whifs of coffee through its spout and bring the two strangers together at the kitchen table.

Essie found herself studying the doctor. Ollie Pryor had said no doctor would travel sixteen miles out in the country in the middle of the night. Especially to treat someone who was black. Once Dr. Grey had realized someone needed his care, he had asked no questions. He followed Essie at 70 miles an hour across 84. Trust. He was laden with trust and it seemed he never once hesitated.

She poured their coffee, the room warming as morning light came through the east window. "Dr. Grey, I'm appreciative of your commitment to your work." She hesitated, unsure of what to say, a hem hawing that was alien to the farm girl from Pinetta, Florida.

Robert Grey sipped his coffee and looked at Essie over the rim of his cup, his eyes in a questioning glance. "But, of course. It's what I do," he said gently, the small crease between his eyebrows deepening somewhat. "Did you expect anything else?"

Essie wrapped her hands around her coffee cup, the warmth comforting her. "Actually, I wasn't sure."

"Sure about what?" He leaned forward and placed his elbows on the table, waiting for more.

The fire popped and sent embers up the chimney. The sparks flitted like racing fireflies. At the window, a wren pecked along the sill, a shrill note following her as she traveled around the entire window looking for breakfast. Essie watched the busy bird a moment before finding Robert Grey's dark eyes. "Wasn't sure you'd drive all this way to treat a… a black woman."

The doctor stilled; then a smile emerged. As his grin grew, the area around his eyes crinkled, exposing something good; a nibble of laughter that lingered across his face. "Oh? Minnie's black?" he asked.

Essie stared at the doctor as he leaned back, his face a study of quiet intelligence. His calmness was soothing. She leaned in. Oddly, she, too, smiled across the table, uninhibited. Unafraid of her thoughts in the presence of this man, she shot out, "Are you patronizing me?"

"No," he said. "I'm educating you." He held her eyes with his own, a steady, but unchallenging inspection of Essie Donnelly, perhaps a glimpse into her mind.

Essie eyed the man across from her. She could whip him verbally or otherwise; it was that hard woman inside of her. The patina protecting her had been formed over a long period of time, an oxidation that locked in the insecurities that lurked there. She hid those insecurities well.

"My gratitude, Dr. Grey," she said, her eyes never leaving his face. "I will recognize your statement as such."

The doctor who wore the boxer shorts nodded. "Let's go take Minnie's temperature." He stood and tossed another log on the fire and, with a measured tread, he walked into Minnie's bedroom.

The room had warmed, the chill removed by the fire in the hot cook stove and the flames coming from massive oak logs in the fireplace. Essie poured herself another cup of coffee, her only thoughts of Minnie and how soon she could recover.

Chapter Nineteen

Minnie's temperature hovered at 99 degrees. "Minnie, can you hear me? Please open your eyes. This is Dr. Grey." He tucked the light quilt around her shoulders and rubbed her cheek. Minnie stirred, her breathing even.

Essie eased beside Dr. Grey and pressed her hand along Minnie's forehead and felt the cool skin. "It's Essie, Minnie. Are you going to wake up for me?"

Minnie nodded and one eye popped open, then the other. "I heard a man's voice." Her eyes flitted from Essie to Dr. Grey. "Who are you?"

Robert Grey picked up Minnie's hand and squeezed it gently. "You've been quite ill, Minnie. I'm Dr. Grey. Your good friend Miss Donnelly and I have been trying to get you well. How do you feel?"

Minnie closed her eyes. "I feel very tired. I's want to sleep."

"That's quite all right. First, let's drink something. I'm going to have Essie make you a hot cup of tea. And, if you feel like it, maybe a piece of toast."

Eyes still closed, Minnie nodded. "I'm thirsty all right."

"You've had some high fever. You're dehydrated and glasses of water will help a lot."

Essie picked up the quart Mason jar. "I'll get some fresh water." She left the room and hurried to the back porch. When she passed through the kitchen, the two young boys were sitting quietly at the kitchen table. "Good morning," she called. "I'll be right back."

Cold morning air rushed across the porch and the pump handle seemed frozen. It squeaked loudly as she lifted it and then pressed it down. A gush of cold water splashed into the jar and all along the wooden shelf. The yard rooster pranced across the barnyard, his high arching tailfeathers glistening in the bright morning sun. There was no sign of Ollie Pryor.

Back in the house, Essie opened the kitchen cupboards, one by one, looking for tea. "You boys know where Minnie keeps tea?" She glanced across the kitchen to the two sleepy-eyed children.

"Yes, mam. They's tea in that tin can by the coffee pot." Pitch pointed to the wood stove. Essie gathered the can of loose tea and measured it out.

"I'm thinking you're hungry. That true?" Essie poked some fat pine into the wood stove and the hot ashes flared up into small flames.

"Oh, yes, mam. We's always hungry." Their faces beamed with expectation, their smiles wide. The older boy, Pitch, looked like his father, his limbs lanky, a thin face with large ears. His club foot seemed foreign to his otherwise perfect body.

Orland, only eight years old, was quite small, his body compact but agile. Essie turned from the stove. "I'm hungry, too. Do you like pancakes?" Essie thought of her childhood and the food the farm produced. They never went hungry, never wanted for much of anything. Their mother Edith swirled around the house from morning till night, dusting, sweeping, cooking and, of course, entertaining. Her buying trips to Tallahassee and Atlanta to spend Hubert's money provided them with fine things; China, silver and crystal from Europe. Her realm as the farm's hostess was well known in Madison County and anyone who was invited to the Donnelly's was sure to swoon at Edith Donnelly's extravagances.

The tea brewed for a few moments, sweetened and poured into a chipped cup without a saucer. Essie carried it to the bedroom where Dr. Grey packed his black bag. "I'd like to write some prescriptions for Minnie. Do you think you'll be able to get to Boston? She needs these medications today."

"Is there a pharmacy in Boston?" she asked, while helping Minnie sit up. "Let's drink this tea, Minnie. I put some sugar in it—it should taste good."

Dr. Grey, writing on a prescription pad, nodded. "Yes, Ed Cromartie will fill them for you. He's on Main Street. You'll see the sign Cromartie Pharmacy."

"Of course. I'll ride into town. Isn't Warmack's Grocery around the corner on US 84?"

"That's correct. Anything you need, Mr. Warmack will have it. He just returned from the Florida Gulf coast with a pile of fresh fish."

Minnie sipped her tea. "I got to take medicine?"

Dr. Grey closed his bag and sat down on the edge of Minnie's bed. "Yes, young lady. I'd like you to continue on some antibiotics. Also a dose of aspirin every four hours. We want to keep that fever in check." He pointed to her feet. "And that spider bite—we don't want it to fester up again."

Minnie dipped her chin and looked up at the good doctor. Her words were hesitant. "I ain't got no money to pay you, Dr. Grey."

The doctor shook his head. "No need to pay me, Minnie. The most important thing right now is your heart is beating and I see a smile on your face." He stood. "I'd like you to continue drinking water as much as you can. And also rest. Snuggle under those quilts and don't worry about a thing." He turned to Essie. "Miss Donnelly, you've been a very good assistant. I'm impressed with your care of Minnie."

How could she not care for Minnie—a lovely girl who was kind enough to offer help in finding Jewell's daughter. Minnie had come into Essie's life just when she needed her: a lifeline, a path to Jewell's daughter. Bootsie Birthright had had no desire to help, even though she had been the only one with knowledge, other than Essie's dead mother, of Jewell's pregnancy and the birth of a baby. When Minnie recovered, the two of them would begin their search.

"I think it is you, Dr. Grey, who has been the hero of the day."

Robert Grey smiled. "Now, Miss Donnelly, did I really have any choice? As I recall, you assaulted the front door of Dr. Lundy's office and demanded my assistance at 3:00 in the mornin'."

Essie became flushed, her face warm. "And as I recall, you rode my bumper all the way to this farm in order to save a patient."

"I think *we* saved the patient, Miss Donnelly. You were the one who sought out a doctor in a place you'd never been. It is I who am beholden to you for trusting that I could, indeed, help Minnie."

The doctor stayed for breakfast. He was from Ireland. Soft and gentle, he spoke of his homeland and his family.

The pancakes Essie cooked were exactly as her mother had taught her—a little drop or two of vanilla for sweetness. Had she not brought several boxes of food, they would have had no pancakes, nor the bacon from Lon Terry's Tamworth hogs.

The two young boys glanced sideways at Dr. Grey. A white woman came to their house and now a white man sat at their kitchen table. The white woman had cooked pancakes, had provided a jug of syrup and as much bacon as they could eat. Somehow, despite the big grin on their faces, they were able to chew and swallow what they thought was food from heaven.

"I bet you boys are glad it's Saturday. No school." Dr. Grey stirred his coffee.

"Uh, huh. We do likes Saturdays, for sure." Pitch spread butter on a hot pancake. "Got to go to church and Sunday school tomorrow."

"Where is that?"

"Oh, down the road. The Beulah Hill church. Our mama went there 'fore she died," said Pitch. "I asked Jesus to fix my foot when I was three years old, and I's still waitin' for him to give me a new foot." He licked the syrup from the corner of his mouth.

"A new foot?" asked Dr. Grey. "What's wrong with your foot?" He looked down under the table at Pitch's feet and saw immediately the deformed club foot.

Pitch laid his fork in his plate and kicked out his club foot. "See here, Mr. Doctor. My mama said when I was born, my foot got mixed up with another baby's foot and I got the wrong foot."

"I can see that, Pitch. Can you stand up and walk over to the front door for me?" Dr. Grey studied the boy as he walked; a see-saw walk, up and down, as his body tried to compensate for its deformity. "Come here and sit in your chair." Pitch did as he was told, grabbing another bite of pancake as he did so.

Dr. Grey lifted the boy's foot and pushed up his pant leg, exposing the deformed foot. He rubbed along the bone in his calf, grasped the foot and maneuvered it as far as it would go to the right and then to the left. He pulled on Pitch's toes and the boy laughed. The doctor rubbed the bottom of the small foot. "Let me have your other foot, young man." Pitch lifted his right leg and Dr. Grey held both legs together and studied them carefully. He noted the deformed leg was approximately two inches shorter than his right leg.

"Well, now, Pitch, are you still waiting for Jesus to bring you a new foot?" Dr. Grey gave Pitch a serious look, a meaningful look, a look full of compassion.

Pitch squinted his eyes at the doctor. Unsmiling and in an almost whisper, he said, "I talk to Jesus 'bout it ever' day."

"Is that right?" Dr. Grey pulled down the boy's pant leg and returned his foot to the floor. "Well, tell you what, young man. I reckon I'll talk to Jesus about it, too." Robert Grey stood and gathered his things.

In the kitchen, Essie removed the iron skillet from the hot stove and placed it in the warmer. Pancakes lined a plate. "More pancakes if you boys are still hungry." She poured another cup of coffee and walked with Dr. Grey to the front door. "I'll come into town in a bit to fill that prescription and buy some aspirin. I don't know where Minnie's father is—maybe in the barn. Not sure. I will assume Minnie will sleep and the boys will keep an eye on her until I get back."

The back door swung open, slamming into the wall. Ollie Pryor stepped inside, a snarl running across his mouth. "Well, now, looks like the white people done took over my house. I'm telling you to leave 'fore I git a two by four after you." Ollie's big hands hung by his side, his wide shoulders seemed made of oak logs. If he chose, with one swing of a two by four, he could send both the doctor and Essie to their graves.

The morning light streamed through the window and caught Essie's face. Her eyes never moved from the man who towered above them all and who, it seemed at any moment, would pounce upon them, fists swinging. Essie, in a voice soft but impassioned, said. "Mr. Pryor, your dislike of white people may be well-founded. However, it is a mystery to me why you would hold so much hate for a doctor who just saved your daughter's life."

Essie walked over to the stove and removed the iron skillet from the warmer. "Come on, Mr. Pryor, you want to beat up on a white woman, come and get me." Essie raised the skillet and shook it. "Let's get all that hate outta you."

Ollie jerked back, his mouth open to speak. His hands balled into fists as hard as bricks. Like a bull in a ring, he nostrils flared, and he snorted air in hot anger. "I ain't never had no fight with an iron skillet before." He stepped forward.

From the kitchen table, Pitch leapt out of his chair and, with his one-sided gallop, ran to Essie's side. "Daddy, you cain't hurt this white woman. She be our friend." Pitch's thin body trembled. "She done made me and Orland some pancakes just like mama used to." The young boy looked up at Essie. "Miss Essie, don't hurt my daddy with that frying pan."

The big black man's body began to crumble, mounding into a deep hurt, his hard fists melting. He stared at the floor and spoke through broken words. "It's all right, Pitch. I'm… I'm just wantin' to keep us together since your mama died. Minnie done gone away. Now, she's sick." He cleared his throat and looked at Essie. "Things is just so hard. And… and I'm so tired."

Essie slowly placed the iron skillet on top of the wood stove. How could she ever know the pain the sharecropper widower had suffered, his face creased with a deep sadness that had drained his spirit. He hung his head, eyes closed.

Pitch walked to his daddy's side. "They's some pancakes, daddy."

Ollie opened his eyes and placed his hand on Pitch's shoulder. With a cracked voice, he spoke to the room, a humbleness covering each word. "Forgive my harshness and anger. I am not the man you see here." He stumbled. "I… I just want to feed my children and keep us together as a family. That's a very hard thing for me to do since… since my wife… died."

Across the room Dr. Grey stepped toward Ollie. "Mr. Pryor, you're not alone." He glanced at Essie. "Miss Donnelly and I will help in any way we can. The important thing right now is to ensure Minnie recovers and gets her strength back."

Essie nodded. "That's true, Mr. Pryor. We're not here as *white* people. We're here as friends. Dr. Grey is here as someone whose job it is to help someone get well. I'm here to do whatever I can do to make things a little easier for you and your family."

Little Orland walked over to his daddy. "Daddy, if'n you don't eat those pancakes, I will." His face turned upward and his eyes glistened. "They is so good, daddy."

Ollie Pryor pulled his son next to him with his large farm hands. "Let's sit down, son. We'll eat together."

Essie picked up the warm platter from the stove top and placed it on the table. Pancakes dripped with butter and syrup and ran into the thick sliced bacon. "Here you go." She reached over and touched Ollie's shoulder. "Things will be fine."

Outside, the crisp March air swept across the porch and through the trees that bordered the fields, shaking the small wooden house. Two scrawny dogs lay in a hole in the sunlight and slept, their hair glistening from the sun's rays. The yard rooster watched Dr. Grey and Essie as they stepped from the porch and walked across the dirt yard. Essie eyed his sharp spurs again and knew at some point she'd have to shoo him away from her. Even now, he pranced around them, pretending he wasn't looking at them. But he was. His feathers were quite ragged; he was a fighting rooster, for sure.

"I'll go by the drug store and leave the two prescriptions for Minnie. She'll need to be watched carefully." Dr. Grey pulled his coat lapels together and stamped his feet. His nose was red, and his eyes watered from the cold.

Essie nodded. "I'll check on Minnie before I go."

"Ed Cromartie will fix you up." Dr. Grey placed his hand on the door handle of his car. "I'll be back tomorrow to see Minnie."

"Dr. Grey, I'm wondering how long Minnie will need to recover." Essie seemed anxious, fiddled with her coat buttons and bit her lower lip.

"At least a week. She's quite weakened from that fever. Perhaps with medication and bed rest, she'll be up and around in five or six days."

"A week!" Essie shook her head. "Are you sure?"

Dr. Grey reached in his pocket and pulled out a pair of gloves. "What's the matter? Is that a problem for you?"

Essie sighed and nodded. "Not really. Just… just I have somewhere to go."

"Where do you have to go?" There was concern in Dr. Grey's voice.

"Thomasville."

Dr. Grey studied the frown on Essie's face. "What's going on in Thomasville that can't wait? Minnie will not do well without someone to care for her."

Essie jerked her head up and glared at him, her cheeks flushing. "Thomasville can wait and it's none of your damn business what I'm doing over there." She turned and stomped up the porch steps and into the house.

As quick as a bolt of lightning, Essie had become the hard woman, the woman everyone shied away from, the one who had slung manure at lazy farmworkers, the one who had chased a pompous yankee off their land, the one who rode their mule Woodrow through the church doors on Sunday morning and proclaimed the preacher a thief, a man who stole the tithes of hard-working farmers and bought a new Cadillac every year.

Better not anyone get in the way of her quest to find Jewell's child, Essie's niece, and the only thread of the Donnelly family that remained. All she had was Minnie to lead her to the obscure plantation that held the secrets of a girl-child who was taken from Jewell and given away to strangers like a bushel of beans. Essie'd find those baby thiefs and then the iron-hard woman would confront them with a vengeance they'd never seen before.

If she had to nurse Minnie back to health before she began her search, she'd do it. If she had to knock Ollie Pryor on the head with an iron skillet to get him to let Minnie-girl go, she'd do it. There was no stopping Essie Donnelly. *She was a hard woman.*

Rob Grey lingered a moment by his car. The night had been long, and his bones ached, not only from the cold but also from fatigue. He had watched Essie stomp heavily across the yard and into the house. He smiled and thought of Scarlett O'Hara. During the past eight hours, he had decided Essie Donnelly was no ordinary woman. He also decided she was the kind of woman he'd been looking for.

CHAPTER TWENTY

Minnie slept most of the morning, waking only to drink water and sip warm broth. For lunch, Essie made soup from Mason jars filled with vegetables from last summer. She had seasoned it with bacon and onions, but wished she had a few pieces of fresh chicken. Some okra would be good, too.

After giving instructions to Pitch and Orland on keeping Minnie supplied with fresh water, Essie pulled the old Pontiac from beneath a big oak tree and steered out onto the Tallakos road. She passed the Beulah Hill church, where Pitch had told her the bell in the steeple rang every Sunday morning. She made a mental note to listen for the chimes the next morning, which would be Sunday.

It was sixteen miles to Boston. She had traveled the same roads at 3:00 a.m. that morning, taking the curves at dangerous speeds, barely stopping for stop signs, swerving back and forth across the red clay and pushing the old Pontiac unmercifully, its motor grinding noisily. Her daddy would not be pleased.

Boston was a lovely Georgia town, reminiscent of days gone by when automobiles were rare, folks traveling by horse and wagons pulled by mules. Its serenity came from the slow pace of life, a gentle change of seasons where most everything centered on the crops in the fields. Planting time, harvesting time and winter, a time when wood piles were replenished and fireplaces glowed with hot embers.

Boston evolved from a stage coach stop back in the 1800's, often referred to as Parramore's. It was the favorite watering hole for Thomas M. Boston, a wealthy man from the North. As time went by, Mr.

Boston's visits were so frequent that the stagecoach stop became a quaint small town, a southern town that bespoke of church on Sundays, fried okra and collards, barn dances and, best of all, pies made from the many pecan trees scattered proudly in the clay soil of Thomas County, as well as nearby Brooks County.

Essie passed Sam Bruce's grocery on Main Street, saw the green John Deere sign, J. C. Pittman's appliance store and John Burney's hardware. She turned the corner off Main Street and headed east where Warmack's Grocery and Seafood Store was busy with customers buying his fresh seafood. Mr. Warmack traveled weekly to the Florida gulf coast to buy fish, shrimp and sometime oysters. His old converted school bus traveled the countryside in Boston's surrounding counties delivering groceries to the elderly as well as those who had no means of transportation.

Essie pulled up at the Texaco station at the corner of Main Street and U. S. 84 where Bud Jones changed a customer's tire. She rolled down her window. "Hello, there. I'm looking for someone to replace the shocks on this old car. Can you do that? Maybe fix the heater, too."

Bud Jones spun the lug wrench and locked down the nuts on the tire. He looked up. "Yes, mam. You can bring your car by on Monday and I'll take a look at it."

"What time?" Essie smiled at the customer who stood by watching Bud. Across the asphalt, two men played checkers in the midday sun, their flannel shirt sleeves rolled to their elbows.

"Oh, 'round noon would be good." Bud walked around to the other side of the car. The conversation was over.

Essie backed up the Pontiac and swung out on Main Street and drove to the Cromartie Drug Store, where she found Ed Cromartie in his white pharmacy jacket amongst a myriad of paraphernalia associated with dispensing medicine. He was an older man, gray-headed, his eyes wrapped with wire spectacles. His face was friendly, grandfatherly with a warm smile.

"Well, hello," he said. "Don't believe I know you, young lady." He grinned at Essie, then continued counting pills into a tray. She noticed his eyebrows formed perfect half-moons over his eyes.

"Hello to you," replied Essie. "I'm Essie Donnelly, but I'm not from around here."

"That so?" Mr. Cromartie didn't look at her, concentrating on his work. "Where you from, if I may ask?"

"Oh, south of here. In Florida. Madison County."

"That right?" Ed stopped what he was doing and looked up. He appeared thoughtful. "Donnelly? You that woman who shot that escaped prisoner? I remember reading it in the newspaper last summer. Don't forget a name."

The hard Essie came to the surface. "Don't believe that has anything to do with filling my prescriptions, does it?" She held his eyes with her own, her chin lifting slightly. She felt a thud in her chest. She'd be damned if she'd discuss something as malicious as a murder with a stranger.

Ed's face softened while his blue eyes studied Essie. "I'm terribly sorry. You're right—it's none of my business, for sure." He turned away from her and picked up a small brown bag. "Dr. Rob had these prescriptions filled an hour ago. Paid for them, too. Said a Miss Donnelly would be by to pick them up." He reached across the counter and held out the bag for Essie.

Essie dropped her gaze from the druggist's soft blue eyes to the brown bag. "Thank you for taking care of this so quickly. That was kind of you."

She hesitated. "Sorry for being so curt with you. I'm… I'm trying to put that all behind me." She left the counter, but looked back over her shoulder. "That was my sister who murdered the convict." Essie walked on a few steps, then turned around and faced Mr. Cromartie. "It was self-defense."

Essie rounded the corner from Main Street and passed Doc Davis' ice cream parlor, a small brick-fronted building, worn but solid, like Boston, like the people who lived there. She heard someone call her name and turned around. Robert Grey hurried toward her, the wind rustling his dark hair, a smile running across his face as he grabbed her arm. "Come with me to get some of Doc Davis' ice cream. It's the best you'll ever eat." He tugged her along.

Essie's heart stirred. When had she ever been whisked along by such a handsome man, a cool March breeze under a bright sun covering them as though they were lovers, blown together in a serendipitous manner that caused Essie to gasp. *Ice cream? He wanted to buy the farm girl ice cream.*

Her feet half-stumbled across the store's threshold as Dr. Grey pulled her inside. She caught her breath and held tightly to the small brown paper bag of prescriptions. "I… I need to get back to the farm. Minnie's medicine."

Rob Grey looked at his watch. "Minnie won't need another dose until 2:00 o'clock—every six hours." He grinned at her. "It's only noon." He winked at her. "Just the right time for ice cream." He glanced up at Doc Davis' wooden sign and read the listed ice cream flavors.

His head whipped back to Essie. "I'm thinking butter pecan. That right?"

Essie blinked. "Yes… yes, my favorite."

Rob guided Essie to a small metal table and pulled out a chair. "Single or double scoop?"

Essie smelled his after-shave and instantly saw he was clean shaven. "Double scoop." She sat down and her eyes followed the tall doctor as he walked away, a pair of bluejeans on his lanky legs, a navy blue wool sweater over a white collared shirt. *Was this the man who had so diligently examined a patient who was near death, diagnosed her illness, and administered medicine with the greatest precision? No, he was a cocky, handsome man who loved a bourbon in the evening, teared up at beautiful sunsets and dearly loved fried chicken livers. And it seemed he relished ice cream.*

The doctor held two double scoop ice cream cones as he walked across the small parlor and sat at the table. "Here you go."

Essie took the cone and noticed the doctor's hands. They weren't farm hands, no roughness, no calluses. Just smooth and long-fingered. She saw a college ring on his finger. Reading upside down, she saw the words *Virginia Tech.* His fingernails were short and groomed, clean. His hands had not been milking cows, shoveling manure or hoeing corn.

Rob wrapped a napkin around the bottom of his cone, licking his finger as a drop of ice cream smeared across it. "Temperature's dropping again tonight. Please don't knock on my door again at 3:00 in the morning." He leaned back and looked at her.

"Please be dressed if I do." Essie Donnelly liked to banter, liked to keep a step ahead of someone, especially if it was a man. "When will Dr. Lundy return?"

"Oh, I'm thinking as long as those trout are biting he'll take a few extra days. Doesn't matter to me. I like this little town."

"Seems friendly. Nice folks." Essie wiped her mouth. "Know anybody at the bank? I need to handle some finances."

"Yep. Those folks at the Jarrett Bank will fix you up. See Ferris Jarret." Rob hesitated. "On second thought, see Bill Davis over at the Peoples Bank. Tell him I sent you. Treated him for a sinus infection last week."

Essie nodded. "You think they'd mind if I used their telephone?" She promised Sam she would call him once she arrived in Boston. Here she was, a day later, sitting with a man who had bought her ice cream.

Sam. Faithful Sam. He believed she'd never find Jewell's baby. After all, Essie had no information to aid in her search. All she had was a young black girl who said Jewell's picture looked identical to a girl she had seen at a plantation in Thomasville. *What plantation?* She couldn't remember. How could she remember from one or two summers ago?

Essie had brought Jewell's picture with her. Tonight, she would pull it out and show it to Minnie again.

Dr. Grey stuffed the last of his cone in his mouth and patted a napkin across his chin. "Oh, yes. I'm sure there's a telephone you can use. Or, if you like, you can come over to Dr. Lundy's office and use his."

Essie stood and clasped the medicine bag to her chest. "That's okay. I'll use the bank's telephone. You're very kind and thank you for the ice cream."

"I might come out and check on Minnie later if everything's quiet around here." He pushed the door open for Essie and they stood together and once more she caught a brief scent of his after-shave.

Essie gave a little smile and headed for the Pontiac. From her left, the noise of a truck caught her attention. The truck was familiar. Beat up, old and rusted, the front bumper askew, the red color dull and faded like an old barn. The man driving was also familiar; he had been at the store with the sign that read "whites only."

CHAPTER TWENTY-ONE

At the Peoples Bank, Bill Davis sat in his office reading a newspaper. The noon-day sun streamed through his windows, causing a glare across the top of his bald head. He looked up when he heard the bank's doors open. When Essie looked his way, he waved.

Bustling through his office door, he walked toward Essie, his hand extended. "Hello. Let me introduce myself. I'm Bill Davis, the bank's owner. What can we do for you today?" He pumped Essie's hand and motioned her to his office.

"Thank you," Essie said. "I'm Essie Donnelly from Madison County, Florida." She sat in a chair across from the dapper man and tried to remember if the Community Bank of Madison County was as friendly as the Boston bank. "Although I don't have an account here, I'd like to cash a check. I have proper identification." She glanced at his telephone. "I would also like to use a telephone here at the bank, if that's possible."

"Madison County? Why, I'm quite familiar with your county. Have friends there. You said your name was Donnelly?" He dipped his chin and waited for her reply. His voice was deep, his words slow and coated with a muddy slag that drew his words into more than the syllables that were intended.

Essie took a breath. "Yes. Donnelly."

It was at that moment that Essie saw the bank owner begin to fidget, pick up a pencil and nervously tap it on his desk. His eyes flitted from her to the telephone, to the street outside his window and then back to the tapping pencil.

He pushed his words out. "You wouldn't happen to be the Donnelly woman who shot and killed an escaped prison inmate down that way, are you?" He was wide-eyed and anticipating Essie's answer. He jabbered further. "That was a big story up this way. Newspaper full of pictures." He leaned back in his large leather chair and rocked slightly. Waiting.

And here it came. Essie Donnelly's hard edge, the edge that for evermore preceded her penchant for a fight. Oh, if the bank owner only knew, he would never have said the word *murder.* Would not have invaded Essie Donnelly's fervent protection of her sister and her sister's life.

Essie stilled and felt the familiar emotions. Her hurt was as deep as the Withlacoochee River, her sorrow as tender and fragile as hummingbird wings. And here it was. As evenly and staccato as a dead woman. "Mr. Davis, your interest in a murder down in Madison County amuses me. I find your concern over a prison inmate who assaulted two genteel, helpless women to be misguided. What is it you'd like to know? Where the bullet entered the scrawny bastard who waved a butcher knife at my sister and me?"

Essie stood and hovered over the bank president's desk. "Why, one bullet shot off the man's ear and the other one went straight through his heart. The bloody ear ended up on the kitchen ceiling and we didn't find it for weeks. When I found it, I fed it to the chickens." She took a breath, slowly, never taking her eyes off Mr. Davis. "Now, tell me, what does your bank have to do with an ear being fed to the chickens?"

Essie turned on her heel and sauntered through the double doors of the bank, never looking back. She headed for the Jarrett Bank, still grasping the brown paper bag holding Minnie's prescriptions. She decided if the owner of the Jarrett Bank said as much as one word about the murder of a prison inmate down in Madison County, she would most certainly pull her daddy's .38.

The Jarrett Bank was as friendly as the People's Bank, the single teller nodding to her as she walked across the small lobby. The bank closed at 1:00 on Saturday and Essie saw signs of closing down the receptionist's desk and the three small offices on the edge of the lobby. The bank president's office was dark, the door closed, the blinds pulled.

"Yes, mam. How can I help you?" The teller was a thin man, ruddy-faced, with a long nose that almost reached his wide lips. His eyes bulged with large blue eyes that seemed full of anticipation. He licked his lips and waited.

Essie told him the same thing she told the Peoples Bank. "Good morning. I'm visiting Boston for a few days and would like to cash a check. I have proper identification."

"Why, of course. Just write it out and let me see your identification."

Essie did as she was told, writing her signature with a flourish and pushing the check across the polished wooden counter. She pulled her driver's license from her handbag and laid it in front of the young man. She glanced at the teller's name, which was imprinted on a small piece of wood leaning on the counter. *Bob Smith.*

Mr. Smith efficiently counted out seventy-five dollars into Essie's waiting hand. "Here you go, Miss Donnelly."

"Thank you." She gave him a half-smile. "By the way, I need to make a long distance call, collect, of course. Do you have a telephone I can use?" Her brown eyes swept the area behind Mr. Smith and rested on a telephone on a desk lining the back wall.

"Why, sure." Bob stepped over to the desk, picked up the phone and placed it on the counter in front of Essie, its long cord stretching eight feet or so.

"Appreciate it." Essie dialed the operator and gave her the information for Sam's office telephone. When Sam answered, the operator spoke: Long-distance, collect call from Essie Donnelly. Will you accept the charges?"

"Yes, mam." Sam's voice was anxious. "Yes, mam, I sure will."

"Hello, Sam." Essie grasped the telephone closer. She heard his breathing. "I've arrived safely in Boston, but Minnie became quite ill—from a spider bite, I believe. I had to fetch a doctor and he was able to get her fever down and give her medication. Looks like I'll be here in Boston for another week."

"Essie! I knew this adventure of yours would become complicated."

The irritation in Sam's voice carried over the telephone line and settled in a big heap in front of Essie. "Please, Sam. This is something I must do. We've already talked about it."

"I know. I know. I'm just so concerned that you'll find no trace of

Jewell's child and you'll come home brokenhearted. How could you possibly think a young black girl who works in plantations all over Thomas County could lead you to the child? You're basing all your decisions on Minnie's recollections of a girl she *thinks* looks like Jewell. How can you place any credibility in that information?" The attorney's perspicacious nature was flying high.

Essie turned her back to Bob Smith and dipped her chin into the telephone receiver. "Sam, my heart is already broken. I lost my precious sister and if there's any chance that girl is her daughter and she's out there for me to find, I'm gonna find her. That's all there is to it."

Sam sighed. "I guess I'm being the lawyer that I am, needing more proof, more evidence that this may be Jewell's daughter. I just... I just think it's a wild goose chase and you're gonna to be very disappointed in the end and it will all be for nothing."

Sam. Black and white Sam. No gray areas. Just the facts. No guessing, no maybes, no pie in the sky. He was solid, his mind a steel trap, with no room for whims. And he thought Essie was pursuing a whim.

"Tell you what, Essie. I think I'll drive to Boston tomorrow. Where's that farm located? Is it the Pryor farm?"

Essie raised her voice. "No, Sam! There's no need for you to do that. I'm fine and certainly capable of taking care of myself."

Sam chuckled. "Essie, everybody in Madison County knows you're able to care for yourself. That's not the problem. I'm worried about your emotions. You're still not over Jewell's death. You've been grieving since last July. You practically skipped Christmas. You holed up at your daddy's fish camp for four months. Hadn't been for DooRay, no telling what..."

"Stop it, Sam. You've got your mom and dad, your brothers Bill and Mike and all those damn Washington cousins and uncles and aunts. Who have I got?? I've got DooRay and Murphy, that damn one-eared goat. Do you really think I'd ignore the chance that I could find Jewell's child?"

She slammed the receiver down and grabbed the bag of prescriptions. "Thank you," she bellowed at Bob Smith as she turned and left the bank.

CHAPTER TWENTY-TWO

At 1:00, Essie turned onto Green Street, then U. S. 33 toward Barwick. The Pontiac easily rounded a bend on Hodges road, then curved onto Okapilco Church road to Tallakos. Essie slowed at a cemetery where an unpainted church snuggled in the trees, its steeple soaring proudly into the cold March sky. The tombstones at the cemetery seemed haunting, a calling to a caring heart. She pulled off the highway and steered down the clay ruts leading to the cemetery and turned off the engine.

The sunlight glinted off the chrome of the car and sent spears of light into the darkness of several large oak trees. Had anyone been sitting on a cloud above the cemetery, they would have seen the auburn hair of Essie Donnelly lift in the breeze, seen the soft brown eyes searching the tombstones, seen the lithe frame of the thirty-three year old gracefully walking through the grass and lifting her lovely face to the heavens. She had momentarily left the hard woman behind and had become the tender woman who was born and raised on a farm in Madison County and had lived her life devoted to family.

She walked among the tombstones: *Lizzie Wright, Edward Manning, Frank People, Diamond Christian.* Diamond Christian: an alluring name that captivated her imagination. The tombstone carried only the birth date, perhaps meaning Diamond Christian was still alive. Essie wished she knew more about the enchantment that surrounded the name—almost a *come-hither—there's-more-to-know* feeling consumed her.

As a writer, she found herself taunted by simple seductions of names and places, her imagination coloring each thought with fetching details. Had she been wrong to cancel the book contract with the literary agency and publishing company? Her lifelong desire to write had culminated into a compelling novel—or at least the book publishers thought so. *Watermelon Queen of Madison County* had enticed the editors to proclaim Essie as a *fresh new voice* in the literary world.

From the graveyard, she walked to the church, and, as she stood in front of it, she could almost hear the choir, the resounding words of the preacher's sermon echoing out into the church yard and into the heavens.

Essie felt herself falter, a humbling that tightened her chest and caused her to gasp for air. In the next moment, she fell to her knees and began sobbing into the cold Georgia clay. *Please, God, let me find Jewell's child.*

Chapter Twenty-Three

At the Pryor farm, smoke puffed through the chimney and caught the cold late winter wind. Bound together, they lifted into the cloudless sky and rushed east. The temperatures had barely climbed above freezing and caused Essie to shudder as she hurried across the yard and up the wooden steps. To her left, a dark blue Chevrolet sat near the well house, its rear end smeared with Georgia clay. The windshield had a crack in it that ran across the passenger side of the glass. The radio antenna pointed up, the furry tail of a squirrel dangling in the breeze at the end of it.

Inside, Pitch and Orland sat at the kitchen table studying their Sunday school lessons. Across the room, on the floral couch, a woman dressed in bright purple stared slit-eyed at Essie, her mouth straight across like a fat clothespin, an unsmiling rectangle.

Pitch and Orland dared not breathe, their eyes concentrating on their study books. A Bible lay opened between them, a faded red bookmarker stretching down the pages. The only sound in the room was an occasional snap from the burning wood in the fireplace.

"Hello, boys. Minnie okay?" Essie pulled off her coat and draped it across the back of a chair. She took a few steps across the room, to the floral couch, to the statue of a woman who was as black as a tar bucket. The smile on Essie's lips vanished when the woman stood, her head almost touching the ceiling, her massive arms folded across her chest.

"Don't nobody talk to those chilluns while they's studying God's word." Her words flew around the room like boomerangs, echoing and rattling the windows. "And that means you, white woman!"

Essie's body flinched. The purple suit covered yards of body flesh, topped with a feathered purple hat that balanced itself on a large head, a head that swiveled back and forth between Essie and the boys.

"My name is Essie, not *white* woman," said Essie, the hardness seeping into her body and mind. "Are you a family member?" She studied the woman's face, the large wart on her chin and felt her legs twitch in a prelude to flight.

The woman puffed herself up and the slit-eyes took in every inch of Essie. "My name is Sister Areba Wright and those chilluns are my God-chillens. I guess you'd say I'm family." She smacked her lips and continued staring at Essie.

Essie also puffed herself up. "Well, Sister Areba, it would please me greatly to make you a nice, hot cup of tea."

Sister Areba stilled, the clothespin mouth wavering somewhat. Her voice boomed once more. "I'd be pleased to have a cup of your tea. Sugar and cream." She sat her huge frame back down on the couch, the purple color of her clothing clashing wildly with the orange and red flowers of the couch fabric.

It wasn't long before Essie served Sister Areba tea, just like she wanted it. The cup and saucer were both chipped and cracked, but the tiny roses on the teacups were pretty and made up for the China's imperfections.

The woman, a thin cream mustache along her upper lip, leaned forward. "Well, now, white woman. You been here taking care of these boys as well as their sister, I hear. Ollie tells me you done a real good job of nursing. 'course, I hear a real doctor was here doin' most of the work." Sister Areba sipped her tea, her large fingers unable to hold the dainty cup handle.

"Minnie is doing much better. Dr. Grey from Boston was able to reduce her fever." Essie glanced at the boys. "You boys been looking after Minnie?"

Pitch looked up from his book. "Yes, mam. She drink real good. She sleep, too."

The boys' Godmother hissed. "Study!" The stern face turned to Essie.

"Ollie tells me you done cooked in his house. Done poked wood in that cookstove all morning long. Didn't know no white woman knowed how to cook on a wood stove. Them boys show you how?" Sister Areba stared lazily at Essie and nodded slightly, the wart on her chin a beacon of surliness.

In her most kind voice, Essie replied, replacing her teacup in the saucer. "Forgive my ignorance, Sister Areba, but I fail to understand the difference between me and you. Just because I'm a white woman doesn't mean I'm unskilled when it comes to a wood stove." She paused. "Nor would the fact that you're black cause me to think you don't know how to set a fine table."

At that moment, a loud pop from the fireplace filled the room. At the kitchen table, both boys jumped, their eyes rounding into surprise. Across the room Sister Areba's large chest swelled, pulling air into her lungs, an obvious preparation for the ominous retaliation that would soon follow. What the huge woman deemed as a suitable retort would perhaps be in the form of a thrown teacup.

Across from her, Essie did not move. Her eyes were steady. Had she just insulted the woman?

Sister Areba's words came slithering out like a poisonous snake. Barely audible, they struck Essie like sharp fangs. "You come to my house tomorrow after church. I show you my fine table. I show you my fine wood stove." The black woman stood and leaned over Essie, her face only inches away. "And I show you this black woman can cook a huner'd times better than any white woman."

She straightened herself and handed the teacup and saucer to Essie. "I'll be goin' now". She looked over to the kitchen table. "You boys be ready at 9:00 sharp in the morning. Make sure you know your lesson."

Both boys nodded and said "Yes, mam."

Essie walked to the door and opened it. "Thank you for your visit, Sister Areba."

The big woman stopped at the door and looked down at Essie. "We black folks is real kind folks. Even to white peoples."

Chapter Twenty-Four

Minnie's room lay in a cool darkness, no fireplace heat, the window covered with a thick muslin cloth. Essie tiptoed to her bedside and looked down at the sleeping young woman. Minnie's face was peaceful, her breathing soft. Essie reached out and rubbed her cheek. "Hello, my friend," she whispered.

Minnie's eyes opened and she smiled at Essie. "I'm glad you're here, Miss Essie."

"I wouldn't be any place else." The skin on Minnie's face was cool. No fever present. Dr. Grey would be pleased.

"I'd like to sit up. My back's hurting. Kinda sore from all this lying down, I guess."

"Yes, let's get you sitting up. I've got some medicine for you. Dr. Grey said to take it at 2:00 o'clock."

Essie reached down and placed her hands and arms around Minnie's shoulders. Together, they worked her into a sitting position. "Oh, it feels good to sit up."

"Good. Are you hungry?" Essie smoothed the covers and sat on the edge of the bed.

"I could eat a bite, for sure. Some hot tea, too." Minnie smiled. "I had a dream. I dreamed we done found your niece and she was so happy to see you. She knowed you would come some day. Somebody from her real family."

"A dream? Where were we in the dream? Thomasville?"

Minnie scrunched up her face. "Cain't say for sure. I jus' 'member her face. How happy she was. She squeezed you so hard." Minnie paused and looked across the room, thinking. "And roses. I 'member lots and lots of roses. They was everywhere. All colors. Yellow, pink, red, white and even some lavender ones. In my dream, I started laughing 'cause we all fell into a big pile of roses. They smelled so good. Like candy."

The tears in Essie's eyes spilled over and ran down her cheeks. "Minnie, was it just the three of us in that dream?"

"I 'member other peoples, but I didn't see their faces real clear."

The two women sat quietly, the wind rattling the window. They heard the yard rooster crow. From far off, a cow bellowed. Essie left the bedside and pulled back the curtain, mid-afternoon sunlight falling across the bed. "Let's get that medicine in you. I'll be right back."

Essie pulled a clean Mason jar from the shelf above the stove and walked out onto the back porch. She lifted the pump handle and began priming it. In a moment, cold clear water spewed out and into the jar.

From behind her, Essie heard a ruckus, a loud shuffling of feet and then a stab into her leg. The yard rooster had caught her, blindsided her with his knife-sharp spurs. She kicked wildly, catching him in the breast, but he came again, turning sideways and lifting his body in the air and aiming for her thigh. He found his target and Essie felt sharp pain as his spur sliced her skin. Blood oozed through her pants on her upper thigh as well as her calf.

She threw the Mason jar and grabbed the broom leaning on the wall of the porch. She swung it wildly, missing him each time. The rooster flew off the porch and into the yard, his feet lifting and prancing in the dirt. He moved in circles, cocking his head and giving short squawks that seemed to say *I am king of this yard.*

Next time, rooster. Next time. Essie limped into the house. "Boys, I need your help. Get me a pair of scissors." She fell into a kitchen chair, her heart beating wildly. "Get a few rags, too."

Pain ran up and down her leg, while blood pumped through the cuts on her leg. Feeling weak, she placed her head on the table. She heard Pitch and Orland scrambling around in the kitchen. "Yes, mam. We's comin', Miss Essie."

A knock at the door went unanswered. Essie didn't look when she heard footsteps cross the room. She didn't move when she heard Dr. Grey's voice. "Miss Donnelly, it seems you may require my services." Essie didn't answer. She had fainted, her body listless, her mouth open.

"Pitch! Orland! What's happened here?"

Pitch limped quickly across the room carrying a pair of scissors and a few rags. "We reckon that rooster done got Miss Essie." The boy's voice trembled as tears filled his eyes.

Rob Grey lifted Essie and carried her to the couch. "Take one of those rags out to the hand pump and run some water on it. Hurry. And watch out for that rooster."

Pitch did as he was told while the doctor rubbed Essie's face and spoke to her. "Essie, come on now. Everything's gonna to be okay." He turned to Orland, who stood cowering by the wood stove. "Orland, run out to my car and bring in that black bag in the back seat. If you see that rooster, you run lickity split back into the house. You hear?"

Orland came alive and said, "Yes, sir. I can do that for the doctor." He ran to the front door and into the yard. In a flash, he was back and carrying the medicine bag.

"Thank you, young man. You did a good job." The back door slammed and Pitch walk-hopped to the couch carrying a wet rag. "Thank you, Pitch."

Dr. Grey snapped an ammonia capsule and passed it quickly under Essie's nose. Then, he dabbed her cheeks with the cold rag. "Here you go, lass. Let's open those big brown eyes of yours."

Essie murmured, "Gonna shoot that rooster." She opened her eyes and saw a smiling Dr. Grey. "What are you doing here?" She tried to sit up.

"Hold on, Essie. You fainted. Let's take things slow. Looks like that rooster attacked you pretty good."

"A rooster has never made me faint before." Essie seemed confused.

Dr. Grey motioned for the scissors. "Well, if you think about it, you've had no sleep and I don't recall you eating any breakfast this morning. I only remember a butter pecan ice cream cone around noon." He leaned over and began cutting Essie's pant legs. "Let's take a look at these wounds. From the amount of blood, I'm thinking we've got some mending to do."

The doctor ran the scissors up the entire length of fabric, exposing a nasty deep hole in Essie's thigh. He lifted her left leg and turned it enough to see the wound on her calf. "Hmmmmm. Both these wounds are significant."

The doctor opened his bag. "You boys check on your sister for a while. I've got some work to do."

Dr. Grey pulled out a syringe and other medical paraphernalia. The smell of alcohol filled the room. Cotton balls soaked in blood fell to the floor. He filled the syringe with a numbing medication. He had some sewing to do.

"Ouch!" Essie cried. "What are you doing?" Her face contorted with pain.

"Stopping the bleeding. Sewing up your leg." He smiled at her. "Saving your life."

Essie's eyes softened as she watched Dr. Grey's gentle hands cleanse the wound. She again smelled the warm fragrance of his Bay Rum aftershave when he moved closer to her and began to cut her entire pant leg off. She saw him reach for the syringe, moving his shoulder where she couldn't watch him. She felt the needle prick and closed her eyes.

The good doctor hummed as he worked, a song she recognized. Patti Page's *Old Cape Cod.* Essie's mind drifted. *If you're fond of sand dunes and salty air, quaint little villages here and there, you're sure to fall in love with old Cape Cod.*

Essie awoke with a start. Across the room at the kitchen table, Dr. Grey sat with Pitch and Orland. Their voices were soft, but she heard their words as well as frequent laughter.

"What did you do with that pig, Dr. Rob?" Orland's young voice was filled with wonder.

"Well, first I collected my prize. After all, catching a greased pig takes a lot of skill. I chased him for miles. Skinned up both knees, got slapped in the face by blackberry briars, then fell in a creek and scraped my elbow on a rock. Couldn't play softball for a week it hurt so bad."

"What was your prize for catchin' that pig?" Pitch asked.

Rob Grey leaned back in his chair and rubbed his chin in deep thought. Finally, he leaned closer to the boys, and said in a conspiratorial whisper, "A treasure map that showed where gold was buried. I haven't found that gold yet, but I'm still looking."

The boys giggled uncontrollably, their eyes filling with happy tears. In a solemn moment, Pitch spoke softly. "That why you be a doctor, to help little boys who done catch a pig and got all skinned up?"

Orland nodded his head. "That right, Dr. Rob. You done help all little boys. You gone fix Pitch's baby foot?"

"Well, I help everyone I can, but especially little boys who need help." Rob's eyes held Pitch's for a long moment and wondered if he was a doctor who was skilled enough to give the boy the help he needed.

In the cold barn, Ollie Pryor stretched out across the floor of a stall, his breathing deep and regular. He had searched for a run-away sow all day, since daybreak, with no luck. His boots were muddy, sticktights lined his pants. The sow's litter was due any day; the piglets necessary to sell at auction for money to buy seed. Without the sow money, he'd have no crops. No crops meant no food for his family.

CHAPTER TWENTY-FIVE

"Oh, no! Minnie's medicine!" Essie called from the couch. "What time is it?"

Dr. Grey left the kitchen table and hurried to the couch where Essie lay. "No worries. She's had her medicine and is doing fine. It's you I'm worried about."

Essie frowned. "Me? There's no need to worry about me." She tried to sit up and winced with pain.

"Oh, no, you don't. Just stay right where you are." Rob Grey pushed gently on Essie's shoulder. "You've had a fight with a rooster. I had to put eight stitches in you. Four on your thigh and four on your calf."

"Oh, my. So that's what I'm feeling." She leaned back on her pillow and took a deep breath. "Surely, a rooster can't do all that harm."

"fraid so, young lady. Not only do you have two lacerations, but also bruising."

Essie lifted her eyebrows. "I say that rooster is headed for Sunday dinner."

"I'll agree with that." The doctor reached in his bag and pulled out a thermometer. "Let's take that temperature. We need to be on the lookout for any infections."

The reading was normal, a relief to Robert Grey. "How about something to drink? Hot tea would be soothing, don't you think?"

Essie nodded. "Of course. But what about Minnie?"

"My dear lady, Minnie is well taken care of. She's eaten and is resting comfortably. I'm getting ready to fry up some ham for the boys. Make some biscuits and ham gravy." The doctor fluffed Essie's pillow and tucked the blankets around her. "After dinner, we need to get those bloody clothes off you or at least what's left of them. I had to cut off one pant leg to get to the wounds."

Essie lifted the blankets and saw a bare leg. "Those were my favorite pants."

The good doctor busied himself at the wood stove. His expertise at biscuit making was impressive. About a dozen rounds of dough were stuffed in an iron skillet, ready to go in the oven. Another skillet was filled with with ham gravy, salt and peppered to perfection. Pitch and Orland carefully watched the man who could not only make little boys well, but could also make biscuits. Their anticipation of a good meal was evident in their shining eyes.

Beyond the kitchen, the back door swung open and a bedraggled Ollie Pryor stepped inside, a cold wind following him. His eyes were red and weary. A gray stubble of beard ran across his face and covered a grim mouth.

Rob shoved the skillet of biscuits into the oven and called out. "Mr. Pryor, come sit. It's dinner time." He walked to the table and pulled out a chair.

"Hey, daddy," said Pitch. "Where you been?"

Ollie shrugged and walked wearily across the kitchen to the table. He sat, his shoulders slumped. "Cain't find that old sow anywhere. Went through a bog over at the Spires place, clear across the Bickaway plantation and couldn't find her anywhere." He covered his eyes with his hand. "Reckon I'll go out again in the morning."

A thundering sound from the front door filled the small house, a pounding that reverberated around the room so loudly that Pitch and Orland both covered their ears and closed their eyes.

Ollie jumped from the table and scrambled across the room, his boots clomping and sounding like a big fat mule in flight. "What's going on here?" He flung open the door and was nose to nose with Frank People.

Frank People, a neighboring farmer, lazily leaned against the door frame. "I say, Ollie, you missing anything?"

Ollie scowled. "How come you bust down my door like that?" His words roared hotly at Frank. "Ain't right to scare me and my family like that."

"You ain't answered my question yet," said Frank. Frank crossed his arms and waited.

"What you mean am I missing somethin'," Ollie barked. "Git yourself home."

Frank smiled. "I'd be glad to and I'm takin' your big ole sow wif me."

"My sow?" Ollie pushed the scrawny man aside. "You got my sow?" Ollie jumped off the porch and marched to Frank's old rusted truck. Inside the bed of the truck, all four legs tied tightly together, lay the sow Ollie had searched for all day. She raised her head as if to ask *am I in trouble.*

"Well, I'll be. Sure 'nuf is my sow. Where'd you find her?" Ollie grinned at Frank, then slapped him on the back.

"Didn't find her nowhere. She found me. I was in my barn when she come lollygagging in like she own the place. I give her some corn and locked her in a stall. And here she be. Didn't like me tying her up like this. Had to get my son to help."

"I sure do thanks you, Frank. Can you drive your truck over to the pen and we'll unload her? Don't want her to give birth in your truck, now do I?"

"I'd like to sleep with you tonight, Essie." Dr. Grey pulled up a chair and opened his medicine bag.

"Sleep with me?" Essie balked.

Dr. Grey laughed and shook his head. "Wait! That didn't come out right. Let me rephrase that. I'd like to spend the night here and watch over my two patients. I'll make you a pallet in Minnie's room and I'll sleep here on the couch. That way I can monitor your temperature and administer Minnie's medicine." He looked up and smiled. "Keep that fire going, too. Freezing again tonight."

Essie closed her eyes while Dr. Grey changed the bandages on her leg. She felt his fingers rub antibiotic salve into her skin, heard the adhesive tape as it pulled from the spool. Heard the scissors clip the tape and then felt it smoothed across the gauze that covered her wounds. Once again, the doctor hummed as he worked, apparently a long-held habit that comforted not only him, but also his patients.

It was an Elvis Presley song, *Love Me Tender.* Essie was certain if he sang the words, he would have perfect pitch, a sweet tenor that captured a girl's heart. She listened to the melody and, in her head, sang along.

She opened her eyes and, at that moment, he looked at her. A lingering, soft gaze with dark eyes that seemed to penetrate her soul. She couldn't seem to move, spellbound by a tenderness that swept away fragments of her inborn hardness and flung them into a deep dark cavern. For an instant, she sensed an awakening, a minuscule sliver of hope that she could be a different kind of woman. That she could leave behind the hardness that had consumed her all her life.

CHAPTER TWENTY-SIX

Indeed, the temperatures plummeted. The early morning light revealed a heavy frost covering the tin roof of the tumbledown house, as well as the barn and outbuildings. Smoke spiraled up into a bright cloudless sky, where a skein of Canada geese winged north, an occasional honk from the front of the vee, *follow me, follow me*.

A half dozen chickens scratched in the dirt yard, the rooster nearby sounding a yuk, yuk, yuk. Ollie's sow rooted in her pen and grunted loudly, her enormously fat belly almost dragging in the dirt. She would give birth soon.

Inside, the house was warm. The fire had been fed all night by the good doctor. His care of his patients had been exemplary, no fevers, no infections. At the wood stove, he boiled water for grits. Nearby, the iron skillet held more of his divine biscuits, each one waiting for a dollop of blackberry jelly.

Dr. Grey rummaged the shelves for coffee. Even at six feet tall, he had to stretch to scour the top shelf, where at last he found a tin of coffee. Behind him, he heard a shuffling of feet and turned to see Essie warming herself by the fire. "Good moring. How's that leg?"

Essie smiled. She had watched Dr. Grey make her pallet the night before. He had meticulously given Minnie her medicine, put the boys to bed, stoked the fire and stayed up late trading stories with Ollie Pryor.

"Doesn't hurt too much. You must have done some magic on those ugly cuts."

"Ah, you've been a good patient." Dr. Grey pulled out a chair from the table for Essie and sat across from her. "I've got coffee brewing."

Essie's hair tumbled around her shoulders, a tangle here and there. Her cheeks flushed with sleep, her eyes luminous. She wore a soft green robe, its collar made of velvet. He found himself wanting to straighten a lock of hair that had fallen across her forehead. *Perhaps he had meant what he said. Maybe making love to Essie Donnelly was not an impossible dream. There was no doubt he had found her captivating. But first, before even a kiss, he wanted to know her heart.*

"Coffee sounds nice." Essie yawned and looked around the room. "No clocks? Boys need to be ready for Sunday school by nine o'clock. Sister Areba Wright will be picking them up."

"It's 7:30. They have time for a good breakfast. Who is Sister Areba Wright?"

The smell of coffee reached Essie's nose. "Coffee ready?"

"Oh, yes." He jumped from the table and poured their coffee, checked the biscuits and stirred the grits. He ended up at the kitchen table, where he decided he hadn't been this happy in a long, long time.

"Sister Areba. Well, it seems she's Pitch and Orland's Godmother and has a vested interest in their Christian education. I met her yesterday afternoon when I returned from Boston."

"I guess Sister Areba fills in for their dead mother."

"I agree. It is—"

A knock at the door broke the quiet morning. "It's too early for Sister Areba," said Essie.

Dr. Grey picked up his coffee cup and walked to the door. When he opened it, the morning cold swept in, along with a tall, blue eyed stranger. Sam Washington glanced at Essie, then back to the dark-haired man in front of him. Without hesitation, he sauntered over to the kitchen table and found Essie staring at him, eyes wide and no smile. "Good morning, Essie. This a bad time?"

CHAPTER TWENTY-SEVEN

Sam Washington's *modus operandi* was simple: he lived his life exactly as he pleased. Thankfully, his mother and father, as well as life on the farm, had taught him about good character, a trait that made him a stellar attorney in Madison County. He faltered only once: he defied Judge Earp and went to jail for thirty days.

He would have paid the hundred dollar fine, but he was the most stubborn of the Washingtons, even more so than his brothers Bill and Mike. Assigned to a prison work farm for thirty days for contempt of court, he became even more contrary, walking off a road crew, through the woods and ending up at Essie Donnelly's farmhouse.

The depth of his rebellious character soared when he traipsed through the back door of the Donnelly house, wandered up the stairs and stripped naked before plunging into Essie's soft bed.

He never intended to be charged with contempt of court in Judge Earp's courtroom, nor go to the prison farm for thirty days. Most certainly, he did not intend to show his naked butt to Essie Donnelly. The encounter, however, proved to be the catalyst that sent him falling head over heels in love with Miss Donnelly.

"Sam!" said Essie. "I can't believe this!"

Sam backed up a step. "Now, Essie. You're just forty-five miles up the road from Madison. I thought we could drive over to Thomasville for lunch and—"

"No!" Essie huffed. "And, yes. Your timing is awful."

Sam glanced at Dr. Grey. "Obviously."

Rob Grey waved his arm. "My presence here is strictly professional."

Sam quietly studied the tall dark haired man. "Who are you?"

"Dr. Robert Grey. I am Miss Donnelly's physician as well as Minnie Pryor's."

Sam stepped forward, extending his hand. "My name is Sam Washington. Miss… Miss Donnelly's… attorney."

Confused, Sam turned to Essie. "Why do you need a doctor?" His gaze covered her and the green robe she wore. "You seem fine to me."

Essie leaned her head into her hands. "Go home, Sam."

Dr. Grey cleared his throat and spoke with authority. "Miss Donnelly was attacked by the yard rooster. Two lacerations on her left leg. The wounds required four sutures each."

Sam took a quick peek at the makeshift bed on the couch, the pillows and blankets in disarray. "Two small lacerations required you to spend the night?"

A slight smile played along Rob Grey's lips. He found himself humored by this man who had obviously chased after a woman whom he deemed *his.* "The wounds needed bandages changed every…"

"I can… can change bandages. Where are the Band-Aids?" Sam's eyes flitted around the room. "I probably could have sewn up those cuts, too. Sewed many a hound dog's ears." He raised his eyebrows, challenging the good doctor. "You… you can… go now."

Rob's expression became thoughtful. "It's a little more complicated than that."

The prosecuting attorney in Sam Washington shot back: "How's that? Explain." His voice was firm. He was in the courtroom and was expertly grilling the defendant.

"Enough!" Essie jumped from the table. "Sam Washington, you get yourself back to Madison County." She shook her finger only inches from his face, her words low and somewhat menacing. "I'm being well cared for by Dr. Grey. So is Minnie."

Sam watched Essie's finger, an admonishing finger that promised more fury would follow. He took a deep breath. "Yes. I can see you're being well cared for." His glance at Dr. Grey was full of resignation. The lawyer from Madison County would, indeed, go home.

Without so much as a backward glance, Sam covered the few feet to the front door, opened it and trudged down the porch steps. He fired up his new 1957 Bonneville convertible and roared down Tallakos road and headed back to Madison County.

CHAPTER TWENTY-EIGHT

Sam, in blind retreat, had pushed his Star Chief Bonneville down the highway at top speed, barely missing a wandering cow that decided to cross the road at the exact moment his speed hit sixty-five miles an hour. *By God, if Essie wanted him to go back to Madison County, that's exactly where he was going. And he wouldn't be back.*

Obviously, the doctor was a refined man, educated. A blue blood, for sure. His accent had been strange, *a foreigner,* who had never milked a cow, farmed tobacco nor run with his hound dogs chasing a fox in the middle of the night.

Dr. Grey's demeanor had been one of self-assurance, a man who was decisive and confident. A man who had held Essie's bare leg and sutured her wounds. Perhaps Sam could challenge the doctor to a duel, proving a Madison County farm boy could hold his own against an obvious cityslicker.

Sam's court calendar was full. Stan Barnwell's trial for attempted murder had been moved to Suwannee County by Judge Earp and trial would open at 9:00 Monday morning, which was tomorrow. Sheriff Simmie Moore had proclaimed the citizens of Madison County too riled up by the influx of three members of the New York mob to ensure a fair trial.

Jewell, Essie's sister, had shot the mob member's brother, George Barnwell, in self-defense, causing his big brother to invade Madison County with revenge on his mind. Barnwell got more than he bargained for when he underestimated the folks who lived in Madison County. The New Yorker had called them 'nothing but farmers,' a remark that would soon be abated.

Setting fire to the Washington's barn with Sam inside had led to charges of attempted murder. Sam, along with his brothers Bill and Mike, had handled the provocation with the utmost integrity, leaving little doubt that the New York mob was up against some very gutsy 'farmers.' Of course, Mike's .38 and Bill's sawed off shotgun were blatant deterrents when the bad guys came calling.

Sam would give Essie her space. Her quest to find Jewell's child was an honorable one, although not conducive to their relationship. He resolved to let her go, with the hope that she would soon return to Madison County and to him.

Chapter Twenty-Nine

Tranquility returned to the unpainted house that sat in the middle of a hundred acres off Tallakos road. Sam's unannounced visit had turned the quiet Sunday morning into a sea of emotional turmoil. Dr. Grey had vehemently affirmed that his professional services were above reproach. Essie had declared Sam a hothead and sent him skedaddling back to Madison County.

Essie carried a tray into Minnie's room, a teapot and a warm biscuit with a hefty smear of blackberry jelly. "Ah, I see you're awake. Good morning."

"Oh, yes, mam. The sun come shining in and done woke me up real good." Minnie stretched and leaned back on her pillow.

"I've got you some breakfast." Essie placed the tray at the end of the bed and poured Minnie's hot tea, stirring in cream and sugar. "Not only does Dr. Grey give you medicine, he makes biscuits for you."

"Dr. Grey! He done save my life, for sho'." Her eyes shining, Minnie bit into a biscuit, a dab of jelly smearing her chin.

From her luggage, Essie pulled the framed photograph of Jewell and sat on the edge of Minnie's bed. "Minnie, this is the photograph you saw in my parlor in Pinetta. Remember?" She tilted the picture and sunlight bathed Jewell's face, an angel's face.

"Oh, I sure does, Miss Essie. I know you said that be your sister, but I know it's my friend over in Thomasville."

Essie nodded. "What makes you say that, Minnie?"

Minnie quietly studied the photograph. She ran her finger along Jewell's hairline, then across her eyebrows. "Miss Essie. It's the eyes. I 'member my friend had the kindest eyes, like they was straight from heaven. And her smile. Her smile done make all my troubles go away. And when she hugged me, I felt her heart beating. A good heart beating with pure love, I say."

Minnie looked up at Essie. "Please believe me, Miss Essie, when I say this photograph is my friend at the plantation."

Essie took the picture and placed it back inside her suitcase. "Let's go to Thomasville and find her, Minnie. You and me. We'll scour every crook and cranny of every plantation until we find her."

Minnie's face sobered. "Miss Essie, do you know how many plantations they be in Thomas County?"

Essie shook her head. "No, I don't. How many?"

"Oh, my. They's Pebble Hill an' Melrose. And Sinkola, Millpond... then they's Dixie, Fair Oaks, Foshalee... we cain't forget Inwood and Mayhaw. Oh, and what about Ring Oak and Winnstead. Oh, I almost forgot Boxhill and Greenwood... yes, and then they's...."

CHAPTER THIRTY

Sister Areba didn't bother to knock. Her six foot frame, again covered in purple, was like a runaway locomotive when she shoved open the door and charged into the room. Pitch and Orland cowered at the kitchen table, their Sunday school book and Bible in their hands. Their Godmother was loving and kind, but her enormous size and bellowing voice was no different than the boogeyman. As if her size was not enough to scare them, her purple lipstick conjured up memories of Halloween goblins. A thick smear of purple covered her thick lips like road tar and glowed like a bauble at the county fair.

"Lawd have mercy! You boys git up from that table and find your coats. We gots to go. I'm singing in the choir today. Praise the Lord."

Pitch and Orland sprung from the table at Sister Areba's command. Pitch limped to the fireplace where his coat lay warming. "Yes, mam. Sister Areba. We coming."

From the bedroom, Essie carried the breakfast tray to the kitchen. "Good morning, Sister Areba."

The towering black woman lifted her chin. "I seed you done spend the night agin." Her eyes cut to the blankets and pillows on the couch.

"I certainly did. So did Dr. Grey," Essie replied.

Sister Areba jerked her head. "What you say? Two white folks done spend the night in Ollie's house!" She clucked her tongue and swiveled her head from side to side. "Reckon you folks is gone take over this whole place."

"Now, why would we do that, Sister Areba? We're just helping out.

That's what folks do." Essie stared at the purple lips, the purple hat and purple suit. When her gaze fell to the woman's shoes, she wasn't surprised to find more purple. *Size 12.*

"Sho nuf it's the Christian way, missy, but Ollie done told me one time he don't like white folks. And the last time I looked, you was white as sifted flour. Cain't see one speck of dark on yo self nowhere." She caught her breath. "Seem to me like company start to stink after a few days." Her eyes rounded into large circles, a little purple shadow on the lids. "Might want to load up that car a yours and go on up the highway."

Essie laughed. "Please don't be concern—"

"This ain't no laughing matter. I see Ollie done be in the barn all the time you is here."

Essie pulled out a kitchen chair and sat down. It seemed Sister Areba's worry over the Pryor household had gone far beyond what Essie considered reasonable. She didn't want to offend the woman, nor did she want to be berated for her presence in the house. After all, Minnie was ill and needed care. The family's food supply had been almost non-existent until she arrived with a carload of canned goods, meat and bread.

If Ollie Pryor wanted her to be gone, all he had to do was say so. She'd leave alright, but she'd take Minnie with her if she wanted to go. In her mind, Ollie had been relieved that his daughter had received medical care. He had also welcomed the food she brought.

"Sister Areba, I appreciate your concern for this family. Your care of these boys and your duty as their Godmother cannot be overlooked." Essie noticed her words had hardened, become firm with an uneasy indifference. She'd not let Sister Areba reign over her, no matter how tall she was, how insistent she was and no matter how much purple she wore.

Essie continued, "It is also my duty as a Christian to offer my heartfelt support for Minnie during her illness, as well as offer my guardianship over this family while I'm here."

She stood and walked over to Pitch and Orland, a wet cloth in her hand. She reached out and wiped their mouths. "I do believe I see syrup on your chins."

When Essie stepped back, she looked directly at Sister Areba. "You look lovely today."

Sister Areba nodded and with a gruff voice said, "I sing alto. They need altos in that choir. Got too many sopranos." She turned and walked through the door and out on the porch, the boys following behind. She looked over her shoulder. "Ain't no white woman knowed how to run from a rooster. Black woman ain't never git caught unawares when they's a rooster 'round."

She roared off in her blue Chevrolet, the gray squirrel tail on the antenna whipping 'round and 'round as though it was alive.

CHAPTER THIRTY-ONE

Sunday afternoon softened into a gentle dusk, the sun easing behind a stand of tall pines at the end of a field west of the unpainted house. The chickens eyed their roosts in the henhouse, their eggs gathered earlier in the day. The rooster sounded his yuk, yuk, yuk as he pranced behind his hens and ushered them inside. The rooster's attack on Essie had crowned *him king of the roost;* it was *his* barnyard.

Ollie had been with his sow, aptly named Henrietta, since daylight, certain she'd give birth before another day passed. The man's dedication to his farm was widely known, one hundred acres of fields, some trees and a small pond on the south edge. He had sharecropped the parcel for twenty-eight years, a hard twenty-eight years, especially since the death of his wife.

Since Essie's arrival at the Pryor farm, Ollie had hibernated in the tack room of the barn, a more or less defiant stance against all the *white* people in his house. Despite Essie's heartfelt care of the family, Ollie's pride was too deep to acquiesce to the existence of what he considered *charity*.

After his introduction to Sam Washington, Robert Grey had not returned to the little wooden house on Sunday evening. On Monday, Essie took the Pontiac to Bud Jones for new shocks as Jack Woodard at the Pinetta Garage had advised her to do. She admitted she was attached to the Pontiac, probably because it had been her father's. Sometimes, when she drove the back roads of Pinetta, the windows down and the smell of cut hay in the air, she'd talk to Hubert Donnelly and tell him she missed him.

Although she had spent her life wanting to leave the farm, she realized the farm, as well as the sprawling two-story house, was her heart. Perhaps her youth had prevented her from recognizing the beauty of her life among the fields of peanuts, corn and tobacco. Seemingly, youth had caused her to dream of far-away places, which, in retrospect, was an ordinary way of thinking given her isolation in the middle of three-hundred acres of farmland.

Essie didn't think she was a troubled woman, but merely sorting things out in her life. Her dream of becoming a writer had metamorphosed into a novel, *Watermelon Queen of Madison County,* followed by an agent who thought her writing was worthy of publishing. A contract followed and then... then Jewell died and Essie's writing became obscure in her thoughts, replaced by the discovery of the existence of Jewell's child. The search for Jewell's child had replaced Sam. Wonderful Sam, who had adored her since high school and then fell in love with her all over again. Sam, who had been enamoured with her no-nonsense demeanor, knowing underneath was a woman he loved.

In Boston, four old men, their faces as wrinkled as a brown paper bag, played checkers in the sunshine at Bud Jones' garage. They wore colorful flannel shirts and bib overalls, their presence a tribute to their status as Boston's checker aficionados. One knew the world was right if these old men gathered at Bud's and shared their intellect with Bud's customers. Their farming days were over, hastened by arthritis and worn out bodies that had lifted too many hay bales and plowed too many fields.

Bud didn't talk much; he grunted and jumped around hunting tools, his hands greased black from his work. "Mr. Jones, I'll be back after a while." Essie left the checker players arguing over a play and meandered down past Earl Mayo's furniture store and J. C. Pittman's appliances. She slowed at the appliance store and noticed a refrigerator, gleaming white, in the store window. The Pryor house needed a refrigerator, but, of course, they had no electricity.

The rattle of a vehicle caught her attention, a sound that was somewhat familiar, grating to her ears. She turned and caught the faded red color of an old truck as it pulled to the curb in front of her.

The front bumper of the truck hung lopsided, almost touching the pavement. A voice called out. "Well, now. There's that sharpshooter gal done shot up my coffee urn and spilt coffee all over my store. I reckon you owe me some money."

The red beefy face of the man grinned at Essie, his teeth the color of old corn, his left eye half-closed. He opened the truck door and stepped out onto the pavement.

Essie stared at him as he walked around the truck and onto the sidewalk in front of her. When she spoke, there was not a shred of hesitancy in her words. "Seems to me you have a bad memory, mister. You forget I almost shot you in that fat belly of yours." She stepped closer and slipped her hand into her coat pocket. The man's eyes followed her hand.

"My memory is excellent, Annie Oakley. You done brought that nigger girl into my store. Can't you read? That sign said *whites only*.

Essie sent a somewhat menacing grin. "My memory is good, too. Believe I tore down that sign."

A few quiet moments passed. "Oh, it's back up where it belongs. 'cept I changed it to 'no niggers.' A dog leapt up from the bed of the truck, the word "nigger" an obvious response to a command he'd been taught. He growled, like there was a rudder in his throat, revving louder when the man waved his hand at Essie.

Essie replied in a pleasant manner, a southern thing even if you were having a conversation with the devil. "Looks like I'll have to go back down to your store and take that sign down again. I hope you'll have some hot coffee for me and my friend." At that moment, Essie placed her hand in her coat pocket, pushing her fingers forward. The man jerked, eyes widened.

The Pinetta farm girl's eyes narrowed, her cussing self materializing like a summer thunderstorm, dark and menacing. "My friend and I will pray for you, mister. For you and your friends. It's quite obvious to us that that brain of yours is mighty small, incapable of decency and respect for others. One day you won't be able to hang that sign of yours." Essie glanced at the panting dog, then back to the corn-fed belly of the man. "Don't threaten me with your dog."

A stream of tobacco juice splattered on the sidewalk at Essie's shoes. "Look out, little lady. My friends and I ain't gone be too far away." He ambled to his truck and climbed inside, his eyes never leaving Essie, nor her coat where her hand rested in her pocket.

Essie watched the old truck pull out onto Main Street. She chastised herself for leaving her gun in her car.

CHAPTER THIRTY-TWO

Tuesday came and went and still the doctor had not visited his patients. On Wednesday, the third day of April, Essie meandered into Boston again, driving the Pontiac down Main Street, heading south. She crossed Railroad Avenue and to her right saw the Carnegie Library, an impressive building with large columns, which seemed to represent the importance of a library in such a small town.

Built in 1914, the library had become a shining star in Thomas County, a result of Boston's citizens raising local funds for a building site. Who would have dreamed that the sale of Mrs. Rosie Henry's cakes would have paid for those big white columns in front of the building. The Twentieth Century Club, a community organization, had acquired grants which had manifested into the fine library in the small Georgia town, a town that had begun as a stagecoach stop.

Essie parked along Main Street, walked up the library steps and through the double doors. The smell of old books was comforting, a memory of reading into midnight, then until daylight. Her mother never knew she read the entire night, closing her book just in time to leave for school. Essie felt a pang of regret. Had she honored her book contract, perhaps *Watermelon Queen of Madison County* would be on bookshelves everywhere. Perhaps even on the New York Times bestseller list.

Essie smiled at the woman who sat at a nearby table. The woman, a pretty brunette, said. "Good morning. Don't believe I know you. I'm Louise Huddleston. You from around here?"

Essie shook her head. "No. Just visiting." She continued walking to the fiction aisle and wondered if Ms. Huddleston thought she was rude. She had not bothered to say *'I'm Essie Donnelly from Madison County, Florida."* She couldn't bear to talk about *the murder* nor *the ear.* It seemed the citizens of Boston were adept at reading the *Thomasville Times-Enterprise*, a daily paper, where supposedly sensational accounts of the murder of George Barnwell had been published for months the previous summer. The paper had depicted Jewell as a sweet, southern belle, who had never shot a gun in her life. Those who read the details of the murder could never know the trauma the shooting had caused Jewell.

A tall thin woman with short dark hair browsed the fiction section and almost bumped into Essie. She apologized. "Oh, my. I'm so sorry."

"That's quite alright. No worries." Essie moved along and pulled out a novel by Carson McCullers, one of her favorite authors.

Only a few feet away, the woman commented on the novel. "I've read that book several times. It never seems to get old. Since I'm a 5th grade teacher, I find it refreshing to read adult books." She laughed. "I'm Laura Sanders." She reached out her hand and squeezed warmly.

"Hello. It's a pleasure to meet you. I'm Essie Donnelly. I'm from out of town."

"How lovely to meet you," she said. "We love for out of towners to enjoy our library."

The woman moved farther down the aisle and, thankfully, did not mention anything about a murder in Madison County.

Essie left the library and stopped at the Sam Bruce Grocery, where she purchased more bacon, as well as bread and milk. From there, she entered Cromartie's Drug Store for more aspirin and perhaps to apologize to Mr. Cromartie for being so rude to him when he inquired about "*the murder.*"

When Mr. Cromartie saw her, he seemed to shudder a tad, shrinking back into the space behind the counter. Essie called out. "Good afternoon, Mr. Cromartie. I hope your day is going well." She sent a warm smile.

The druggist returned her smile with his own. "It's been a grand day." He moved closer to the counter, "Say, did you hear about Dr. Grey?"

"Dr. Grey? My goodness, no. What's happened?" Essie held tightly to the bottle of aspirin in her hands, an uneasiness washing over her.

Mr. Cromartie straightened his glasses and licked his lips. "Well, I hear the Archbold hospital over in Thomasville called him to service. Said they had an outbreak of flu over there and every bed was filled. So he rushed over there Sunday afternoon to help out. I hear he's returning to Boston tomorrow."

The beating of Essie's heart slowed. The good doctor was doing what he was supposed to do… *and whatsoever house I enter, I will enter to help the sick.* Minnie and Essie were well on their way to recovery, Minnie from her spider bite and Essie from the rooster attack, the need for Dr. Grey's skilled hands were no longer necessary. Still… Essie found his presence calming. Admittedly, when the doctor had entered the Pryor's lives and household, he brought with him a welcomed energy. Perhaps that was what Irish men were famous for—their kindness and care for others. And there was another thing: Dr. Grey was quite charming.

From Boston, Essie ambled back to the Pryor farm along clay roads, passing the regal stands of pecan trees and plowed fields, across a small creek and then right on Tallokas road. She daydreamed about the novel she had written, yet remained unpublished. She felt her writing gave her power. She could make new things familiar and familiar things new, and all with words. Her intellect mixed with her soul when she sat before her Royal typewriter and, with just a few taps of the keys, made literary music.

True to his word, Sam had not returned to Boston after his surprise visit. Nor, had Essie called him. His objections to her quest to find Jewell's child had been harsh and unrelenting, a protest that came between them and simmered for weeks, then blew up into a maelstrom of mutual resentment. Her love for Sam was unmistakable, yet it quivered in a dark uncertainty.

Essie slowed at the turn to the farm house and saw the pink and orange of an April sunset in the western sky. It was her belief that the burdens of the poor were laid down at sunset, while the broken hearts of those saddened by loved ones lost evaporated into the darkening sky.

Had Essie not been daydreaming, she would have noticed the dilapidated red truck that trailed her only a mile away, moving stealth like and brimming with quiet peril.

CHAPTER THIRTY-THREE

The chill of a late March frost had given way to April breezes filled with the fragrance of blooming oleanders that lined the south side of the house. Early Thursday morning, the sun hiding behind tall pines, a sublime Henrietta delivered eleven piglets. The sow grunted and squealed, then stretched out in her pen and squeezed out tiny three pound pigs, all alive. Ollie worked nearby, using hay to clean them up, all the while talking to Henrietta. "You done good, ole girl. These is mighty fine baby pigs. Gonna git some good money at auction."

If Ollie had a friend, it was Henrietta. The old sow had been around for years, giving him a litter twice a year, litters that provided money for seed and fertilizer. Without his pigs, he couldn't farm.

The treacherous rooster left the hen house and jumped on the top rail of a wooden fence, emitting his first crow of the morning. The sound rang out like a bugle at reveille; the day could not begin without his say so.

Inside the house, Essie readied breakfast before the boys caught the school bus. Pitch sat in front of the warm fireplace, waiting for breakfast. "Miss Essie, I done had me a dream."

"A dream?" Essie picked up her coffee cup and sat down beside the boy. She rubbed his back and felt his thin shoulder bones. His twisted foot rested on the hearth, a reminder that he would never run a race or play basketball.

"That's right. I dreamed my mama done baked me a birthday cake." He looked up at Essie and grinned. "It was chocolate. And it had twelve candles on top. They was blue." His sad eyes turned back to the fire. "They weren't no presents, but that cake was mighty fine." He paused. "It was a good dream."

Essie squeezed the boy's shoulder. "That was a good dream, for sure, Pitch. A chocolate cake is the best." When she glanced at the boy, she saw evidence of tears. "When is your birthday, Pitch?"

The boy waited a long time before answering, fiddling with a thread hanging at the end of his sleeve. He swallowed hard, a sniff of his nose, and, with a croak in his voice, said. "It's today, Miss Essie."

The fire popped, sending sparks up the chimney. Essie stood and placed a small log on top of the burning embers. "Your birthday? Today?"

"Yes, mam. Mama said I had just missed April Fool's day. She said she didn't want no April Fool's baby." He chuckled. "I reckon she got one anyway."

They laughed together in the early morning, just the two of them, the hard woman from Madison County who searched for a girl who looked just like her sister and a boy with a clubfoot talking about his mama's chocolate cake.

The knock at the door was gentle, hesitant, as though reluctant to disturb the worn house. It came again, soft and muffled. The creak of the porch boards sounded almost musical, the notes of a visitor asking for entry.

Essie crossed the room and opened the door to find a smiling Dr. Grey, his medicine bag swinging in his right hand. "Ah, I think it may be too early for a call, but my patients are important to me. I'm after gettin' you examined."

All at once, the good doctor was in the house, pulling off his jacket and looking for a coffee cup. "Right, I'm anxious to know how you're feelin'." He poured his coffee and strode across to the fireplace and sat by Pitch. "C'mere, lad. I've missed ya." He pulled Pitch against him. "It'd be nice if we'd get pancakes this mornin', now wouldn't it?"

Rob Grey glanced to the kitchen where Essie poked wood into the stove. "Can you reach that big crock on the top shelf?" he called.

Essie smiled. "It's good to see you, Dr. Grey. I'm wondering if we didn't make pancakes for you, if you'd visit at all."

Booming laughter filled the room. It was evident Dr. Grey brought an abundance of energy to the little house, energy perhaps defined as happiness. "Tis true, Miss Essie. Feed me pancakes and I'll change the bandages on your rooster wounds as well as examine Minnie. By the way, I'm thinkin' we'll get Minnie a movin' 'round today. Get her in the sunshine." He chuckled. "Maybe have her do a little jig fer us."

From the doorway, a sleepy Orland stumbled into the kitchen. "Miss Essie, you making us some pancakes?"

"Dr. Grey seems to think so, Orland. Go out on the porch and wash up. There's some water in that big enamel pan. Don't forget to use soap." She rubbed the top of his head as he passed through the kitchen.

Essie dumped flour into the large crock. "Do you think Minnie can travel by next Monday?" *Yes, Thomasville. Jewell's daughter.*

Robert Grey frowned. "If she has no fever and her strength improves, I'd say so."

"I'll be anxious for your assessment of her this morning." Essie glanced at the black-haired Irishman. "I'm doing fine—no need to bother with these rooster wounds."

"Ah, no, lassie. We've got to clean those wounds and apply medication. Put on new bandages." He winked at Essie. "Are ye troubled by me seein' your bare leg?"

"Of course not," barked Essie. "Men have seen my bare legs before," she said hotly. She stumbled. "Well, you know… at the lake. Swimming and such."

"Eh, so I understand." Rob sent a smile her way. The farm girl's tousled morning hair was lovely, as were her pink flushed cheeks. He watched her add milk to the flour, as well as eggs. "Put a dab of vanilla in those pancakes," he called. "They'll taste like puffs of angel wings."

Essie stared at him for a long moment. His black eyes shifted from the pancake bowl to her. He leaned back in his chair and crossed his legs, his eyes laughing and pulling Essie Donnelly in just a little closer.

Essie slammed the spoon into the pancake bowl. "I'll check on Minnie." She wiped her hands and threw the dish towel across her shoulder, then disappeared into the back bedroom where Minnie lay sleeping.

"Minnie, are you awake?" Essie tugged on Minnie's foot. "Let's get you up and eat some breakfast with us." She pulled harder. "Dr. Grey is here."

Minnie stirred and opened her eyes and stretched. "What you pullin' my toe for?" She turned over and grinned at Essie. "You said pancakes. I's so hungry." Minnie threw the covers off her thin body and set up. "Wid lots of molasses on 'em."

Essie pulled the chamber pot from under the bed. "Here you go, Minnie. I emptied this thing early this morning, before daylight." The Pryor house lacked all the modern conveniences. At Essie's mother's insistence, the Donnelly house had indoor plumbing installed in 1952, a welcome change. Edith was too much of a queen to make the long walk to the outhouse and, most certainly, found the chamber pot equally inconvenient.

"Thank you, Miss Essie. You so good to me." The girl stood and straightened her nightgown. "Dr. Grey's here? He gone give me some medicine?"

"I don't know," she said irritably. "Just dress and come eat."

Minnie's eyes widened. "You okay, Miss Essie?"

"Fine, Minnie. Just fine." Essie left the room and closed the door behind her.

At the stove, Rob busied himself with a hot skillet while pancake batter dripped from a large pitcher. He hummed softly, a potholder in his hand. The spatula scraped across the pan and a pancake flipped in the air.

Across the room, Pitch and Orland watched with wonder. Their eyes followed the sailing pancake and they held their breath as it dropped back down into the skillet. "Mr. Rob, you done make magic. Can you flip one a those pancakes our way?" The boys laughed and held their mouths open.

Rob made some silver dollar sized pancakes and stacked them on a nearby plate. "Ready, boys. Open up!" With an uncanny marksmanship, a pancake sailed into Pitch's mouth; another followed for Orland. They giggled uncontrollably, their little faces upturned with anticipation.

"Okay. Let's get some on your plate with some butter and syrup. Clock's running. That school bus will be here in fifteen minutes."

Essie watched from the hallway. The Irishman was more than a doctor. He dispensed medicine along with a big piece of his heart, a gentle touch caused pain to vanish and, with just one look, he commanded trust and respect.

Chapter Thirty-Four

"Ah, Miss Minnie, I deem you well enough to dance an Irish jig." Dr. Grey wrote a few notes in his journal. *No temperature. Normal blood pressure. No swelling. No rash. Lymph nodes normal.* "I'd like to see you out of that bed and gettin' a little exercise, maybe a walk 'round the barnyard a few times. Drink lots of water. Don't want to get dehydrated."

Dr. Grey closed his medicine bag and stood. "I'm after going back to Boston, now, you see. Dr. Lundy will be returnin' on Monday and I best put his office to his liking." He slipped into his jacket. "I'll return later today to treat your wounds, Miss Essie. I've a few patients on the appointment book for this mornin'."

The two chatted for a few moments on the front porch, then Essie watched Dr. Grey cross the yard and walk quickly to his car, ever mindful of the yard rooster. He turned the engine and then rolled down his window. "See you later." He laughed when he saw the rooster skitter across the yard like a road runner, his wings flapping wildly. A few yards down the road, Rob Grey's arm shot out the window in a joyous wave.

Essie stared after the car a long time, her thoughts mostly of the good doctor. She considered him a reflective man, perhaps acquiring knowledge through lengthy, quiet observations. Maybe it was his wise passiveness that drew her to him: he was a *thinking* man.

The boys ate the entire platter of silver dollar pancakes, though be it with a fork rather than Dr. Grey slinging them across the kitchen into the boys' mouths. Their bus stop was a quarter mile down

Tallokas road, at the bottom on the hill, where nine children gathered at 8:40 every weekday morning to attend a schoolhouse designated for the colored population. Miss Mosley, heralded as an outstanding teacher, was a serious, thin woman who held great authority over her brood. She taught first through sixth grade, which included the Pryor boys. Miss Mosley held a special place in her heart for Pitch, who played with unending vigor at recess, his body moving like a metronome when he ran across the playground.

A chill remained in the air all across southern Georgia, including Brooks County, which was busy with planting corn, peanuts soon to follow. Essie called to Minnie. "Find a warm sweater, Minnie, and let's go look at those newborn pigs." At Dr. Grey's instructions, Minnie needed to regain her strength; it seemed touring the pig pen fell into the category of exercise.

"Oh, Miss Essie. This sunshine feels so good." They stopped on the back porch and pumped a jar of water, cold and clear. Chicken poop lay like pebbles throughout the yard and they stepped gingerly across the winter brown grass. Essie carried the broom for rooster protection, while her eyes scanned the barnyard.

At the hog pen, Ollie poured corn into the trough, Henrietta grunting happily as she crunched the ears like they were candy. Ollie's affection for his big sow was evident in the care she received. The piglets lay in a pile like big potatoes, squirming in and around each other, their mama keeping a watchful eye on them.

"Look at Henrietta's eyelashes, Miss Essie. They's so long. She be a pretty girl pig, for sure."

Ollie 'harrumphed' his way from the hog pen to the barn's tack room, obviously still smarting somewhat over the houseguest who seemed to have invited herself into the Pryor home without *his* permission. Now that Minnie's health was improving, he would ask Miss Donnelly to leave. *For the second time.* And to leave *without* Minnie.

In three or four months, after the piglets had been weaned, he'd fatten them up to about two-hundred and fifty pounds and take them to the Hancock farm, where Mr. Aiken, the sharecropper, would commence with a hog killing. *November. Yes, in November, he'd load them up. Then, he'd fill his pockets with money.*

Essie and Minnie continued their walk around the yard, under the giant walnut tree, then along the field of planted corn. "See that plowed field over there, Miss Essie?" Minnie pointed west, along the Tallokas road. "Daddy gone plant some peanuts real soon. We's roast 'em and boil 'em. They's so good."

Minnie pointed to another field. "They's watermelons planted over yonder."

Essie laughed. "Just like at my farm, Minnie. You know, we're a lot alike." Essie turned and tugged Minnie's sweater together. "You stay warm. Dr. Grey won't like you catching a cold." The young women walked without speaking, the end of the day becoming soft, with tender twilight easing into the sky.

"Dr. Grey says you can travel soon and I'm thinking we could drive to Thomasville next Monday. You know, after we get the boys off to school."

"Hmmmm. I be fine by Monday. We go to Pebble Hill plantation first, 'cause I got me a friend there. Ain't seen him since last summer, but I ain't forget him. Yes, sir, Mr. Herbert a good friend."

Essie slowed her walk. "You know, Minnie, I loved my sister more than anything in the world. Tell me one more time—the girl you saw? Was she truly like the picture of Jewell?"

"Yes, 'em, Miss Essie. They's twins, for sure. 'member, that dream I had? The dream when we's all jumping in a pile of roses, all colors of roses and they smelled sweet as sugar?" Minnie stopped her walk. her voice lowering into a secretive softness. "Miss Essie, I ain't never told you this, but I can see things."

"See things? Like what?"

"In my dreams. My dreams is real." The black girl closed her eyes and lifted her beautiful face to the cloudless sky. "Yes, mam. I sure do see yo' sister."

Essie made an egg pie for dinner, its crust soft and buttery and filled with fresh eggs from the henhouse, chopped bacon and small spring onions. "You boys smell what's in the oven?" Essie grinned across the table. Pitch's face shone with anticipation. "It smell good." Orland nodded in agreement.

"Oh, yes," said Minnie. Her dark eyes moved to the stove as she sniffed the air. "Something delicious, for sure."

The knock on the door was loud and commanding. A voice rose

up: "Is there a lad named Pitch living in this house?" Everyone stared wide-eyed at the front door, which was suddenly kicked open, resulting in loud squeals all around the table. There stood Dr. Grey, his hands holding a large white box.

"I'm after findin' a boy named Pitch!" His voice boomed. "Where are ye, lad?" He stomped across the room and circled the table. "Ah, let me see if there's a lad named Pitch at this table." Dr. Grey's eyes narrowed and roamed around the table, a shrewd glance at each expectant face.

A little voice, hesitant with a small tremble, piped up. "I be Pitch Pryor."

"Don't be gawkin' at me, lad. C'mere, I say." Rob Grey placed the white box on the table. "C'mere!" The boy jumped from the table as commanded and ran to the box.

"Yes, sir. I's here." Pitch's body shook with anticipation, his mouth hanging open, his hands clasped tightly behind his back.

Ever so slowly, the doctor opened the box and peered inside. "Willywigs!"

Pitch leaned over the box and squinted his eyes. "That there's my name wrote on that cake!" He leaned in closer. "P-i-t-c-h," he read. "And "*Happy Birthday*!" Pitch sucked in his breath and threw his hands over his mouth. He jumped away from the box and see-sawed his body around the table, around the room, into the kitchen and back again, like a bucking pony let out of his stall.

"I say we light these candles, lad." Dr. Grey glanced at Essie. "Miss Donnelly, would you be so kind as to light this lad's candles?"

Essie pulled the matches from the shelf above the fireplace and dutifully lit the blue candles. The small flames flickered above the grand chocolate cake, above Pitch's name, above the words *Happy Birthday*. It was then that Dr. Grey's voice rang out, a high tenor, as melodic as a meadowlark. "*Happy Birthday to you…*" They all sang, at first with a soft tenderness, then jumped into the rousing verse a second time, before collapsing in laughter.

The cake, baked by Mrs. Henry in Boston, a woman whose reputation for her scrumptious cakes ran far and wide, both in Brooks and Thomas County, was devoured except for one piece. They left it for Ollie Pryor, who sat alone in his little home in the barn, absent from his family and wanting the white woman gone.

A Georgia moon is like no other. As though a constant sentry watching a sleeping earth, it rose over the freshly plowed fields east of the shack of a house, its light growing like the opening petals of a flower.

The Irishman and the farm girl left the warm house and settled into a cool April evening. Robert Grey eased onto an overturned bucket on the Pryor's front porch, across from Essie, who sat in a worn wooden rocker, a sweater around her shoulders. "Miss Donnelly, your idea of a cake for Pitch was a splendid one. The boy will remember his twelfth birthday."

Essie smiled at the man who had magically provided a three layer chocolate cake with twelve candles to a boy whose mother was not alive to bake him one. "You fulfilled a young boy's wish, and I thank you for that."

"It was your idea and we must give thanks to Mrs. Henry. From the moment I knocked on her door, she rushed into her kitchen and, in a mere two hours, produced a grand cake for Pitch. Glorious, I say."

"Boston is a lovely town with good people."

"I've enjoyed my stay here. When Dr. Lundy returns, I shall be disheartened to leave."

"You're leaving? Where are you going?"

"Not far. The Archbold hospital in Thomasville."

Oddly, Essie felt relieved the doctor would remain nearby. He had been a constant support since her arrival in Boston, since Minnie's illness. "Not far at all." In the moonlight, Essie studied Dr. Grey's profile. A handsome man, indeed. "Tell me, Dr. Grey. Ireland is a long way from Boston, Georgia. How is it that you're filling in for Dr. Lundy?"

He chuckled. "That is quite the story, now. My uncle migrated to the United States from Ireland some years ago and had spoken of so many opportunities available to a young man like me. So, eighteen years ago, I visited him in Baltimore, where he was an orthopedic surgeon at Johns Hopkins hospital." Dr. Grey took a deep breath, as if recalling details. "Of course, I was impressed with just about everythin'. In no time, I was an American citizen enrolled in medical school." In the moonlight, his eyes glistened. His words held profound humility, a softness that came from within.

All at once, Dr. Grey slapped his knee. "Bejabers! I have some good news! While at Archbold these past few days, I had a conversation with a Dr. Christoph Meyer, who heads up the orthopedic department. It seems he is willing to take a look at Pitch's foot. Can you believe that?"

Pitch's foot? The boy with the lopsided body? "A surgeon?" asked Essie.

"A bone surgeon, I say. I'd like us to take the boy for an examination as soon as possible.

Like a wet woolen blanket, a dark cloud moved over the full moon and left the porch in deep shadow. "Do you think Ollie will allow that?" Essie asked.

Rob jumped from his bucket seat. "He must! Can you imagine what could possibly be done for that lad?" The doctor paced the porch. "Why... why, Pitch could play basketball. He could do things he's never done before. And what about those prayers of his? Asking Jesus to bring him a new foot?" Rob threw out his arms in question.

Essie nodded in agreement. She sat motionless, the rocker still. Then, barely audible, "Minnie and I are leaving Monday for the Pebble Hill plantation to search for my sister's child." She looked up at the doctor. "But, I'll be back."

Dr. Grey studied Essie's face and, even in shadow, saw her consternation. She had that look about her, that look of otherness, of eyes that saw things much too far and of thoughts that wandered off to the edge of the earth.

"Of course," he said.

CHAPTER THIRTY-FIVE

Had gale force winds of forty knots blasted the front door of the farmhouse, the winds could not have been more powerful than Areba Wright's entry into the small front room of the house. "Pitch!" she hollered, a voice hovering near one hundred decibels. "Orland!" The purple woman slammed her hands together. "You studied up yo' Sunday school lesson?"

The boys ran from their bedroom, each carrying their Bible and Sunday school lesson book. "Yes, mam. We know all our verses," said Pitch.

"That's good. The Lord be proud of you boys." Areba's purple body moved into the kitchen, a loud creaking of the floor as her weight bore down on the wooden boards. The hat she wore was wide and floppy, a garden of flowers along the edge of the brim, with leaves studded inbetween. Her dress swished as she walked, bouncing the purple ruffles to and fro along the skirt.

"Where's yo daddy?" She opened the back door and hollered into the yard. "Ollie, you get yourself out here. You know it's Founders Day at the church. You done got to put on your deacon clothes and lead the choir."

At that moment, the yard rooster crowed and flapped his wings. *Come on out, purple woman. I'll chase you to the other side of the Holy Land.*

From the barn, Ollie ambled out across the barnyard, giving no mind to the nearby rooster. "Yes, 'em. I knowed what day it is." He wore a dark brown suit almost the color of cow manure. A tie, brighter than a Georgia sunrise, lay perfectly on top of a white shirt.

"I ain't leadin' no choir," he mumbled.

"Now, you sho is Ollie Pryor. It done be your turn and the preacher said so. You just git yourself ready 'cause I'm singin' me a solo this morning. *Praise the Lord*," she roared. She stepped off the back porch within twelve feet or so of the rooster. She shook her finger at Ollie. "An' you know who's playing the piano? That Richardson girl. You know, Sister Juanita's daughter. She never been married and she's lookin' for a husband. I'd say you is sure 'nuf available."

Ollie growled his way to the porch and turned around and faced Areba. "Now, listen here, Areba. I don't care if Lena Horne done asked me to marry her, I ain't marrying no woman, not even Miss Horne." He spun around and stomped into the house.

Areba, all six feet of her, lumbered up the steps to the back porch, her long skirt following. She heard the flapping of Spur's wings and a gutteral caw from his skinny throat. When she turned around, Spur was soaring through the air, his feet aimed for her ruffled skirt. When he hit the purple chiffon, his two and one half inch spurs tangled in the fabric, twisting and turning, looking for her mammoth legs. Areba grabbed him by the neck and slung him out into the yard. "You is a dead rooster. I come back after church and you goin' in the pot."

Without fanfare, Areba straightened her skirt, marched into the house, picked up her Bible and said, "Come on. We gotta go. They's food in the car."

Essie and Minnie had dressed for church and stood silently while Areba and the boys filed through the front doorway and to the tank of a Chevrolet with the squirrel tail on the antenna. As soon as the purple woman was out of earshot, Essie and Minnie cackled. "Oh, my. Spur done attacked the wrong woman, would you say?" said Minnie.

"Minnie! Did you see all the chicken feathers in her skirt?" Essie said, through peals of laughter.

"I sho did. And she gone be in front of all those people singin' a solo. Oh, Miss Essie, it's gone be a great day!"

The women gathered their bibles and hurried to the Pontiac, snickering to themselves. Across the yard, Ollie eased his truck onto the clay road and, with much reluctance, began to think about Celista Richardson, who had never been married. But, she could play the piano with fiery fingers, much like Jerry Lee Lewis, who had just released '*Whole Lotta Shakin' Goin' On.*'

The Beulah Hill church set on a slight rise at the edge of a thick woods. From the main road, a narrow clay lane lined with deep ruts passed the cemetery and ended up in the church yard, where the congregation had parked their cars and trucks. Even a mule and wagon were among the vehicles, the reins of the mule tied to the bumper of a car. A decrepit Ford tractor had nudged in between two pine trees, its red paint long turned to a rusty orange. A vast slew of worshippers congregated at the church steps, their Sunday-best clothes brushed and pressed.

On Founders Day, a grand celebration of the church's history as well as its heritage, would take place after the day's sermon. Food was prepared the night before and early on Sunday morning, and would be served to every man, woman and child on this glorious day.

Inside the church, Minnie and Essie walked down the aisle and found space in the third pew on the right, in front of the piano, in front of the place where Areba Wright would sing her solo. And, where they could see the chicken feathers stuck in the purple chiffon of Areba's long flowing skirt.

Ollie sat on the front row on the left of the aisle, his boys beside him. They were a family. When Ollie turned around and looked for Minnie, his eyes fell on his daughter and he glared. *Why are you sitting with the white woman?*

Essie had visited black churches before, but it was evident no white woman had visited the Beulah Hill church. The congregation's stares were not hostile, nor were they friendly. Their eyes followed her with a fervent curiosity, their whispers filling the pews like a soft falling snow.

The pastor, a giant of a man, stood firmly in the pulpit, a Bible held between his arm and chest, next to his heart. His cheeks were rounded and protruded like a chipmunk's, while his lips stretched across his perfect white teeth. He smiled lovingly at the parishioners, his eyes glistening.

"We gather in awe of the moving of God in each of our lives," he boomed. "Today, let us reflect on our challenges with an eye on the divine instructions we receive through the written words of the Bible." He held up his Bible, high to the rafters. *Amen!*

At the piano, a woman sat primly, her eyes downcast, unmoving. The pastor called to her. "Sister Richardson, it would delight all of us if you would begin today's chorus of songs."

That was Ollie's cue to stand and walk to the front of the church. His duty as leader of the choir was upon him. "May we begin?"

In united splendor, the voices of twelve choir members burst forth: *Bringing in the sheaves, bringing in the sheaves, we shall come rejoicing, bringing in the sheaves.*

A robust rendition of *He Lives* followed, Ollie's arms pumping to the beat of the music, his foot tapping, a thin film of perspiration forming on his brow. The song ended and a quiet anticipation settled over the pews.

From the back of the church, head held high, the flowers on her hat in full bloom, Sister Areba Wright walked slowly down the aisle. Miss Richardson played softly, the congregation unmoving as though stricken with apoplexy.

When Areba reached the front of the church, she turned in a grandiose twirl and faced the spellbound parishioners. From the piano, Miss Richardson's fingers flew down the keyboard and Areba burst forth with *Wade in the Water. Wade in the water, children, wade in the water. God's gonna trouble the water…"*

Her voice thundered into the room, the chorus behind her whipping their voices into perfect harmony. Soon, the entire congregation swayed in song. *Wade in the water, children…* The rafters seemed to tremble. God was in their House and He was receiving praise through song.

In the third pew, Essie and Minnie clapped their hands and, with mounting glee, watched Areba's twirling purple chiffon skirt with its gargantuan ruffles. Her body rocked back and forth, forcing itself into a purple whirlwind and releasing Spur's feathers into the air, up into the rafters, closer to the heavens. It was a joyous sight.

On a nearby pew, Essie and Minnie, awestruck by the vision of Areba's performance as well as Spur's floating feathers, found themselves weak from laughter. *Yes, it was a great day.*

At 2:00, the pastor ended his sermon. "Now, you folks are dismissed. I believe you women have lots to do, so let's all work together. Time to enjoy some wonderful food!" He waved the congregation from the church and hunted down a cool glass of water.

Essie and Minnie organized the dessert table, where eight-layer cakes were iced to precision, pies glistened with the juice of blackberries and apples. Banana pudding was piled high with lightly toasted meringue. Nearby, a large platter of oatmeal cookies were stacked six inches high, next to a bowl of divinity candy.

Minnie leaned over the table. "That's Mrs. Henry's chocolate cake. This one here is Annette Jones' sweet potato pie. Oh, and I see Rhunette's cookies." Desserts famous around the community crowded the long table.

"Minnie, why don't we go ahead and slice these desserts. That way, they will be easier to serve."

"Oh, no! Miss Essie, ain't nobody slice a dessert that's not their own. It's tradition." Minnie arranged three sharp knives near the pies as well as a several pie servers. "You touch Vickie Booker's pie and she will stomp you to the ground." Minnie was not smiling.

Essie stared wide-eyed over Minnie's shoulder. "Here comes Areba. You think we're in trouble of some kind? She's walking like a mad elephant."

Minnie turned around and saw the purple lips of Areba's moving in resolute concentration. "Oh, she mad alright. You reckon we laugh too much?"

"No, no. I don't think she saw us laughing." Essie moved slightly closer to Minnie, behind her back, away from the danger that was headed their way. "Should we run?"

"You girls get over here?" Areba roared.

Essie and Minnie shivered and shrunk back as far as they could go without knocking over the dessert table. The purple skirt seemed to be alive as it came toward them, the chiffon fabric billowing out like an unleashed umbrella.

Areba crossed her arms and towered above them. "Ain't nobody touch them cakes and pies." She glowered at them suspiciously.

"Yes, mam, Miss Areba. We jus' keeping the flies away." Minnie ducked her head.

Essie stepped from behind Minnie. "Yes, mam. We're taking good care of these desserts." She couldn't help it—her eyes dropped to the long, purple skirt. "You're lovely today, Miss Areba."

Areba's purple mouth softened. "Thank you, Miss Donnelly." Areba straightened her hat. "It would please me greatly if you ate some of my macaroni and cheese." She dipped her chin. "And my carrot cake."

"I've been looking forward to your cooking, Miss Areba." Essie smiled sweetly, then averted her eyes when an orange feather floated near Areba's ear.

At twilight, only a few stragglers remained on the grounds of the church, some walked through the cemetery and around the many tombstones. Only crumbs remained on the wooden tables, the empty pans and plates removed and returned to their homes on nearby farms.

Essie and Minnie gathered the boys, whose tired bodies slumped into the backseat of the Pontiac. Ollie pulled out a few minutes ahead of them and slowly steered the truck down Tallokas road toward home.

"I like your church, Minnie," said Essie. "Your pastor's sermon touched many hearts today, especially the part about facing challenges in your daily life and how we can find guidance through a relationship with Jesus. That takes a lot of burden off us, doesn't it?"

"It sho' does, Miss Essie. Life ain't easy, now, is it? Why, if'n we turn to God, we will surely be blessed." She yawned and rested her head on the car window. "It was a long day." She suddenly turned to Essie. "Did you see daddy talkin' to Miss Richardson? Yes, mam, he sure did. Kinda smiled a little bit, too."

Essie laughed. "All I saw was Miss Richardson's eyelashes flashing your daddy. Her eyelashes were as long as Henrietta's."

CHAPTER THIRTY-SIX

It wasn't a scream, more like the howling of an animal in agony; an otherworld cry that escalated, stopping only to breathe and then beginning again. The gutteral sound raced through the Pontiac's open windows as it turned off Tallokas and into the farmhouse yard. Essie slammed on the brakes, slung open her car door and ran past the house and to the barnyard, where Ollie Pryor knelt with his head in his hands. He swayed his body back and forth, the shrieking continuing until he collapsed into the dirt.

"Mr. Pryor, what has happened?" Essie knelt beside Ollie, a hand on his shoulder. "Please tell me."

"Poor Henrietta," he moaned, pulling his face away.

Essie stood and crept closer to the hog pen, where Henrietta lay, her throat cut, blood seeping into the mud. Around her lay her eleven piglets, all dead, a bullet hole in each one.

"What's wrong?" called Minnie from the back porch.

"Go back into the house, Minnie! Keep those boys away!" Essie looked around the barnyard. The two dogs lay unmoving. Spur hovered under the porch steps, along with two hens.

"Dear God," breathed Essie. "Who did this?" She ran back to Ollie. "Ollie, who is the sheriff in Brooks County?"

"Sheriff," Ollie moaned. "Ain't no sheriff gone come from Quitman 'bout a dead sow."

"But, Ollie, this is a crime." Essie stared at the dead sow. Henrietta seemed to be smiling, the line of her jaw sweeping upward toward her ears. So pink and smooth. Her long lashes swept outward where a fly buzzed and then landed on her eyelid.

Yes, who? Who did this? Who would shoot eleven piglets and then slit the throat of their mama. Essie wandered around the yard and found six brass casings strewn about. The bottom of the casings were stamped with 30.30. *A malicious act by someone full of hate. Fat Belly.*

The house lay in semi-darkness, a lantern burning on top of the wood stove, its flame seeming to send a message in Morse code. Tall, then short; wide, then narrow; dancing as it slowly burned the kerosene.

"What we gone do, Essie?" whispered Minnie. The thin black girl sat on the floral couch, a blanket wrapped around her. Essie could see the lantern flame reflected in her wide eyes. "Daddy ain't never gone get over this. He done collapsed like I never did see before."

The shock and anger had long passed for Essie. She had spent the last hour watching the clock move to midnight, her mind sharp. "Minnie, you go on to bed. There's nothing we can do tonight."

"Poor daddy," said Minnie, the blanket dragging behind her as she walked to the bedroom.

At 12:30, Essie slipped out the door, cranked up the Pontiac and headed south on Tallokas road, then the road to Quitman. At Quitman she picked up highway 333 and crossed into Florida onto highway 53 and then 150 to Pinetta. In an hour she was at the Washington farm in Pinetta.

She turned out the headlights and slowly drove down the lane, around Julia Washington's azalea bushes and parked under a large pecan tree west of the house. The dogs never barked; they knew the old Pontiac and the woman who drove it.

Next to the house, Essie eased along until she stood beneath Mike Washington's window. "Mike," she whispered. His window was open; the sound of a soft snore, almost melodious, rose up. "Mike," she called again.

A shuffling in the bed, a few mumbled words, and Mike sat up. "Is… is somebody there?" he cried out.

"Mike, it's Essie."

"Essie? What in the world are you doing, Essie?"

"Come outside and I'll tell you." Essie ran to the backdoor of the house and waited. Of the three Washington brothers, Mike was the youngest at twenty-six years old, the brother who loved adventure and any reason to load up his .38 and set things right in the world. He went to college as well as worked the farm like his brother Bill.

Outside, he buttoned up his shirt and slipped on his boots. "I thought you went to Georgia."

"I did, but I'm back." Essie pulled on Mike's arm. "Come over here so we can talk." She led him to the Pontiac and they eased inside. "Mike, I need your help."

"Help? What kind of help?" He brushed his hair back with his hand. "Do you realize it's the middle of the night?"

"Yes, I do." She shifted in her seat and faced him. "Mike, there's this bad fella I ran into on the way to Boston. We had a little altercation at his roadside store when Minnie and I went in to get some coffee. Remember, the late cold that moved in about a week ago? The heater was out on the Pontiac and we needed something hot to drink and to warm up a bit."

Mike groaned. "I know what you did, Essie. You took that black girl in the store with you, didn't you? And there was a sign that said 'whites only'."

"Well, the sign's not there now." Essie let out a long breath. "Well... I did take Minnie inside with me, but that's not all. When I asked for coffee for Minnie, that fella pulled out a shotgun and placed it on top of the counter. Said he didn't serve coffee to niggers."

Essie closed her eyes and leaned her head on the back of the seat. "You know, I always carry daddy's .38 with me." She opened her eyes and grinned at Mike. "I thank the Lord daddy taught me how to shoot." She let out a yelp. "Of course, that fella didn't know that, or he'd never have pulled out that shotgun."

Mike hung his head. "What all did you shoot, Essie?"

"A hole in the coffee urn."

"What else?"

"A coffee cup."

"Then what?"

"You don't need to know all this, Mike. I'm just here to tell you that fella followed me to Minnie's daddy's farm and killed a big ole sow and her eleven piglets. And his two dogs. All this while we were at church all day yesterday."

Mike seemed to shudder. "Now I know why you're here, Essie." He found her eyes in the dark. "I know you have a plan."

Essie nodded and waited a long moment. "That I do, Mike. That I do."

CHAPTER THIRTY-SEVEN

Here's what I think, Mike." Essie furrowed her brow, deep wrinkles lining her forehead. She licked her lips and began stroking her chin. Essie Donnally might have been a farm girl from Madison County, but her ability to assess a situation, especially a complex one, was remarkable. Had she been called to fight a war, she would have risen to a general in the army. Decisive and commanding, Essie was afraid of nothing.

Her decision to drive back to Madison County was a good one. Together with Mike Washington, *Fat Belly* would rue the day he slaughtered Henrietta and her eleven piglets. "Mike, we cannot let Sam know about this."

"I understand. Can't let mama know either." Mike grinned. "Essie, I'm more afraid of mama than anybody."

"And your brother Bill doesn't need to know. Let's keep this between us."

"Well, heck, Essie, exactly what are we gonna to do? We can't kill this guy, you know."

Essie laughed quietly. "I'd certainly like to kill him, but let's do the next best thing."

Mike leaned back and stared at Essie. "And exactly what would that be?"

Essie gazed out through the windshield of the Pontiac, to the quiet plowed fields where the moonlight swept the straight furrowed rows and, at daylight, would turn over its sentry to the rising sun. "I want Ollie Pryor to receive compensation for the loss of his pigs. For the villainous act of trespassing in order to cause harm."

Her voice rose. "The abominable behavior of *Fat Belly* cannot be overlooked or go unpunished." *There she was; that hard woman, the same one who had protected her sister Jewell her entire life, the same one who challenged the pastor and his wife for their unChristian behavior, the same woman who stood up against a New York mobster who came to Madison County looking for trouble.*

She turned back to Mike. "I want you to follow me to Georgia. Bring your favorite gun." Her voice was soft, resigned.

"Okay, Essie. But I've got to be back home before mama gets up."

"You'll be home by sunrise. Let's go."

Essie parked on the farm lane and waited for Mike to start up the farm truck. It was 2:30, a night where no sleep was needed, a night where a heartbeat came fast, but steady. In her rearview mirror, she saw Mike pull up behind her. She shifted into first gear, turned on her lights and then suddenly braked. In front of the low beams, Bill Washington stood in the middle of the lane, his arms crossed and a face that was not happy.

Bill Washington, the oldest brother, the Washington brother who could be depended on to follow rules, a pragmatic thinker who was inherently calm and forthright. A brother who was a no-nonsense man who would never dream of traveling to Georgia to confront a hog killer in the middle of the night.

Bill approached Essie's car. His voice was low, "You and Mike conspiring in the middle of the night can't be good," he said matter-of-factly. He waved at Mike and turned back to Essie. "Care to tell me what's going on?"

Essie squirmed in the car seat and grasped the steering wheel. When she finally had nerve enough to look Bill in the eye, she spoke with unruffled authority. "Mike and I are going to take care of a little business."

Bill gave Essie a condescending smile. "That's obvious." His hand rested on the door frame of the car. "I think what I need is a little more detail, Essie. After all, it's the middle of the night, you're supposed to be in Georgia..." Bill looked back at Mike. "And Mike's... supposed to be... in bed." He lifted his eyebrows in question. "I'm all ears."

Essie's body slumped and she nodded her head. "There's a problem up in Georgia."

"What kind of problem?"

"There's this big fella I ran into when I stopped at his little roadside store on the way to Boston. We didn't get along too well because I took Minnie into the store with me. There was a sign above the door on the outside that said Whites Only." Essie paused. "You know that doesn't mean anything to me. If I wanted hot coffee, I was getting us hot coffee."

"Couldn't Minnie have stayed in the car? This is a segregated South, Essie."

"I wanted her inside where it was warm. There's no heater working in the Pontiac and the temperature had dropped near freezing."

"What happened next?"

"This big fella pulled out his shotgun."

"And?"

Essie averted Bill's eyes and glanced at the clock on the dash. "I happened to have daddy's .38 in my coat pocket."

"Oh, Essie! He could have shot you and Minnie." Bill looked away, the line of his jaw hardening into anger.

Essie nodded. "Yes, he could have. But when I shot the coffee urn and the cup he was holding in his hand, he realized what a good shot I was. After all, I shot right through my coat pocket. Dead on."

If it hadn't been dark, Essie would have seen Bill's face pale. He didn't speak for a long time. "So what's this problem you're getting ready to remedy?"

Essie looked at the clock again. *2:45 a.m.* "That fella found out where I was staying and followed me to the Pryor farm. While we were at church all day yesterday, this fella came and slit the sow's throat and shot her eleven piglets. Shot the two dogs, too." Essie voice quivered.

"How do you know it was the man at the store?" Mike walked up behind Bill and leaned on the car.

"Because he was that mean. He didn't get to shoot me and Minnie, so he shot the pigs instead. Also, he confronted me on a street in Boston. Threatened me."

"Why not let the sheriff handle it? What county is that? Brooks?"

"Yes, Brooks County. The farm's sixteen miles from Boston. Mr. Pryor said the sheriff wouldn't care one bit about a black man's pigs."

The three fell silent. From the woods, an owl called, another answered. At that moment, a cloud passed over the moon and left them with darkened faces. Bill sighed deeply. "Give me a minute to get my gun."

Chapter Thirty-Eight

They passed over the Florida state line into Georgia, Essie in the lead. Following her were the Washington brothers and two guns. The men traveled in the family's farm truck, a blue Ford that had carried hay and cow feed and now was on a mission of revenge.

Their Christian hearts kept the two men centered; their integrity well known throughout Madison County. There was, however, a huge dose of compassion within them, a compassion that compelled them to help the downtrodden, those who did not have a voice, those who, through no fault of their own, were thrown into a life of hard times.

Neither Bill nor Mike would hurt another human being; they would, however, even the odds when it came to the underdog. They felt it their duty to protect the unfortunate from the apple-rotten characters who unleashed their evilness upon the world.

The tiny store was dark except for a single light bulb on the outside of the building, right above the sign Whites Only—the sign that *Fat Belly* had restored to its rightful place after Essie demanded he take it down. And take it down, he did. Essie had stood behind him, her .38 in her coat pocket where two bullet holes proclaimed she would, indeed, put a third hole in her coat pocket if she needed to do so.

Essie, Bill and Mike parked a quarter of a mile down the highway, in a small cutout in the woods, a place where they could not be seen by passing traffic. It was 4:00 a.m. as they walked along the edge of the woods toward the store. Once they were closer, they could see a small house trailer jammed up against the back of the store, smoke coming out of a stovepipe at one end.

"Looks like he lives in that trailer. Probably has direct access to the store that way." Bill stepped closer, his ears tuned to any sounds. Behind him, Mike scoured the area around the trailer, then walked around the corner of the store. The lone lightbulb shone on the front of the store, where moths flickered in chaotic dance.

Essie kept her eyes on the small window at the end of the trailer that faced them. If a light came on, they'd look for cover and decide what to do. She motioned to Bill to follow her. At the front of the store, they stood at the entry door. "Let's see what kind of lock's on this door," she said. When she and Minnie were in the store, she didn't remember seeing any kind of sliding lock on the inside.

Bill pulled a small flashlight from his pocket and studied the doorknob. "Not sure about this," he said. "Why don't we go around back. Surely, this isn't the only exit from the store, as well as the trailer." They edged back to the trailer where they found Mike snooping around.

"Only one small window," he whispered.

"Let's figure some way to get him to come out of his trailer." said Bill.

"Like what?" Mike asked.

Essie held up her hand. "Let's go over to the edge of the woods."

The three hovered about twenty yards away, behind a clump of gallberry bushes. Then, without warning, Essie begin to howl like a tomcat looking for some evening fun. She threw her head back and from her throat came a long, loud, doleful cry. Bill and Mike stood wide eyed, only a moment away from running back to their truck and heading back to Pinetta.

"Well, take a look, boys." She pointed to the trailer and the light in the small window. "Looks like Fat Belly is awake."

It wasn't long before they heard the opening of the store's front door. "Come on." Essie ran to the back side of the trailer, Mike and Bill behind her. They plastered themselves against the side of the trailer and waited quietly, hardly breathing, as Fat Belly walked only a few feet past them. He stood on the edge of the woods, a flashlight beam running across the ground, back and forth, looking for the howling tomcat.

Essie emitted another mournful cry, raised her pistol and waited. *Fat Belly* jerked around and his flashlight beam caught Essie, Mike and Bill. He was unarmed, in his long johns and barefooted. "Wha... you bitch," he sputtered. He looked from Essie, to Bill, to Mike. "What's this? A lynching?"

Essie stepped forward. "That depends," she said, audibly clicking the gun's safety off.

"On what?" snarled Fat Belly.

"On how well you know your math."

"My math? You crazy woman, you! I'm calling the sheriff!" Before he took a step, Essie threw a few bullet casings at his feet. Confused, he shined the flashlight to the ground where the casings lay, then looked up and sneered at Essie. "Ain't nobody gonna cry over a nigger's dead hogs, now is they?" He laughed and shook his head. "If I was you, I'd head on outta here and take those two bozos with you."

Calling the Washington boys *bozos* was the beginning of Fat Belly's downfall. In an instant,, they both surrounded him, Mike grabbing a handful of his hair and Bill kicking his legs out from under him. Bill turned his flashlight beam on and held it inches from the man's face. "Mister, whether you know it or not, you're outnumbered. Get up! We're gonna have a conversation." The Washington boys pulled up the big man and pushed him to the front of the store.

Inside, the man was told to sit in the wooden chair next to the pot-bellied stove. His expression was belligerent, his eyes black with hate. The faded long johns he wore were dirty, a button missing, allowing his belly to protrude. "Guess you people know your days are numbered." He glared at Essie. "Especially yours, Annie Oakley. That gun in your pocket ain't gone be enough to stop me."

Essie, the hard woman, pulled a chair in front of Fat Belly, sitting down and leaning back. She crossed her legs and sent the man in the red long johns her most abominable stare. Mike and Bill had melted into a dark corner of the store. They had seen the persona of the hard woman before and knew *Fat Belly* was in for a ride like he'd never had before.

Essie uncrossed her legs and leaned forward, her forearms resting on her knees. Her face was masked; a perfect poker face. "We're not gonna kill you." She paused. "At least not today, anyway. Maybe tomorrow though." She jerked her head at Mike and Bill. "See those fellas over there?"

The man's eyes shifted to the Washington brothers. He looked back and nodded.

"Those two are gonna try to keep me from stripping you naked and staking you to the ground. But right now, all three of us are gonna provide you with an opportunity to keep all your limbs, your tongue, your testicles and your eyeballs."

In the corner, Mike and Bill squirmed. Mike became instantly nauseous and looked away. Bill's face twitched.

A small, unbelieving smile played across Fat Belly's lips. His eyes narrowed while he studied Essie's face. "You cain't do all that."

"Why not?" Essie asked, matter-of-factly, a steadiness in her words, like she was discussing a recipe for potato salad.

The big man shifted in his chair. Nervous, he twisted his hands together. Again, he glanced at Mike and Bill, perhaps a little bit of pleading in his glance. "Folks don't do that to people, that's why not."

Essie leaned back. "Folks don't slaughter a farmer's pigs, either. Just because they want to."

Becoming flustered, Fat Belly cleared his throat. "Those niggers deserved having their hogs kilt."

Essie grinned wide. From her coat pocket she pulled the .38. "Well, mister, guess what? I think you deserve to lose your testicles. When you slaughtered Mr. Pryor's hogs, you did so with hate and malice. I'm thinking I'm gonna to do the same thing to you."

Essie stood and looked down at the man. "Mike! Bill! Let's get him tied up real good. I see some rope hanging up on that wall over there."

"Now, wait a minute here," said the big man. "We can work this out."

"We're not so sure we want to work it out," said Essie. She motioned to the boys. "Get that rope, boys."

"Now, see here." Fat Belly raised his hands, palms open. "This is against the law."

"So was killing Mr. Pryor's hogs." Essie moved closer to Fat Belly and leaned into his face. She spoke in a whisper. "Those hogs were to be sold at auction. The money was to have bought shoes for two little boys. Seed for crops. Food to keep a family from starving. Parts to repair their tractor." She never blinked. "When you killed those hogs, you took more than their lives, you took a family's life."

Red-faced and sweating, the man fidgeted in his chair. "I can pay that nig—Mr. Pryor back." He gestured over to the back of the store, to the small doorway that led into his trailer. "There's a safe in there. Let me open it and I'll give you some money."

"How much?" asked Essie.

"A couple hundred," he said.

"A couple hundred for a big sow and her eleven pigs? What about her future litters? What about the trauma and heartache you caused this family? What about those two dogs—they were part of the family."

Eyes downcast, the man nodded. The muscles on his face contorted and, without looking up, he said. "You can have everything in the safe." Then, "That is, if you don't cut off my testicles."

Essie shrugged. "Show us where the safe is."

The Washington brothers followed Essie and Fat Belly into the trailer. The man pulled a small safe from a corner closet, spun the dial and, in seconds, the door of the safe swung open. He backed away, his body slumped, his chin tucked down on his chest.

Bill counted three thousand, two-hundred and forty-seven dollars when the last bill was laid on top of the stack of money. "Do you think this will cover it, Essie?"

"It's a start." She glanced at the stack of money, then pulled the .38 from her coat pocket. She rubbed the barrell and fiddled with the safety and then twirled the gun gently. "I want to make something very clear to you. When we leave here and your testicles are intact, that doesn't mean we won't be back. My advice to you is to stay clear of the Pryor farm. Is that understood?"

Fat Belly's eyes roamed the room, to Bill, to Mike and then to Essie. In a trembling voice, he replied. "I don't plan on going anywhere near Tallokas road."

"And that includes your friends. Correct?"

He nodded. "Yes, ain't nobody gone go near that farm."

Chapter Thirty-Nine

On Georgia highway 333, Mike and Bill headed south to Madison County, to the Washington farm, sliding in just at daylight. They eased down the clay lane and looked for lights in the farmhouse kitchen. It was dark; their mama still in bed. It was going to be a good day.

Essie had driven north from Quitman, back to the Pryor farm, the money in a feed sack beside her, all three thousand, two hundred and forty-seven dollars. To the east, an orange glow announced a new day. At the farm, Essie walked across the farmyard and pulled herself up on a fence rail and gazed out over the fields. She watched wild turkeys walking along the rows, probably pulling up new corn. A hawk screamed above her and soared over the plowed land, its wings leisurely moving up and down. An early morning symphony, as the sun rose higher and found the little farm on Tallakos road.

In a while, to the north, the sky had lightened into a hydrangea blue, dotted with puffy clouds shaped like double camellias. The sound of a tractor motor drifted across the barnyard, then the smell of diesel as it moved out of the barn, Ollie behind the wheel and a blade mounted on the front of the large machine. He didn't see Essie and continued to drive down to the hog pen. He pushed the hogwire fence over with the blade, then scraped the bodies of the pigs into a pile. From there, he pushed them about an eighth of a mile to a hole he had dug the night before. The farmer slowly covered the hole with dirt, then leveled it.

Ollie's ride back to the house was slow, an end to a disheartening task, one that only he could do. When he rounded the corner of the barn, he saw Essie standing in the middle of the barnyard, a feed sack in her hand. He didn't acknowledge her, shoved in the clutch and parked the tractor, turning off the puffing motor.

"Guess what you're going to do today, Mr. Pryor?" she called. She smiled and walked a few feet toward him, waiting for him to climb down off the tractor.

"Can't imagine," he said, with a disinterested tone, and walked away from her. His shoulders were slumped, his gait slow. He was a beaten man.

"Got something for you. Come over and get this feed sack." Essie moved a few feet and held out the bag. He didn't look at her or he would have seen she was happy. She dropped the bag and walked away.

On the back porch, she pumped water into an enamel pan and watched the black man amble to the feed sack. "What you got here?" he asked, leaning over and lifting the bag.

"Look inside," she called, drying her hands.

Ollie stared at her a long time, his eyes filled with sadness, a permanent hurt that wrapped itself around him and wouldn't let go. He lifted the bag and peered inside. Minutes went by until finally he looked up at Essie. "They's money in this here bag."

Essie stepped down off the porch and stood only a few feet away. "That's your money, Ollie," she said quietly.

"My money?"

"Your money."

His look was stern. "Tell me more, Miss Essie." He looked down into the bag once more.

Essie, the hard woman, lifted her eyes. "I was able to determine who killed your hogs and paid him a visit. I asked him to make restitution and he asked if three thousand, two-hundred and forty-seven dollars would be adequate. I replied 'yes, it would.' So there you have it."

"This is all mine?"

"To spend as you like."

Ollie Pryor's chin quivered, a sob escaping into his hands. His shoulders trembled. "I… I don't know what to say, Miss Essie. I ain't been too nice to you and all. Why you do this for me?"

Essie could have told Ollie the truth: that she had taken his daughter into a *whites only* store, shot a hole in a big coffee urn and then shot a cup from the hands of a man who pulled a shotgun on her. She could have told him it was this man who slaughtered Henrietta and her piglets and the family's two dogs. She could have told him about Mike and Bill, about the potential removal of testicles and a severed tongue. But, she didn't. Her smile was sweet as she walked over and hugged Ollie Pryor. "Because you're a good man, Ollie."

Part Two

The Plantations

Chapter Forty

The old south in Thomas County, Georgia, was destined to be discovered by northerners late in the 19th century, by men of great wealth who deemed it the best quail hunting in the world, along with the perfect place for their lavish lifestyles.

The county had been proclaimed the winter resort of the South, its social circles filled with some of America's richest families. Their opulent lifestyles were commonplace, a myriad of cultural and economic diversity that allowed them the best of southern hospitality.

The City of Roses, as Thomasville would become, was a city of golden heritage, its architectural elements some of the most beautiful in the South, antebellum as well as postbellum homes that stood in memory of a bygone era. A drive down Pinetree Boulevard, a perimeter road around Thomasville, provided the visiting northern families a *country* drive, where they could breathe the pine scented air, far away from the polluted cities of the North.

It was Thomas County's many plantations, like Pebble Hill, Greenwood and Melrose, that required their grand, extravagant lives to be serviced by the Negro population of not only Thomas County, but also Brooks and Grady counties.

Minnie Pryor had worked at many plantations since the age of thirteen, performing various duties, depending on the social events at the time. She became adept at dishwashing, floor scrubbing, and general cleaning. Soon, as she became older, her duties became more refined. She learned to serve at the splendid galas, which were held almost daily, especially during quail hunting season, in the sumptuously rich dining rooms, surrounded by extraordinary ornate plaster trim and the fine details of renowned architects who followed the Greek Revival style.

Sometimes, Minnie served out-of-doors, under moss covered trees and in expansive gardens as far as you could see. Minnie was in demand, especially at Pebble Hill, where she had worked for three years, not only in the winter resort season, but also during the hot summers. It was her lovely face and genteel manner that enamoured her to her employer, which was quite an asset when a plantation hired its employees.

The old Pontiac ambled along on Highway 84 toward Thomasville, a peaceful ride west. "Oh, it gone be so good to see Mr. Arthur and Mr. Herbert," said Minnie. "I ain't seen 'em since Christmas when they's had a big Christmas party. Why, everybody in the world was there. Even the President."

She took a quick breath. "Yes, mam. That bald headed man was so nice to me. He sure did like a deep dish apple pie. He said his wife, Mamie, would make him a pie and he'd eat the whole thing. Can you imagine?"

Essie slowed the Pontiac at a Georgian Northern railroad track where they watched a train head north, its boxcars noisily clacking by, each one painted a different color. "Did he visit often?"

"I'm not sure. I knowed I just saw him last year at Christmas. One of the guests played the piano in the music room and he say, 'Play *America the Beautiful.'* Well, that piano music filled the room and the President sang along. So pretty." Minnie giggled. "Then you know what, Miss Essie. The President walked over to his wife and picked up her hand and held it. And, he say to the piano man to play '*Smoke Gets in Your Eyes*' and he look into that woman's eyes and sang that song to her." Minnie quieted and became thoughtful. "That whole room done gone quiet."

The young black girl gazed at the passing fields. "You know, Miss Essie, I 'member somebody tole me that man was in a *perdickerment*. He had a bad heart and didn't think he'd run for president a second time." She turned to Essie. "Now, what do you think about that?"

Essie pondered Minnie's question. "I think you were very fortunate to have met him and Mrs. Eisenhower."

"That be for sure. He done love roses, too. And everybody knowed he loved golf the best. He played at that big ole country club every day. Somebody say to me that man said, 'If I can get up this hill, I'll run for president again' and he sure 'nuf did."

They neared the red hill region of southern Georgia, unending fields of peanuts flying past, the plants only a few inches high. Minnie hummed, happy her daddy had not said anything about her traveling with Essie. They had left clean laundry for the boys and a pot of vegetable soup for dinner. "I be back soon," Minnie had said.

Minnie chattered on, the twenty-three year old captivating as she flitted her hands this way and that and told stories of working on the plantations of Thomas County. She quieted a moment, thoughtful. "You know, Miss Essie, I know somethin' be the truth."

"What is that, Minnie?" Essie glanced at Minnie. So lovely and so in need of a life away from the farm in Boston.

"The truth is this. Dr. Grey done be sweet on you, I say. I see it in his eyes. He cain't stop lookin' at you. Those eyes of his just twinkles somethin' fierce when he watchin' you."

Essie frowned and thought about Minnie's observation. Indeed, Dr. Grey had shown her his tender side, a man who had found her alluring and seemingly wished for a reciprocation on her part. In her quest to find Jewell's child, her focus had been just that, not on a handsome Irish doctor. She would admit, however, he was quite appealing.

Then, there was Sam Washington. *Wonderful Sam.* Sam, who was not happy with her at the present time. She had not heard from him since the Sunday he stomped away from the Pryor farm and told her he would not be back. Nor had she called him. It was true: her dedication to the search for her niece was foremost in her mind. "Well, I doubt we'll see him again since he's at the Archbold hospital for a while. He mentioned Dr. Lundy would return to Boston today."

Minnie squinted at Essie, her expression one of disagreement. "You think that man gone let a beautiful, smart woman like you get away from him" She shook her head back and forth. "Yes, mam, Miss Essie, he gone find you wherever you be and that be true."

Newly planted cotton fields stretched for miles, their rows arrow straight, broken only by an acre or so of giant pecan trees with new spring leaves. A tractor traveled down the road in front of them, the farmer waving them past with his hat in his hand. The tractor's tires were orange with Georgia clay, as was the harrow he pulled behind.

They continued along, almost leisurely, leaving behind the community of Boston. Minnie occasionally hummed, and sometimes sang a line from an old hymn… *in the sweet bye and bye, we shall meet on that beautiful shore.*

They passed a road sign: *Thomasville, Georgia. Population 15,200.* Minnie stirred in her seat and seemed thoughtful, finally expelling a deep sigh. "Miss Essie, I sure am wondering about your niece. And your sister." She turned and leaned closer to Essie, lowering her voice. "I think 'bout that baby's daddy. I wonder where he is. Reckon he knows where his baby is?"

Essie felt the muscles in her throat tighten. *The daddy. Autrey Browning. She knew where he was. In a grave in Texas. She had loved Autrey Browning all her life.*

"The father of the baby is dead, Minnie. He died last fall. A few months after Jewell."

They rode in silence, perhaps thinking of unspoken questions. Essie had lived through the pain of Autrey's death; she had not, however, come to terms with his brief affair with Jewell.

Near downtown Thomasville, the air seemed to change, a sweetness that was familiar. "What is that I smell, Minnie?" They slowed on South Broad Street and Minnie told Essie to turn on Wright Street.

Minnie slapped her knee. "I's wonderin' when you gone smell the Flowers Bakery. Yep, right on time. They taking bread out of the ovens right now. Oh, lawdy. And, on Fridays, 'round 8:00 in the mornin', they be baking cinnamon rolls. Oh, that just makes me want to lie down on Wright Street so I can smell every little whiff of that bread."

Essie rolled down her window a little farther. "My goodness! I've never smelled anything so good." Essie pulled the Pontiac to the curb and the girls closed their eyes and sniffed the air. The skies above Thomasville drifted into a late afternoon blue, the clouds forming into angel wings as they flew east toward the oceans.

"Minnie! Where are we sleeping tonight?" Essie sat straight up in the car seat as her head swiveled from side to side, as if lost and looking for something familiar.

"Now, I got that all figured out, Miss Essie. They be a guest cottage over at Pebble Hill and when I works a long weekend gala, I sleep there so I can be available for anything that's needed. We'll talk to Mr. Herbert—you know, he's my friend I was talking to you about."

"That's good to hear. Let's drive over there and talk to him. Which way is Pebble Hill?" asked Essie as she pulled onto South Madison Street to West Jefferson, where they passed the Thomas County Public Library and stopped at a traffic light.

There was no answer from Minnie. She stared out the car window, not moving.

"Minnie! How do we get to Pebble Hill?" After a moment, Essie leaned over and peered out the car window. "What are you looking at, Minnie?"

It took only an instant for Essie to see the same thing Minnie saw. There he was: *Fat Belly*. He strolled down the Jefferson Street sidewalk as if no care in the world, a cigarette in his mouth and a green cap that read *John Deere*. He had yet to see them, but, sooner or later he would. The sight of the old Pontiac might as well have been a comet soaring right past Thomasville, announcing she was there. Essie pondered her recent conversation with Fat Belly. She had been clear, as had Mike and Bill Washington. S*tay away.* Seeing him in Thomasville was happenstance, a fluke. No need to worry.

"Let's go, Minnie. Which way to Pebble Hill?"

CHAPTER FORTY-ONE

Pebble Hill lay six miles directly south of Thomasville on Highway 319, where the gilded age of the powerful and prominent had gathered for decades. The plantation, a magnet for sportsmen from all over the country, as well as formal parties and fox hunts, carried with it an air of majesty, a place where one left behind a piece of their heart.

The Pontiac meandered down the lane to the main house, past magnolias, dogwoods, persimmon, and live oaks. From the distance, great stands of long-leaf pines soared one hundred feet into the air. Birds flitted in and out of the trees as if in a welcoming song, noisy and beckoning.

They found Mr. Herbert mulching rose bushes with pine straw, the scent of pine sap strong, almost alluring and somehow healing. The bushes were scattered along the path to the main house and mixed with an occasional dogwood. Herbert sang as he worked, a raspy tenor, "*I got a home in Beulah land that outshines the sun...*" His hands worked steadily, his back hunched over to the ground. His hair sprinkled like steel shavings across his scalp, Gray and close to his head.

"Mr. Herbert! It's me, Minnie." Minnie ran and threw her arms around him. "Mr. Herbert!" She squeezed him hard. "I done missed you so much."

Herbert Roundtree, the caretaker of the plantation owner's Walker hounds, leaned back and his happy eyes took in Minnie. "Well, there's my girl. Minnie, it's been too long, honey. This place ain't been the same with you gone." The old man shuffled his feet in a clumsy jig. "Nope. Not a bit a fun since you left."

Herbert squinted his eyes, peering at Essie. "Who you got here, Minnie?" He walked a few steps closer to Essie, holding out his worn hands.

"I'm Essie Donnelly, Mr. Herbert. Hello."

The thin man smiled and studied Essie. His face was smooth, no wrinkles, his skin the color of the dark brown in a box of Crayons. His eyes set beneath eyebrows that were the same gray as his hair and shaped into perfect arches. "I suppose you're Minnie's friend?"

Essie glanced at Minnie. "That I am. A good friend."

Mr. Herbert spoke eloquently. "They's nothing like a good friend, is there?" He looked back at Minnie. "Come here, girl."

Minnie obeyed as though Herbert were her father. She picked up his hand and held it. "Mr. Herbert, can I tell you a little story?" She waited wide-eyed, expectant.

"Oh, Herbert is always ready for a story. Let's hear it." He let go of her hand and the tall, skinny man tottered away to a wooden bench. "Come on, girl. I's too tired to stand up so long." He groaned as he sat and reached out for Minnie's hand. "Pebble Hill ain't the same without you."

"How's Mr. Clyde doin'?" Minnie loved the stableman and the horses, a prize herd that had won trophies from all over the country.

"Clyde's doing just fine. Got a few new horses from Kentucky last week. Mrs. Poe's as happy as can be." Herbert looked off into the distance, a remembering. "Been here thirty years taking care of the kennels. I reckon Mrs. Poe'd rather hear a pack of hounds running than eat when she's hungry." He laughed. "She's quite a woman, that woman."

"She been mighty good to me," said Minnie.

Herbert took off his cap. "Now, what's this story you gone tell old Herbert?"

Essie moved in closer and sat on the grass in front of the bench. Shade from a large live oak covered them. Festooned with Spanish moss, the tree stood in dignified repose, a relic that never tarnished.

Minnie began slowly. "Mr. Herbert, my friend Essie," she turned and smiled at Essie, "is looking for her niece. Her niece done be adopted out when she was just a baby and when I seen a picture of

Miss Essie's sister, I thought it was my friend here in Thomasville."

Essie pulled out a picture of Jewell and handed it to Minnie. "This here is a picture of Miss Essie's sister." She placed the photograph into Herbert's waiting hands.

He studied the picture a long time. "Hmmmm. She sho is pretty." He pulled the photograph closer. "I don't believe I 'member this girl, Minnie. Maybe she done visited here, but I don't recall. So many folks come and go." He handed the picture back to Minnie. He looked up. "Reckon Miss Alice might know?"

Alice Massey, Mrs. Poe's personal maid, was a woman whose fingers were in everything that went on at Pebble Hill. She knew who did and did not attend the church services held at the Piney Grove Baptist Church, which was built especially for the Pebble Hill employees. One could expect a lecture from her if they missed a service, especially on Sunday morning. Miss Massy required participation in the choir as well as daily scripture readings. She was well loved.

"She might know. We'll find her and see." Minnie stood and glanced at the big house. "Mr. Herbert, you think maybe Miss Essie and I can stay at the Overflow Cottage for a few nights? Or maybe the Waldorf House. I knowed they's extra beds 'round here for all the help comin' in for the quail hunts and all."

Herbert slapped his knee. "That's a fine idea, Minnie. You go on over to the Overflow Cottage. Ain't nobody coming in til the end of the week. 'course you know the rose festival is comin' up. You best check in with Mrs. Poe 'cause I'm thinking she'll want you right 'side her. They's lots and lots of peoples gone be here."

"Thank you so much, Mr. Herbert."

Closer. They were getting closer. Then again, there were the other plantations they'd have to visit if Pebble Hill did not provide the clues they needed to find the girl... *Melrose, Sinkola, Millpond, Dixie, Fair Oaks... Foshalee, Ring Oak, Winnstead... Box Hill, Greenwood...*

The most important question: *The girl? What about the girl? It was quite possible she had no desire to be found.*

Chapter Forty-Two

It was four in the afternoon, the sun dipping low in the sky, hardly seen behind the towering long-leafed pines. There could not be a more peaceful place, its lovely gardens beginning to bloom with spring flowers, a flush of color that rivaled a rainbow.

The Overflow Cottage was perfect. Austere in its furnishings, it was clean and neat, almost puritanical. The beds were comfortable and made up with lovely quilts showing pheasants and birds among bright greenery. A square oak table sat at each bedside, a Bible in the small drawers. Braided rugs, oval in shape, ran along each bed, on top of rough plank floors.

The photograph. Was it that simple? Show the photograph of Jewell to everyone they met and hope for a name, a lead to where she lived, to whom she belonged. *An adopted child?* Did she know she was adopted? Were her adoptive parents approachable? What if it wasn't her niece? How would she know otherwise? There had to be a way to find the girl Minnie had seen. Had talked to.

"Minnie, I'm going to drive into Thomasville to the courthouse tomorrow. We passed it on North Broad Street"

"The courthouse? What's at the courthouse?" Minnie lay on her bed and sighed. "This bed sure feel good."

"Minnie! Your spider bite! The scar's almost gone!" Essie leaned over and studied Minnie's leg. The girl had almost died. Hardly breathing, a high fever and delirious, she had lingered on the brink of death in a small room at the back of the Pryor farm house.

"Dr. Grey done a good job, didn't he? Hadn't been for him, I'd probably be in some grave somewhere." She laughed. "Oh, and Miss Areba would be singing at the funeral, *Take My Hand, Precious Lord,* a big purple hat on her head."

"Do you think Spur's feathers are still floating around?"

Laughter filled the small room while the sun eased farther down the sky, making way for an April night.

Essie lay down on the bed opposite Minnie, her eyes closing. "I shall forever be grateful to Dr. Grey for his care of you, Minnie."

"Yes, em."

The room darkened, shadows pulling in the night. *I'm here, Jewell. I'll find your baby for you. She's here somewhere; I know it.*

A soft tap at the Overflow Cottage door awakened Essie and she sat up. "Who's there?"

"It's me. Herbert. Got you some dinner."

"Come in, Mr. Herbert." Essie jumped up and shook a sleeping Minnie. "Minnie. Mr. Herbert has brought us some food."

The tall black man held a tray filled with leftovers from the Pebble Hill kitchens. He placed it on a small table at the front of the cottage, where a small kitchen with a stove and refrigerator faced a parlor-like room lined with bookshelves holding a myriad of books. Pictures of hunting dogs hung along the walls, all of them framed in rustic wood.

Minnie and Essie dutifully sat at the table. Hungry, they admired the tray from the Pebble Hill kitchens. Slices of tender pork with gravy and mashed potatoes were piled on a large plate, surrounded by fresh green beans and cinnamon apples. A plate of hot cornbread sat nearby, butter melting and running down the bread.

"I spoke with Mrs. Poe, Minnie. She's so glad you're back. She'd like to see you in the morning after she eats breakfast. She said to visit the kitchen for your meals." He glanced at Essie. "I told her about your friend. Mrs. Poe say to me to have your friend visit the kitchen, too."

Herbert frowned. "By the way, Mrs. Poe said they's no baby been adopted in Thomas County in years. No need to waste your time lookin' here for that girl in the picture."

Essie stared at Herbert, unbelieving. "I'm wondering how Mrs. Poe would know that, Herbert," she asked softly.

Herbert shrugged. "Mrs. Poe. She done know everything."

CHAPTER FORTY-THREE

Mrs. Parker Poe was a well-respected pillar of the Thomasville community, a member of the Historical Society and countless other philanthropic organizations, which kept Thomas County and its multitude of plantations in the limelight in not only America, but in the world. Only five feet tall, the well-bred woman lauded Thomas County's pristine long-leaf pine forests as the quail hunting capital of the world, its roses the most grand, and its citizens the epitome of southern hospitality.

At Pebble Hill, the sportswoman's Jersey cows were held in high esteem, her Walker hounds and thoroughbred horses receiving accolades from far and wide.

To her wide circle of friends throughout Thomas County and, for that matter, North America, she was simply known as Pansy. A pragmatic woman with a good business sense, her position as owner/headmistress of Pebble Hill had been a love story from the beginning. She held in her hands the culmination of the magnitude of heritage that dwelled in Thomas County. If Pebble Hill was a monarchy, she would definitely be its queen.

Pansy was a humanitarian, a visionary who had the wealth to honor the past and embrace the future of Thomas County. If you knew Pansy Poe, you knew a renaissance woman whose spirit was unleashed in everything she did.

"I declare, Minnie. You're back! It has been difficult to imagine Pebble Hill without you. You look wonderful." Mrs. Poe was dressed in knee patch jodhpurs, a matching jacket and a knit cap. Regardless of her petite frame, Mrs. Poe could handle any horse she rode, as proved by her skill in polo.

Minnie dipped her head. "I sure have missed Pebble Hill, Mrs. Poe."

Pansy slipped on her riding gloves. "I guess you know the rose parade and festival are this coming weekend. We'll have lots of folks here beginning Thursday. I'm hoping you can stay and serve at all meals, as well as be available for anything else that might come up." She smiled warmly. "Folks always take a shine to you, Minnie. Remember when the President asked you to sing along with him?"

Minnie sent Mrs. Poe a shy smile. "I sure did like Mr. and Mrs. Eisenhower. They be fine folks."

"The Duke and Duchess will arrive on Thursday evening from New York. Alice tells me their suites are in pristine condition." Mrs. Poe paused thoughtfully. "I'm wondering if the Duchess' favorite flower was the yellow day lily or that wonderful antique rose… the Madame Isaac Pereire?"

She flitted her hand through the air. "No worries. Alice will remember." Alice Massey, Pansy's personal maid for many years, filled many duties at Pebble Hill, one of which was remembering the likes and dislikes of their varied guests. Alice kept a small journal and recorded details about the Plantation's most renowned house guests.

Mrs. Poe smiled at Minnie. "Please stay in the overflow cottage while you're here, Minnie. Of course, the kitchen is open most all the time." Dressed to ride, Pansy Poe walked briskly from the room and headed for the stables, where her stablemaster, Clyde, had her favorite horse waiting.

At the cottage, Essie tidied the small rooms and stepped outside. To her left, the grand house seemed castle-like in the early morning mist. It was magnificent in every way, not so opulent as it was stately, a place that exuded great wealth. She gazed a long time at the architecture, the tall windows, the detail of the roof lines.

She heard the barking of the hounds as well as horses nickering from the stables. Peacocks strutted at the edge of the woods. Majestic, they disappeared behind a stand of beech trees only to be flushed out by a yardman with a rake in his hands. The plantation hummed along in a quiet beauty. Everywhere Essie looked there were pastoral vignettes of brick barns and stables, of blooming shrubs mixed with lilies and ivy. Across the way, the Piney Grove Baptist Church, built for Pebble Hill employees, sat serenely under the oaks, its steeple calling one to worship. Nowhere did she see anything that wasn't groomed or out of place.

Essie felt herself missing the farm. Missing DooRay and his goat Murphy. Even the neatly plowed fields seemed at this moment to hold a loveliness that she could not explain. The porch. The porch where she and Jewell had made a lifetime of memories.

Her breath caught. At once, she wanted to cling to something. Anything. She reached out, her hand grasping only air. *She was alone.* Her search for Jewell's child was more than finding the girl Minnie had seen. She was searching for something more. Sam Washington had said it so well: *Until you find yourself, Essie, you'll never be happy.*

She heard a shout. Minnie crossed the lawn, waving and smiling. "Good morning, Miss Essie. I thought you was going to sleep all day!" The slim girl was beautiful, her body swaying as she walked, her face beaming in the morning light. "I brought you some ham and biscuit."

What could she do for Minnie? Could the girl's life be anything but plantation work? Did she want anything more than what she had? She was intelligent but unaware. Essie watched the girl approach. Minnie could be anything she wanted to be.

"Thank you, Minnie. I made coffee. Let's have a cup before I leave."

"You're still going to that big courthouse?" Minnie almost skipped along the path to the cottage. Her skirt did not keep her long legs from swinging to and fro.

"I plan to, yes."

Inside the cottage, they poured coffee. Essie noticed the cups were from England. Fine China. A floral pattern that reminded her of a meadow.

"I'll be back later this afternoon."

"I be busy here. Mrs. Poe done told me the Duke and Duchess of Windsor will be here on Thursday night. She say she like for me to stay in the big house 'cause I knowed everything about her kitchen and dining rooms." Minnie laughed. "Miss Essie, please don't tell my daddy this, but sometimes I serves alcohol."

CHAPTER FORTY-FOUR

Essie pulled out on Highway 319, the highway that led to Thomasville. She had not slept well, her thoughts ricocheting in every direction. Carefully, she had appraised her past conversations with Bootsey Birthright, during which her anger returned. The conspiracy between her mother and Bootsey, her mother's best friend, had resurfaced in her mind. It was nothing short of subterfuge. Sending a pregnant Jewell to Atlanta in secrecy, lying to everyone, including her husband. And to Essie. Telling everyone that Jewell was at a finishing school in Switzerland.

Such a sham, an extravagant ploy to keep Edith Donnelly's pretentious position in the community above reproach. She had told her husband that Jewell must go to a finishing school in order to marry well. Reluctantly, Hubert had agreed, given Edith an untold amount of money. Money sent, not to the fictitious finishing school, but to Bootsey Birthright in Atlanta for the care of Jewell.

Essie had assumed Jewell's baby had gone through a formal adoption process, but in a cross-examination of Bootsey's recounting of that time eighteen years ago, she had surmised that was not necessarily the case.

Perhaps Bootsey had just *handed over* the baby, handed it over like it was chattel of some kind. If that were true, would there be records of some kind?

The Thomas County Courthouse, a massive building on North Broad Street, sat auspiciously in the hubbub of Thomasville's morning. Designed by architect John Wind in the Greek Revival architectural style, the courthouse was built in 1858, and had remained an impressive sight in downtown Thomasville for a hundred years. Essie parked nearby and walked a half a block until she was climbing the steps and entering the double walnut doors into the courthouse.

It was her inclination to call Sam and discuss with him her thoughts regarding the so-called adoption of Jewell's baby. His position as an attorney would certainly provide some kind of guidance at this point. It was, however, not an opportune time to talk with Sam; he still smarted over her leaving Madison County and going on this *wild goose chase,* as he called it.

Essie tried to think logically. If the baby was *given* to a couple, would they have recorded her birth? Of course, they would. Life required documents, especially birth certificates.

It was the summer of 1940 when Jewell had returned to Madison County. She had been away for almost a year. It was also the summer she had almost drowned, leaving her with an oxygen starved brain and an inability to think cognitively, a loss of memory that washed away the birth of her child.

On the second floor of the courthouse, Essie approached the Department of Vital Records, a vast collection of births and deaths recorded in Thomas County. A woman worked quietly behind the counter, her glasses sitting at the end of her nose, a pencil behind her ear. Her hair had been permed and the curls set tightly across her head, so tightly that it gave the impression her facial skin had been stretched toward her scalp in an unplanned facelift.

"Hello," she said to the woman's back. "What is the process for searching your records?" Essie pulled out a small notebook and pen and waited.

The woman turned around and smiled. "What type of record are you searching?"

"Birth certificate."

"What is the date of birth?" The woman held a pen and was poised to write.

"I don't have an exact date of birth. Just an estimation."

The woman nodded. Essie read her name tag: *Elsie Whitehead.* "What is the name of the person?"

Essie hesitated. "I don't have a name."

Miss Whitehead blinked a few times and took off her glasses. She gazed at Essie, questions in her eyes. "Perhaps you can tell me what it is you're trying to do." She rested her hands on the counter and waited.

I am trying to find my sister's baby. Please help me. "There was a baby," she said. "I think it was a girl. She was born in the summer of 1940, in Atlanta." Essie paused. *Jewell, I wish I had been there for you. We would have taken that baby and brought her back to Madison County.*

"If she was born in Atlanta, why are you searching Thomas County records?" *A good question, of course. The woman didn't know about Minnie and the picture of Jewell.*

"I... I have information that the baby was brought to Thomas County after her birth."

"What information?"

What information? A picture. A young black girl who worked the plantations saw her. Essie picked up her pen and wrote on her notebook. *Summer 1940.* Essie was fourteen years old that summer, loading watermelons for her father in the hot fields, ant bites on her feet, sunburned nose, sweat across her brow. And in Atlanta, Jewell was in labor. Alone. *Edith Donnelly knew. Bootsey Birthright knew.*

"Seventeen years old. The girl is seventeen years old and lives in Thomasville," she said to Elsie.

There was a long silence, filled with nothing but curious thoughts, a wrenching of the heart and a fervent desire to find a young woman. *A young woman who had no name.*

"Shall we start with June 1940 records?" Elsie asked, her words gentle. "I will assume you want to look at all the births recorded. You see, even if a baby is born in another county, the birth can be recorded anywhere." She placed a large binder on the counter. "As long as the information is correct, of course." Her eyes softened. "You have a lot of work to do."

The slim fingers of the woman opened the heavy book. "There is a table from which you can work." She pointed to a doorway that led into a small room. In the middle of the room was a large wooden table and two chairs. "Take one book at a time. You may not take the book from the room once it's released. When you're through with one book, I'll take it and give you another one. Chronologically, of course." She pushed a clipboard across the counter. "Sign your name, please, with date and time."

At noon, Essie listened to the Westminster chimes from the courthouse clock tower, then twelve clear strikes. The chair at the wooden work table had no cushion and her body ached from sitting so long. She rubbed her neck, then stood and walked around the small room.

She had studied June 1940's birth records carefully and found three births that fell into the criteria with which she worked. Her pen moved across her notepad slowly, each name meticulously recorded, along with the date and the name of the mother and father. A birth certificate was a small piece of paper, but it established who you were and gave you the right to citizenship. Essie wondered who delivered Jewell's baby. Bootsey Birthright had said a midwife. Did the midwife complete a certificate of any kind recording the birth? And was the birth properly registered. Her search was a longshot, a stab in the dark.

At 4:00, Essie closed the record book for August 1940. She sat a long time looking out the window, unmoving. Finally, she closed her notepad. Seven names. Seven possibilities. Seven reasons to continue her search.

April breezes swept N. Broad, the afternoon sun in its descent to the west, the aroma of the Flowers Bakery's bread drifting across the city. Essie walked down Broad to her car, her notebook grasped tightly in her hand. From across the street, a voice called out. "Essie! Miss Donnelly!"

Who else could it have been but Dr. Robert Grey? He bounded across the street, the wind catching his black hair. He rushed toward her, smiling. Inexplicably, he wrapped his arms around her in a warm hug. As if it was the most natural thing for him to do, he rocked her back and forth, laughter coming forth in happy bursts. "Oh, a joy to see you, Miss Donnelly. I'm after going to the farm to see you; but, alas, you are here!"

The doctor stepped back and looked at her. "I must inquire how those rooster injuries are doing." He half grinned. "Surely, my good work has made them well?"

Hardly recovered from Dr. Grey's jubilant greeting, Essie found herself delighted to see him. He continued holding her hand and she did not pull away. "My wounds from Spur have fully healed, thank you. You're at Archbold?"

"Oh, yes. There for a while. The hospital is in great need of doctors, you know."

"Where are you staying?"

"At the Hawkins house. A wonderful old house on Dawson Street." He pointed down Broad. "Not far away. They take very good care of me." He leaned closer. "Their breakfasts are wonderful. They served scones this morning."

He pulled her along the sidewalk and they stood in the shade of a blooming dogwood. "It appears as though you have begun your search?"

"Minnie and I are at Pebble Hill for a short while." She looked away for a moment, then back to the handsome face. "I've been at the courthouse searching birth records. I was thinking perhaps a birth certificate had been recorded for Jewell's child. You know, in case the family is in Thomas County."

"I see." Dr. Grey reached out and pulled a strand of hair away from Essie's face. His fingers were warm, a gentle brush of her skin and then a tug at her hair.

"I found seven possibilities."

"Seven good possibilities, I will assume."

Yes, thought Essie. *Seven girls in Thomas County born the summer of 1940. Jewell, did you hear that? Your daughter's here, Jewell. I can feel it.*

"Yes, I think so. I'll continue my search as planned." Essie found herself studying Dr. Grey's face, looking for the twinkle Minnie had mentioned, the longing the good doctor seemed to have for the hard woman from Madison County.

"So your work is going well at the hospital? I imagine it's quite different than Dr. Lundy's office… and the Pryor farm."

"Going well. I have several associates with whom I've worked before—even some from Johns Hopkins. Medicine is really a small community and Thomasville is fortunate to have doctors with such esteemed credentials." He hesitated, thinking, his eyes sweeping her face. "Say, I won't be working tomorrow. How about lunch at The Plaza Restaurant? I hear their steaks and seafood are superb. And, I'd really like to hear more about Pebble Hill. I spoke at the historical society meeting the other day about the influx of the Irish in Thomas

County and met Mrs. Poe. In fact, she has invited me to visit Pebble Hill. She's a lovely woman."

"I've yet to meet Mrs. Poe. Perhaps I will in the next day or two." Essie smiled. "The influx of the Irish? You mean you're not the only Irishman in Thomas County? In Georgia?"

"Not hardly!" He tilted his head back and laughed. "There are Irish everywhere, but perhaps they are not so bold as I." He dipped his chin. "And lunch with this Irishman? Tomorrow? Noon? Meet me at The Plaza Restaurant. It's at the corner of South Broad and Smith Avenue."

Essie looked away, her eyes following a pair of mockingbirds flying past them to a lovely Victorian home down the street. They lighted on the rail of a small balcony above the front porch.

When she turned back to Dr. Grey, he frowned at her and said softly. "We shall have a lovely visit together."

"Of course. Noon."

The clock tower struck the half-hour, the sound somehow melodic, announcing the moving of the sun, a shift of the universe, the passing of time.

Dr. Grey clapped his hands. "I have a splendid idea! Let's go see the Big Oak. It's over three hundred years old. I have yet to see it! It's over on Monroe Street. Let's go!"

Without waiting for her answer, Rob slipped his arm through Essie's and began to walk briskly down Broad, a short way to Monroe Street. They passed the First Baptist Church and the Hardy Bryan House and were out of breath when they turned right onto Monroe, where they found the majestic oak. Standing sixty-eight feet tall with a trunk circumference of twenty-six and a half feet, the tree was mammoth, a natural Thomasville relic that surpassed anything standing in Thomas County.

The doctor and Essie peered upward, their necks craned, their eyes roaming the massive limbs that reached skyward in a welcoming salute.

It was a reverent moment. Since the 17th century, the oak had lived in this spot, had seen the creation of Thomasville and, no doubt, had thrived in the red clay soil of Thomas County. The tree had seen the Apalachee Indians, then the Lower Creek tribe, taken from Thomas County in the sweep of Indians into the Trail of Tears to Oklahoma.

The majestic tree had seen every wild animal imaginable and perhaps even had some of them climb its sweeping branches.

It seemed the natural thing to do. A slow pulling of Essie into his arms, a hand lifting her chin, his lips finding hers. All so slow. A moment where everything stilled. The wind, the sounds, everything was far away, waiting. Essie placed her hands on Rob's shoulders, her toes pushing her body closer, upward where his lips had found hers. *Don't stop. Please don't stop.*

Chapter Forty-Five

Twilight had settled on Thomas County when Essie turned the old Pontiac down 319 and steered back to Pebble Hill. She looked west and saw only a thin layer of sunlight along the horizon. She glanced east and wondered if there was a new moon. Somehow new moons made her hopeful, a promise of something wonderful that sat waiting for her.

Sam. Her heart. Where are you, Sam? The Irishman had kissed her. Not only that, she had kissed him back. *What was her weakness?* Was it desire? Need? A longing for a champion in her cause to find Jewell's child? Sam had given her everything except… except his blessings on her quest to find the baby.

The sobs came violently, like giant waves on an ocean's shore. Crashing and flooding her chest, they came in torrents, with no end in sight. She pulled the Pontiac to the roadside and turned off the motor. *Sam. She must see Sam.*

The plantation lay in quiet repose, a tranquility that seeped from the lighted arched windows of the grand house. The grounds seemed in slumber, the Walker hounds bedded down as were the horses. The peacocks were nowhere to be seen, most likely roosting high in nearby trees. The landscape artist Thomas Cole would have taken delight in the softness of dusk on the plantation, his brushes working quickly to capture the lingering light that fell across the brick barns and the winding paths, creating a beautiful masterpiece.

The overflow cottage was dark except for one light in the front room, where the kitchen and dining room joined together into a cozy place for eating and visiting. Essie began to hear crickets as she walked the path to the cottage, a soft night breeze lifting the hairs at the back of her neck. She stepped inside and Minnie greeted her.

"There you are, Miss Essie. How is everything'? You been gone all day long." The girl smiled and left the couch. "I got us some leftover fried chicken and green beans. And guess what? The cook baked pies today. Two kinds. They's coconut cream and apple. She made banana pudding, but those yardmen done eat it all."

Minnie pulled two plates from the cupboard and uncovered the tray that held their dinner. She looked up at Essie. "I hope you're hungry."

"Oh, yes. Everything's fine, Minnie. It's been a long day. Thomasville is a beautiful city." She washed her hands and sat at the table and began serving their plates. "You know why I went to Thomasville, don't you, Minnie?"

"I been waitin' for you to tell me, Miss Essie. I know you is a private person, but I was hopin' you'd talk to me."

The young women began eating, a slow enjoyable meal in a lovely cottage on one of Thomasville most beautiful plantations. "Minnie, I know we're going to visit other plantations and try to determine if the girl you saw is truly Jewell's daughter." She wiped her mouth with a linen napkin. "But, I was thinking that maybe if that girl is Jewell's daughter, her birth might have been recorded right here in Thomas County."

Minnie was wide-eyed. She stared at Essie. "A birth certificate?"

"Yes! Exactly. Why wouldn't her new parents leave Atlanta and come back to their home here in Thomasville and have the birth recorded? You see, we don't really know where the baby was born. I think maybe a midwife at the girls school. Most likely, whoever delivered the baby completed a birth record of some kind, with all the pertinent information. The baby's name, weight, date and time of birth, parent's name.

"Then, the new parents could file a legal birth certificate. And that's what I'm looking for." Essie slid a piece of pie onto her plate. "I have seven names from the recorded births, Minnie. And I'm going to find each one of those girls."

"My, my, Miss Essie. Those be a lots of girls."

Essie pulled out her notebook and opened it, running her finger down the names. "Alice Winthrop, Deborah Kline, Margaret Bozeman," she called out. "Oh, Minnie, what if Alice Winthrop is Jewell's child?"

"That'd be somethin', Miss Essie."

Essie placed the notebook in front of Minnie. "Do any of these names look familiar to you? The surname—the family name?"

Minnie studied the names, her eyes moving slowly across the page. "No, nobody here I know." She frowned. "Miss Essie, let's don't make this too hard. I say we take that picture and go visit some plantations. We just pay them a visit, say we looking for someone and pull out that picture." Minnie slapped the table with her hand. "That girl's in Thomas County, for sure!"

Seven *girls. Of the seven, how many lived on plantations? How many plantations were there?* Essie's mind tumbled. If she found the girl, what would she say? *Nothing. She could say nothing. The girl was someone else's child.*

Essie reached over and turned out the bedside lamp. Minnie had slept while Essie had studied the names in her notebook. There were no unusual notations on the records she read, just dates and names. All records indicated births in Thomas County. *Bootsey Birthright. I know you know more than you told me. I'm certain you knew the people who took the baby. Maybe mama didn't care about the baby, but I know Jewell did. And, if I had known, it would never have happened the way it did.*

There would be no sleep. *The Irishman.* Did it begin the moment he flung open Dr. Lundy's office door in the middle of the night wearing only his boxer shorts? No. *Nothing* began! He saved Minnie's life. That's what doctors do!

Was it Spur's slashes across her legs that brought the good doctor a little closer to Essie? He was there for all of them: Minnie, the boys, Ollie. *Robert Grey was a physician.* Of course, he cared. Of course, he administered to them.

Robert Grey was a man. Take away his small doctor's bag and he became a tall, dark-haired Irishman whose eyes sought her out; she could not help but notice his admiring glances. When she exposed her bare leg, his hands had gently dressed her wounds, his demeanor that of a doctor. When she sat on the Pryor's front porch with him, he watched the moon with her and somehow she knew he wanted to reach out and touch her.

He had worn blue jeans, a flannel shirt and boots when she had seen him on Broad Street. Such a common fellow, no pretentiousness to be found as he had bounded across the street and snatched her into a giant hug. He smelled of soap. Clean and fresh. She felt a slight roughness of whiskers when his face touched hers, his skin warm.

In the morning, she would call Sam. Tell Sam to come to Thomasville. Tell him to leave Madison County, his law practice, his family, Judge Earp and the trial of Stanley Barnwell. *Why?* Why did she demand he drop everything and come to Thomas County? *Because she was afraid.* She was afraid Robert Grey would capture her heart, would sweep her into an impassioned love affair that was all consuming.

Essie pushed her face into her pillow and fell into a fitful sleep. Her dreams were not of Sam, but of the Irishman.

CHAPTER FORTY-SIX

He was thirty-five, perhaps considered old not to be married and with children. Medical school had robbed his youth with long nights studying, residency and now a full-fledged doctor who spent sixteen hours a day at the Archbold hospital. Robert Grey's life, since Ireland, had become complicated in many ways. Since medical school and residency, he had worked at Johns Hopkins in Baltimore, Mount Sinai in New York and various others medical facilities throughout the northeast.

It was a call from Dr. Lonnie Lee Lundy in Boston, Georgia, an associate of his uncle's, that brought him to the deep South, a place that had captured him since stepping from the Atlantic Coastline railroad in Savannah, then catching a connecting train to Valdosta, then Thomasville. He couldn't say exactly what it was that called to him when he said yes to Dr. Lundy.

"Why, of course, Dr. Lundy, trout fishing is a man's little piece of heaven. You must go to the Blue Ridge. I hear the mountains are beautiful, like Ireland. I'd be delighted to fill in for you while you're away."

The red clay hills of Thomas County had spoken to him of new things, of perhaps finding what it was that he had left behind in Ireland. His uncle had promised great opportunities in America and, indeed, he had found them, found them in the great cities of the northeast. But, nothing like what he found in the South. He had lingered at the Thomasville train station upon his arrival on that cold March day. He roamed the city for a week before he drove to Boston, only forty-five minutes east and began his position for Dr. Lundy.

It was on the third morning of his stay in Thomasville, as he walked down Broad Street, that he had stopped and listened to the clock tower of the courthouse. The chimes seemed to speak to him. He felt as though he levitated, a realization that he would always be Irish, no matter where he was. It was here, in the glorious Southland, with its extraordinary history, that he felt most at home, less separated from his homeland.

And then there was a lassie. Had the good doctor squinted his eyes and observed Essie Donnelly from afar, he would have declared she was Irish through and through. *How could she not be?* Her auburn hair and brown eyes were proof enough. Ah, but the frisky way she had about her said it loud and clear.

After leaving the big oak and sending Essie back to Pebble Hill, he walked briskly down Monroe and turned right onto Dawson Street and the Hawkins house. There was a skip in his walk, as though he heard music in the air, a tune that gave him the rhythm of a *man in love*. Essie had stirred him, stirred him like no lass in Ireland had; nor, for that matter, any lass anywhere.

He bounded up the steps and went immediately to his room on the second floor. His schedule would take him to work for the 11:00 to 11:00 night shift at the hospital and he desperately needed sleep. No sooner had he put his head on the pillow he was fast asleep and dreaming of Essie Donnelly.

The faded pick-up truck had followed Rob to the Hawkins House. Fat Belly had recognized him. *That's the feller who was at the Pryor farm.* The man parked at the curb and turned off the motor. *He's a friend of Annie Oakley's, the woman who threatened to cut off my gonads, my tongue and gouge out my eyeballs.*

CHAPTER FORTY-SEVEN

The City of Roses. Considered the winter resort of the South, Thomasville had also been lauded the Rose City since the early 1920's, a three-day festival in April of every year that hosted acres of roses, as well as the people who loved them. Mrs. W. K. Atkinson, 1957's chairwoman, shared her duties with Ed Kelly, who was the general chairman of the magnificent event. Preparations had begun long before the event was scheduled, the only detail not covered being the weather. No one could predict rain or shine for the festivities that were so eagerly awaited by the citizens of Thomasville, but incredibly, it had never rained during the festival.

The rose shows were judged by a panel of horticulturalists with extremely high standards of excellence, and entries were scrutinized with almost surgical precision. Everywhere, whether at the Plaza Restaurant, the Thomasville Library or the Historical Society, the subject was *roses.* At the corner of Broad and Remington Avenue under the "big top," members of the Thomasville Rose Society fluttered about, their eyes on the prized entries.

The two-mile long parade of roses, with dozens of floats, would begin at the corner of Broad and Clay, where a float covered in roses would carry The Rose Queen and her court through the City of Thomasville for all to see. Most of the girls were seventeen and eighteen years old, still in high school and soon to graduate in June.

The Rose Queen contestants brunched at the Greenwood Plantation where Mrs. Betsey Whitney, a lovely, poised brunette, was their gracious hostess. "Ladies," she called across the large dining room. "Just two more days and one of you will be crowned the Queen of Rose City." Mrs. Whitney's eyes scanned the room and took in the lovely faces of Thomas County's most beautiful young girls, most from Thomasville High School. "Where's Betty Lou?" Her eyes darted down the table. "Oh, there you are! Did you get your hair cut?

Betty Lou rolled her eyes. "I didn't want to, but mama made me."

Beside her, Sandra Larson giggled. "Remember when your mama tried to trim my bangs, and I ran home?"

"All of us know how your mama is with those scissors," said Yvonne Gibson. "She wants all of us girls to have bangs!"

Mrs. Whitney shushed the girls. "As you know, besides the queen, there will be six princesses chosen to ride the Rose Queen float."

Across the room, the young girls squirmed with excitement. "Please, please. Get plenty of rest prior to Friday's event," called Betsey, "especially you, Beatrice. Your mama told me you stay up really late every night." Beatrice Cavender shook her head. "Mrs. Whitney, that's not my fault. Our dog barks all night long and I can't go to sleep."

"Well, just do your best because—"

From the entry doorway into the spacious dining room, a slim man, handsome, with a receding hairline, glided into the room. His brown eyes were warm and laughing, as was his smile. If ever there was a dapper dresser, it was this man. "Oh, Betsey! So sorry to intrude."

"Oh, no, Fred. You're not intruding. Do come in! I'd like these ladies to meet you." Betsey swept her arm wide in a welcoming gesture. "Ladies, I'm sure you recognize Fred Astaire. He's our house guest all this week."

Fred bowed slowly. "What have we here, Betsey?" He glanced around the room and waved to the wide-eyed ladies.

Betsey lifted her eyebrows. "Why, Fred, these ladies are vying for Miss Rose Queen. Aren't they lovely?"

Fred Astaire practically floated to the dining table and held out his hand to the girl seated at the end of the table. "Such a pleasure to meet you. Shall we dance?"

The renowned dancer gently pulled the girl into his arms and began humming a tune from *Puttin' on the Ritz.* His light baritone melted into *'have you seen the well-to-do, up on Remington Avenue...'* He held the girl's hand and danced around her, his feet light and airy as he slowly twirled her around. It only lasted a moment, but the faces in the room were spellbound. So was the dark-haired, green-eyed girl in his arms.

CHAPTER FORTY-EIGHT

Miss Essie! Wake up!" Minnie shook Essie's shoulder. "Let's go find your niece. The day's a wasting. Sun been up for a while now."

Essie stirred, her eyes still shut. She stretched and turned over. "I'm coming."

"I got coffee made and some breakfas' from the big kitchen. This day's gone get away from us if we don't hurry." Minnie pulled back the curtains and soft rays of morning sun fell across the small room.

Across the yard, the peacocks screamed and took off for the woods, the sun catching their brilliant feathers. From the milk barn, a flurry of activity as Pansy Poe's prized Jerseys gave their milk for the day. In the stable, Arthur Massey saddled Mrs. Poe's favorite horse *Mighty* for the horsewoman's morning ride.

Sleepy-eyed, Essie cranked up the Pontiac and let it idle for a while. The morning was cool, a spring that was slow and creeping, like a bud opening and revealing everything that was beautiful inside. She knew the days would become warmer, the cotton planted in March poking up through the red clay soil and promising an abundant harvest in the fall.

She waited for Minnie, who had run to the kitchen and packed a lunch for them. The cook was generous to the young girl, remembering all the times Minnie had peeled potatoes and washed dishes in her large kitchen. Essie watched Minnie cross the long yard, a swing in her gait, like a fawn with long legs and a sweetness about her walk. She considered Minnie a good friend, loyal, dedicated to her Christian beliefs and, most certainly, prided herself as the Pryor family's surrogate mother.

Her role in the family as caretaker of her younger brothers had been thrust upon her at a young age, but she had assumed those responsibilities as one must. Essie wondered if the girl could have a life beyond Boston, Georgia, or even, for that matter, want one. Her potential was there, but perhaps not the opportunities.

Minnie jumped in the car, her face bright, her lips in a wide grin. "Oh, Miss Essie. We gots us some fine ham biscuits with grape jelly. I had to grab them quick 'cause Mr. Herbert was eyeing them for sure."

"They sure smell good. Are those cinnamon buns,too?" Essie peeked under the dishcloth that covered the plate.

"Yes, 'em. Cinnamon buns with icing." All of a sudden Minnie squealed, her eyes opening wide. "Miss Essie, they's four of them. Two for me and two for you!"

They laughed all the way down the long lane, driving away from the grand house, away from the pine forests, the wiregrass and the ghosts of times when Indians ran through the trees in search of wild game and the promise of peace was in the air.

"Minnie, where are we going?" Essie uncovered a cinnamon bun. *Jewell, we're looking for your baby today.*

Minnie became serious. "Now, Miss Essie. You're gonna have to trust me. I's takin' you to Susina."

"Susina?" said Essie. "Another plantation?"

"That's right. Turn left." Minnie sipped her coffee. "South."

Essie turned off the Pebble Hill drive onto highway 319, going south. Early morning mist rose from the woods on each side of the road, the pines tall and majestic. A faint scent of pine seemed everywhere. A hawk flew across the road in front of them and landed nearby, its head swiveling. To their left, the sun rose higher, sending shafts of light through the trees.

"I done be at Susina and workin' for Mrs. Mason last summer. Her name is Rosalie, but everybody calls her Rodie. She tell me to call her Rodie, but I just cain't call a white woman who own a big plantation by her first name. So I just calls her Miss Rodie."

"Do you think you might have seen my niece there?" Essie looked hopeful.

Minnie frowned. "I cain't remember, Miss Essie. I worked so many plantations last summer and around Christmas, too. Susina just be one of them. They's so many people comin' and goin'." Minnie laughed and slapped her knee.

"What's so funny? Essie got caught up in the laughter, the Pontiac speeding south, rockin' and rollin'.

"Oh, my. Miss Rodie, she done be so irritated. They was this movie star who came to Susina so she could study how to be a southern lady. So she watch Miss Rodie, try to talk like her, move like her and be like... you know... Scarlett O'Hara or somethin'."

"What movie star? Did you see her?"

"I 'member she had light hair. Very beautiful woman. Miss Dunway or something like that."

"Dunaway? Was it Faye Dunaway?"

"Yes! That's the name. She gone be in a big movie. About a sunset, I think." Minnie pulled out a ham biscuit and handed it to Essie. "Miss Rodie get so tired a that woman follerin' her around." Minnie jerked her head around to Essie. "Then, that woman left without saying goodbye. Just left." Minnie cackled. "She like *gone with the wind!*"

It took but one change of railcar to arrive in Thomasville from just about any northern city, and a total of thirty-eight hours listening to the clickety-clack of the steel wheels on the tracks. The Atlantic Coastline Railroad brought Heywood Mason and his wife Rosalie to Susina where they became revered community members, the ultimate host and hostess of their grand Greek Revival style house.

At Minnie's direction, Essie steered the car down a long winding lane where azaleas lined the drive and were beginning to bloom. Some white blooms mixed in with pink, all planted near the base of the many dogwoods, whose branches draped over the drive.

The house sat on a knoll, surrounded by large live oaks and in view of Mitchell Pond. Susina meant "plum" in Italian and lived up to its name with the many wild plum trees throughout the plantation.

"Oh, my," said Essie as she gazed across the vast lawn. The house's portico was supported by four two-story, fluted and tapered round columns, another creation by architect John Wind. Almost breathless, her eyes roamed the side porches and the enormous front door of the postbellum home. Underneath the portico was a cantilevered balcony, its grandeur designed by the infamous English architect.

"Go 'round back, Miss Essie. They's a place to park right by Miss Rodie's old car." Minnie rolled down her car window and hollered across the yard. "Grady! Grady! It's me. Minnie!"

From the center of a formal garden, a tall lanky black man waved. His grin was as wide as the Missouri River, teeth big and white against his coalmine dark skin. "That you, Minnie?" His voice was rough, like he had called hogs all his life. He meandered around the shrubs and small trees and, within yards from the car, he began laughing, his thin chest rumbling deeply. "Oh, child. Is it really you? Ain't seen you since last summer."

Minnie jumped from the car and ran into the tall man's arms. "Grady! I'm so glad to see you."

"I thought you'd done gone away forever, Minnie. You doin' okay?"

"I'm fine, Grady. Just worried 'bout you, that's all. Last time I seen you, you had pneumonia."

"Oh, Miss Rodie done take me to the doctor and I's all well now. Don't you fret no more."

"Where's Miss Maudie?"

"Oh, she done baking pies today. Gots lots going on wid that rose stuff. I ain't worked so hard in my life. Look at these here blisters." He spread his large garden rake hands for her to see. "Done lost my gloves."

"My goodness. We need to get you some salve on those. They look awful."

"Don't you worry, none. Mr. Grady gone be fine." He glanced at the Pontiac. "Who you got wid you?"

"Come." She grabbed his sleeve. "I want you to meet my friend."

The pair ambled along the yard to the car, the sun warm on their backs. "I need to tell you somethin', Grady. My friend and I is looking for a girl."

"What girl?" Grady took off his hat and fanned himself. Sweat glistened on his face, and perspiration rings stung his shirt.

"You'll see."

Essie found herself watching the tall man, so tall he could have folded up like an accordian. She got out of the car and smiled. "Hello. My name is Essie Donnelly."

Grady eyed Essie carefully. Wasn't many white women talked to a black man unless they were his employer. He stood tall and waited a moment before speaking. "Hello. I'm Grady."

Essie reached out her hand and felt the blisters on Grady's hands as he held hers in a quick shake. "I like your garden, Grady." They strolled together to the massive kitchen on the back of the house and stood under an oak tree.

Grady nodded and placed his hat back on his head, then glanced at Minnie. "You come back to work at Susina?"

"Maybe this summer. Right now I'm over at Mrs. Poe's. She done asked me to help during rose week. All these peoples is coming. She said some king and queen was coming."

"You told me the Duke and Duchess of Windsor, Minnie." Essie laughed.

"Oh, that's right. They's royalty, all's I know." The girl grinned, her lovely face lighting up the morning.

From the back door of the kitchen, a short, portly black woman eased down the steps. "I thought I heard you out here, Minnie." The woman held a big enamel bowl in her hands. "I sure could use some help 'round here. Mrs. Mason done tell me they's twenty-five peoples comin' to dinner on Thursday night. Woe is me."

Maudie sat the metal pan down on the brick walk and five cats came running up from beneath the house. They gathered around the pan and enjoyed a breakfast of milk and scraps from the kitchen. They were large cats with long fur and tails that sashayed back and forth as they ate.

"Miss Maudie, this is my friend Essie. We's here to show you a picture."

"A picture? What kind of picture?" Her curiosity showed in her face, her eyes opening wider and glancing around.

Essie pulled out the picture of Jewell, wanting to touch the black hair and the soft cheeks. Jewell's green eyes smiled. "This is my sister, Miss Maudie. She died last summer, but she may have left a daughter that... that I didn't know about. Minnie says she saw a girl who looks just like my sister last summer at one of the Thomasville plantations, but she doesn't remember which one. Black hair and green eyes, about seventeen or so." Essie eased the picture forward, her heart beating quickly.

Miss Maudie's hand reached out and Essie saw flour caked beneath her nails and smelled cinnamon and other spices as she pulled the photograph from Essie. The woman squinted her eyes and stared a long time, moving the picture closer. "Hmmmm," she said. "I believe I have seen this girl here at Susina. Maybe last summer. Not sure." She looked up at Essie. "We has so many parties and so many guests."

"Of course. I understand. Perhaps you will remember sometime later." Essie gave Maudie a half smile, "Thank you for trying to help."

"Yes, mam. I tell Mrs. Mason 'bout this girl. Maybe she know her."

"Would you? That would be so kind of you."

Essie and Minnie left Susina Plantation, but not before eating lemon meringue pie under a shady oak. Maudie's crust was light and fluffy, the meringue piled high like puffs of sugar, browned just a little on the top. They said goodbye to Grady and promised they'd be back. "You tell Miss Rodie I said hello," Minnie called.

At highway 319, at the end of the Susina Plantation lane, Minnie pointed left. "We goin' even farther south, Miss Essie. Only a a few miles. Gots to cross into Grady County." She rolled down her window and let the April breezes whip across their faces.

Essie was quiet. "No one seems to know this girl, Minnie."

"Don't you worry. We just gettin' started. We gone find that girl, Miss Essie. I just know it."

At Meridian Road, they turned north on highway 93 into Grady County, only a few miles to Blackshear Road where Fair Oaks stood in grand splendor. The land was studded with pines, oaks and magnolies. Sitting on a gently sloping hill, the house seemed to sit waiting for them. They curved around the lane to the back of the house. Before they got out of the car, they heard a voice. A commanding, deep hollow of a voice said, "You can't park there. Gertrude won't be happy you're on her grass like that." A man with dark hair bounded from the back steps and into the yard. "There!" He pointed. "Park over there."

Essie quickly eased the Pontiac to the far side of the garage where pine straw covered the ground. Squirrels dashed here and there in a mad escape. A dog barked and, from around the corner of the house, a big Irish setter, its tongue lolling out of the side of its mouth, loped toward them like an antelope.

"Stay down, Hero! Leave those ladies alone." Hero evidently did not mind well, as he plowed past the man and skidded to a stop in front of Essie and Minnie. His paws immediately went up onto Essie's chest in a jubilant welcome, while his tongue swept her face.

"Down, Hero," the man yelled. "Down, I say." The dog circled the tall man in a sporadic race for freedom.

Minnie, squeals of laughter breaking the morning quiet, knelt to the ground. "Come here, Hero. It's Minnie." The big dog immediately galloped to Minnie and almost pushed her to the ground. "Hey, big boy. Look at you!" She rubbed his muzzle and spoke gently to him.

"Good morning, ladies. So sorry for the more than zealous welcome. Hero is quite friendly, as you can see." Mr. Brigham Britton, panting from his run into the yard, slipped a leash on Hero. "He'll settle down in a few minutes, I'm sure."

He glanced at Minnie. "I believe I know you."

"It's me, Mr. Britton. Minnie Pryor. I served at your Christmas party last year."

"Oh, that's right. How could I forget you, Minnie? And who is your friend?"

Essie stepped forward. "Good morning. My name is Essie Donnelly and I'm from Madison County, Florida. Just visiting the area."

"Well, welcome to Fair Oaks. I'd invite you in, but Gertrude isn't home. She's over at Glen Arven lunching with Mary Faulk. I'm headed there, too. President Eisenhower's getting ready to tee off at 1:00. What can I do for you?"

A handsome man with dark brown eyes, he wore a knitted golf shirt the color of yellow daffodils, lightweight tan trousers and oxford shoes. He was freshly shaved, and a whiff of aftershave caught in the morning air.

Essie stumbled somewhat. How do you tell a stranger that you're looking for someone you've never met. Someone who may not be anywhere near Thomas County or even in Georgia. "I… we're looking for a girl we think is my niece. She's about seventeen or eighteen years old." Essie pulled out Jewell's picture and handed it to Mr. Britton.

"Oh, my. What a lovely girl."

"That's actually my niece's mother. But Minnie tells me she saw someone who looked just like this picture. I'm wondering if you might know her."

Brigham Britton studied the picture a long while. It was a portrait that had been tinted, showing Jewell's green eyes and black hair. Soft pink had been brushed on her cheeks. "Can't say I know this girl." He looked up. "Why do you think she's in Thomas County? Where was she born?"

Minnie stepped closer. "Mr. Britton, I been working in Thomas County for years and been to every plantation there is and I knowed I seen a girl who looked just like this picture."

"She was born in Atlanta." Essie gathered her thoughts and returned to Mr. Britton, her eyes misting over. "She was born out of wedlock, Mr. Britton. Perhaps whoever adopted her was from Thomas County."

"I see." He handed the photograph back to Essie. "Why don't you come back by Fair Oaks so you can talk with Mrs. Britton. It's quite possible she'll recognize this picture for you."

"Yes, sir. Perhaps we can visit at another time."

"Of course. I'll let Gertrude know."

Brigham Britton watched the car loop around the drive, pass beneath the hanging limbs of dogwoods and veer toward Blackshear road. His heart thudded in his chest as he wondered if Gertrude would recognize the girl in the picture.

Chapter Forty-Nine

They left Fair Oaks at high noon, the sun straight up and warming Thomas County into a perfect spring day. Essie thought about the names she had obtained from the Thomasville courthouse. Seven girls, their birth certificates all recorded in Thomas County. All born the summer of 1940.

Jewell had left the Donnelly farm in December 1939, just after Christmas. A hurried departure. Essie remembered a verbal confrontation between her mother and father, raised voices from the upstairs bedroom that carried throughout the rambling house and settled nervously on that last morning.

And Jewell. Jewell had been teary eyed when she hugged Essie goodbye. "I wish I could go with you," she had said to her older sister. Jewell looked at her with sad eyes. "Me, too, Essie."

Essie had watched her father drive their new Buick down the lane to the Bellville road, saw Jewell wave back at them through the closed car window, the smudge of her sad face hardly recognizable. She and her mother were standing on the porch when she looked up and asked: "Mother, what is a finishing school?" Her mother never answered. Instead, she walked into the house, her shoulders stiff. Essie heard the heels of her mother's shoes on the stairs, heard the bedroom door slam. *Eighteen years ago.*

Had it not been for Bootsey's visit to the farm in the summer of 1956, Essie would not have known about the baby. Such a casual conversation on the front porch of the farm house that day. *Does*

Jewell remember the baby? Bootsey had asked, almost an absent-minded inquiry from the snippy woman who had been her mother's best friend.

The baby? What baby? Then, Bootsey's questioning face. *Oh, surely you knew. Surely your father knew.* A roll of her eyes, a frustrated slap of her hand to her knee.

No, we didn't know. Her mother's deception had been flawless the year Jewell was away; a parade of teas with her friends, her trips to Tallahassee, her glorious porch luncheons with fruit punch in her sparkling crystal. Edith had smiled and laughed and flitted her hands in the air. "I found the most gorgeous dress in Atlanta."

All the while, Jewell hidden away, not at a finishing school in Switzerland, but at an all-girls school in Atlanta; imprisoned, more or less, under the watchful eyes of Bootsey.

Even at fourteen years old, Essie could have helped her sister. *If only she had known.* Her mother had orchestrated a great charade, had gone to the grave with the knowledge she had given away her daughter's baby, her grandchild. Only three years later, during the last week of her life, Edith had lain in the upstairs bedroom surrounded by friends and family, her hair groomed, dressed in her finest nightgown and smiling at those around her as she lay dying. She would have made a great actress.

They returned to Pebble Hill in mid-afternoon and walked to the large kitchen where Maudie, the head cook, and four of her helpers prepared food for the evening meal. Maudie organized the kitchen and cooked for the plantation workers. There was, however, a chef from Cleveland who was hired by the Poe's for their special events. The chef brought his own staff and, together, they prepared fabulous food, the guests delighting in every meal.

During a guest's stay, no China pattern was used a second time, each meal served unique with China, crystal and silverware. Mrs. Poe had a flair for color and arranged the tables herself, giving special attention to the floral arrangements, the flowers chosen from Pebble Hill's vast gardens.

"Minnie, is there a telephone I could use? I need to make a collect call to Madison."

"I think so. Let's ask Maudie."

"Miss Maudie, my friend would like to use your telephone. Is that alright with you?" Minnie asked.

Maudie, hands full of fat onions, jerked her head to the other side of the kitchen. "Over there at the food desk." The food desk, as everyone called it, was piled high with lists of produce and meat, receipts and various paperwork that went along with the busy kitchen. The telephone was half-hidden under a stack of invoices.

"Thank you, Maudie." Essie brushed aside the paperwork and picked up the receiver. She dialed the operator and asked for a collect call to the office of Sam Washington in Madison, Florida. She gave her the number and listened as the telephone rang. After six rings, the operator disconnected. "No answer, mam."

"Thank you. Let me give you another number, please." Essie gave the operator the telephone number for Judge Earp's office. After only two rings, his secretary picked up. "Judge Earp's office."

"Hello, Jeanette. It's Essie Donnelly. How are you?"

"Hello, Essie. We're all doing just fine. I hear you're traveling."

"That's true, but I'll be home soon. I'm in Thomasville at the Pebble Hill plantation." She paused. "Jeanette, I was wondering if you'd seen Sam around. He doesn't answer his office phone."

"He's been in and out all week, Essie. I believe he's over in Live Oak today, working on the Barnwell case. Shall I give him a message for you?"

Essie hesitated. "No, that's not necessary. I'll just call another time."

Essie replaced the receiver and absent-mindedly straightened a few papers on the desk. *Sam. She wanted to talk to Sam.* At the same moment, she wondered if the blond bombshell, Bonnie Lou Hinson, had wormed her way into Sam's life. She felt a tinge of jealousy, a rare thing for her.

Pebble Hill busily prepared for the 36th annual rose festival, a myriad of guests arriving on Thursday from various cities, far and wide. Mrs. Poe's guests were prominent individuals from the world of politics, finance, industrial giants as well as sportsmen who lauded the plantation lands as some of the best hunting places in America.

Minnie dutifully reported to Mrs. Poe's kitchen for her assignments, most likely ensuring her uniform was freshly washed and ironed. The girl brought joy to Pebble Hill.

Despite her vast wealth, Pansy Poe lived her life in care of others, providing a church, school and a medical facility for her workers. Mary Ann Mitchell lived her entire life on the Pebble Hill Plantation, and Pansy considered the black woman as part of her family.

Essie ate a piece of toast and drank a cup of coffee full of cream. Nearby, Maudie washed eggs, placing them in a huge enamel pan. "That cream you drinkin' is from those pretty Jersey cows out there in the milkin' barn."

"I bet you make some wonderful desserts with it, too." Essie smiled at the woman, noticing the colorful apron she wore.

"That I do, missy. We gots to keep these peoples fed 'round here." Her strong arms lifted a crate of bananas. "Guess you know these bananas is going into banana pudding."

Essie laughed. "I'm getting a spoon right now."

Both women examined the bananas and were joined by Mrs. Poe. "Good morning, ladies." Pansy Poe, barely five feet tall, tiptoed higher to look into the large crate of bananas. "Oh, those are lovely." She then turned to Essie. "Well, hello. You must be Minnie's friend." She held out her hand. "I'm Pansy Poe. Welcome to Pebble Hill."

Essie smiled, touched by Mrs. Poe's warmth. "I'm Essie. Thank you so much. I appreciate your hospitality, Mrs. Poe."

"You're lovely as can be, Essie. I hope the overflow cottage is comfortable for you."

"Oh, yes, mam. It's perfect."

Mrs. Poe cleared her throat. "Minnie tells me you're looking for your niece. I truly can't recall a girl of her description in Thomas County."

"We're searching several places in hopes we find her," said Essie. "We don't have much to go on."

Mrs. Poe turned to leave the kitchen. "I hope you find her. Nice meeting you."

"Thank you," said Essie, a disappointment spreading over her. The search for Jewell's child was beginning to look futile.

The *hard woman* from Madison County left the plantation on a perimeter road, one that wound around and eventually ended up on the west side of the vast woods, a ride through some of the best quail hunting acreage in the world. The road was lined with magnolia trees, tea olives and dogwoods. Pebble Hill's manager, Neil Boland, had followed Mrs. Poe's instructions without question. "Plant more trees."

She drove slowly to Thomasville, gathering her thoughts along the way. It seemed since she left Madison County there had been a barrage of emotional trials and tribulations, all of them thwarting her search for her sister's child. Ollie Pryor had not welcomed her with open arms, choosing instead to order her out of the farmhouse by sunrise. Had it not been for Minnie's illness, she was certain Ollie would have prodded her to the Pontiac with his shotgun as soon as the sun touched the horizon the next morning.

The killing of Henrietta, Ollie's prized sow, and her eleven piglets had traumatized the entire family. The two young boys, Pitch and Orland, had cried over the loss of their two dogs, not understanding the hatred that had been thrust upon the family.

Essie chastised herself. Had they not stopped at the roadside store—the store with the *whites only* sign—perhaps Henrietta would still be alive. *And the gun.* Her daddy's gun in her coat pocket had been quite convenient, a means by which she had made a statement to the big man in the plaid shirt and overalls, the man who had pulled a shotgun onto the counter and pointed it in a threatening way. Fat Belly did not have Christ's Beatitudes implanted in his heart and mind. The simple teachings of humility, charity and brotherly love would have had the man pouring a hot cup of coffee for Minnie and he would have done it with a loving heart. Fat Belly's lack of brotherly love had caused the *hard woman* in Essie to come forth with vigor.

And what about vengeance? Is that what she was after when she hailed Mike and Bill in the middle of the night to find Fat Belly and retaliate? *Yes. A mighty yes.* All she had to do was conjure up a picture of Ollie's face when he saw his slaughtered pigs and her anger became unleashed.

Sam had always told her she had to rein in her anger, that she was an angry woman. She agreed.

A bright sky with no clouds sent endless blue across the wide windshield of the Pontiac. She listened to a Thomasville radio station WPAX, the song *You Ain't Nothing But a Hound Dog* blasting the airwaves. She found Elvis' song too energetic for the quiet morning and decided to drive in silence.

Only moments into Thomasville, she smelled the scent of fresh-baked bread in the air, the ovens from Flowers Bakery at work since very early morning. She passed the First Baptist Church on North Broad, the second oldest church in the city, second only to the Methodists who came by wagon in the 1830's and began their traditional beliefs of shunning evil and performing kind acts, as well as abiding by the edicts of God. The churches of Thomasville and their vast memberships contributed to the well-being of the citizens of the city and made life in the Southern city idyllic.

She passed under the Harris oak in front of the Baptist church, an oak tree protected by the preacher's wife, Mrs. Harris, who, years ago, had set in a rocker underneath the tree and had dared the City to cut it down. Continuing to South Broad, her eyes caught Thomas Drug Store, where she reminded herself that she and Minnie needed shampoo and toothpaste. Though mostly healed, she wanted Band-aids for the injuries from Spur's attack, a decision most certainly approved of by Dr. Grey.

A left onto Remington brought her by the WPAX Radio Station, a station originally broadcast, using batteries, in 1929. The stalwart station had broadcast 1957's launch of the Soviet Union's Sputnik, the inauguration of Dwight Eisenhower and, of course, played the music of Elvis Presley. Essie smiled; she had listened to Elvis from its airwaves only a few minutes earlier.

A left on South Crawford Street took her past the Thomasville Municipal Auditorium, then back to Broad, where she parked in front of the Mode Theatre. Twenty-five cents would buy a ticket, popcorn and drink. She read the marquee: *The Bridge on the River Kwai.* Movie posters in frames hung on the brick siding of the building. *Around the World in Eighty Days*, 1957's best motion picture. Yul Brynner, best actor for *The King and I,* his bald head catching the sunlight that warmed the building. There, in the center was a larger poster of Ingrid Bergman, best actress for *Anastasia.* Her eyes were haunting, her lips red and turned into a slight smile.

Essie walked down N. Broad and crossed Jackson to the Thomas

Drug Store on South Broad. It was a lovely building with arched windows, an awning covering the front of the store, which had been in business since 1859. She opened the door and a bell jingled above her. A woman who stood behind a nearby counter called out to her. "Good morning. May I help you?"

"Good morning. Yes, I need a few things. I'll just wander around until I find them. Thank you." The clerk nodded and Essie walked down an aisle with Easter candy displayed on the shelves. She picked up a bag of jelly beans for Minnie and a few other things they needed. Back at the front of the store, she stood behind a man who wore horn-rimmed glasses and held a pack of cigars in his hand. The cashier chatted as she rang up his purchase. "How are you, Mr. Varnedoe?"

"Doing well, Doris. Are you closing the store for the festival?"

"Oh, yes. I wouldn't miss the parade for anything," she said, as she placed the cigars in a paper bag. The man turned and left the store while Essie placed the jelly beans, toothpaste, Band-Aids and a bottle of Jergens lotion on the counter.

"You're new around here. Are you visiting for the festival?"

Essie nodded. "Yes. The festival."

"Where are you staying?" The woman placed the items in a paper bag with Thomas Drug Store printed on the side.

"At Pebble Hill."

The woman raised her eyebrows. "Oh, my. Pebble Hill. How lovely."

From the counter where she stood, Essie glanced at a rack of newspapers, the words *Thomasville-Times Enterprise* emblazoned in large letters across the top of the page. After her purchase, she pulled a newspaper from the stand. "I'd also like to buy this newspaper."

Essie left the store and found a bench in the shade under a small Bradford pear tree just outside the drug store. She unfolded the newspaper and read the headlines: *39th Annual Rose Festival Underway. Judges Selected for Rose Competition*. A picture of six members of the Thomasville Rose Society was printed next to the article. Farther down the front page, an article entitled *Rose Queen Contestants Vie for Coveted Title* was placed above a picture of twelve girls in fancy dresses. In the middle of the picture, a dark-haired girl looked into the camera with luminous eyes and a jubilant smile. She was the spitting image of Jewell Donnelly.

Chapter Fifty

Hello, niece. It's me. Your Aunt Essie. You've never met me, but I knew your mother. Your mother was my sister. Jewell. Essie hardly breathed. Her hands grasped the edges of the newspaper and held them close while she looked into the girl's eyes. *Jewell's eyes.*

I've been looking for you for a while now. I would have looked long before now, but I didn't find out about you until this past summer. Your mother died last year. She died in my arms. She's buried in the Mt. Horeb cemetery, where all the Donnelly's are buried. Your grandmother and grandfather. You would love the farm where your mother and I grew up.

A breeze ruffled the newspaper in Essie's hands. She let go of one side of the paper and reached out and ran her finger along the girl's jawline, across the top of her head, across her smiling lips. *Do you ever think about us?*

The clock tower began its noonday chime, the lovely sound spreading across the streets of Thomasville. Spring was definitely in the air, the year repeating its old story once again and coming to its most charming chapter. A field of blue stretched across the skyline, the thin clouds chased by winds from the west. The sidewalks began to fill with people who wanted a bite to eat, a place to relax before returning to work. The once quiet street turned to jubilant chaos. Cars honked their horns, friends waved to one another while Essie Donnelly sat quietly, mesmerized by the picture of the girl staring up at her.

"Essie!"

She knew that voice. Deep, but lilting, it rang songlike across the street, in and out around the people who scurried down the sidewalk in front of her.

Rob Grey dashed around cars that had stopped at a traffic light, his head popping up here and there, trying to get a glimpse of her, meeting her for their lunch date at the Plaza Restaurant.

The Irishman. The unassuming man who saw past the hard shell of Essie Donnelly, saw past her commanding him to follow her to the Pryor farm in the middle of a cold March night. The man who saw straight into her heart and lingered there, wanting more.

He rushed toward her with a bouquet of flowers in his hand. Essie quickly folded the newspaper and tucked it into the bag from Thomas Drug Store. "Hello," she called, pulling herself up from the bench.

For the second time, he gathered her to him, laughing and talking at the same time. "Oh, my, lassie, but you are beautiful! I saw that lovely face from afar." He pulled away and gave her a little bow. He then stood straight and held out the bouquet of spring flowers. "For you."

They strolled to the Plaza Restaurant and sat outside at linen-covered tables. Their waiter brought them menus, glasses of water and a wine list. He was tall and very thin, young with barely a whisker on his soft cheek. His smile was warm, his accent deeply southern. "Welcome to the Plaza," he said, placing his hands behind his back and standing straight. "Have you been here before?"

Rob shook his head and looked at Essie. "I haven't. Have you?"

"No, I haven't. It's a lovely restaurant." Essie noticed the table settings. "Could you possibly find a vase for these flowers?"

The young man jumped forward. "Certainly." He sped away, leaving Rob and Essie by themselves. She smelled his aftershave; he noticed a few freckles across her nose. She followed his hands as they opened the menu. He saw a wisp of hair pushed behind her ear. When he looked down at the menu, she saw his eyelashes were very black, his eyelids half-covering his blue eyes. When Essie sipped her water, he noticed the pout in her lower lip.

They sat so close, only an arm's length away. Perhaps the good doctor wanted to reach out and grasp the slim fingers of the farm girl. Perhaps the farm girl wanted him to.

The waiter returned with the flowers arranged beautifully in a soft blue vase and placed them on their table. "How kind of you," said

Essie. There were yellow spring daisies, white carnations, a spray of baby's breath, a few blue Iris' and several Peruvian lilies.

"Shall we have oysters? Steamed?" Rob looked hopeful. Surely the farm girl liked oysters.

"Of course. And a salad." Essie smiled. "Do they have oysters in Ireland?"

Rob grinned. "Do they ever! Galway is famous for its native oysters. They're a tad different, you know, than your Apalachicola oysters. They're flat oysters, in a rounded flat shell, but the taste is superior."

"Galway?"

"Aye, Galway. It's in the west of Ireland, lyin' on the River Corrib between Lough Corrib and Galway Bay. All surrounded by County Galway."

"Do I hear a little nostalgia in your voice?" Essie leaned back and watched Rob's face and wondered how much he'd been changed by life in America.

Rob became reflective, a hint of a cloud crossing his eyes. "I cannot lie. Ireland is always in my heart. But, you see, a young man must seek his fortune." He picked at the tablecloth with his fingers, a small smile playing at the corners of his mouth. He looked up at her. "I have no regrets." He took a deep breath and let it out, while his gaze swept over her.

Essie held his eyes with her own. "You seem to be content. You have your work."

"That I do. I cannot deny the satisfaction I receive on a daily basis. Helping those in need." He laughed out loud. "Especially those with spider bites and rooster wounds!"

Essie laughed along. The waiter arrived and refilled their water glasses. "Ready to order?"

"Yes. We'll both have the steamed oysters and a salad." He glanced at Essie. "What kind of salad for you, my lady?"

"A Caesar would be perfect."

"Same for me."

The restaurant began to fill up and the clinking of glass and the low hum of voices settled around them. Essie reached down and pulled out the newspaper article about the rose queen pageant. "I'd... I'd like to show you a photograph."

"Oh? Let's see."

She pushed the newspaper toward Rob and tapped the picture of the dark-haired girl who sat in the middle of the photograph. "I believe this is my sister's daughter."

Rob smoothed the newspaper on the table and peered closely at the picture. "She's a lovely girl." He studied the article. "There's no listing of the names of the contestants."

"No, there isn't. But it's her."

Rob folded the newspaper and handed it back to Essie. "Are you that sure? From a small photograph?" His brow furrowed, doubt creasing his forehead.

Essie was quiet for a long moment, her thoughts far away. It had taken her so long to get here. So long to bury Jewell. That's why she had left the farm and stayed at her daddy's fish camp at Cherry Lake all winter. She couldn't bear to see Jewell's empty chair at the end of the porch. DooRay had taken care of the farm while she ran the Pontiac up and down the dirt roads of Madison County. Running the hurt out of her, she supposed. Yet, when she was still and quiet, the hurt came back. The hurt was here now, right below the surface, a pain that wound itself around her heart and squeezed everytime she thought of Jewell.

Rob saw Essie's confusion unfold in her face. "Do you have plans to… to contact her?"

"I have no plans, really. I… I just want to see her. Hear her voice."

"Will you talk to her?"

Essie frowned and threw a frustrated glance at Rob. "What would I say? Hey, I'm your aunt. My sister gave birth to you eighteen years ago and someone took you away from her and gave you to a stranger."

The tears came, spilling over. Flushed, Essie turned away. "Maybe… maybe if I see her just one time, it will be alright." She heard anger in her words, an exasperation that had manifested itself from the moment Bootsey Birthright had told her about the baby.

Rob spoke softly. "Perhaps so. But, perhaps not." He reached over and picked up Essie's hand. "One never knows the heart of another. How can you possibly know what has gone on in her life? How can you know who she really is if there isn't some kind of communication. Even if it's a casual conversation in a crowd somewhere, stranger to stranger." He paused and leaned closer, whispering across the table. "What if she's looking for *you*?"

Chapter Fifty-One

The sun warmed their table, the sunlight glistening on Essie's hair while she chatted softly, a rarity for the farm girl who had spent her young life cast aside by an aloof mother who did not know she existed. Her mother had favored Jewell, the *beautiful* sister, and had left Essie to her father. Her father had gladly assumed the responsibility of his daughter, who, as far as he was concerned, was supposed to be a boy.

There was no pretentiousness in the man and he went about her care with love and acceptance. Hubert Donnelly had taught her how to shoot all of his prized guns, plant crops, ride horses, and skin out catfish. The fact that she had grown into an intelligent, lovely woman was no surprise to him. It was, however, a shock to her mother. Edith Donnelly had looked at her one day and said, "My goodness, Essie. Take off that awful flannel shirt and dungarees and boots and you might be more attractive."

In her senior year in high school, Essie won the *Watermelon Queen of Madison County* beauty pageant. The *Madison Enterprise* published a picture of her, a tiara on her head and a bouquet of roses in her arms. When her mother saw the picture, she shook her head and clucked her tongue. "Your hair's a mess."

Her father had encouraged her writing and ensured there was plenty of typing paper for the old Royal typewriter. When Essie received a contract from a publisher for her novel *Watermelon Queen on Madison County,* her father had long been in a grave at the Mt.

Horeb cemetery.

"The parade begins at 10:30 in the morning. Will you be there?" Essie ate the last of her oysters, squeezing lemon on them and a little pepper.

Rob dabbed his chin with his napkin. "I'm hoping so. I get off my shift at 8:00. I'll eat a little breakfast and walk downtown."

"It's a two mile parade route, beginning at North Broad and Clay. It's tradition that the pageant float is the last one in the parade."

"I'll look for you," he said. Rob studied Essie's face. Her brown eyes were full of truth, a trust that consumed all that she saw and knew. He found himself thinking of holding her again. He remembered the kiss and wanted more.

"By the way, Dr. Meyer and I will visit Ollie next week to discuss Pitch and his deformed leg. I'm hoping Ollie will be receptive."

"I think Ollie has warmed up to the idea that you're there to help."

They left the restaurant and walked downtown on Broad, crossing Remington Avenue and passing the old Griffin Isaac Harness and Saddle store. They came upon an unusual building on South Broad, where brick, stone, stained glass and wood gave the building an exuberant Queen Anne asymmetrical style. The small metal plate by the door read "Isadora Popper Wholesale Wine and Liquor 1889."

Almost next door, a building in the folk Victorian style with corbelling as its main decorative element, stood before them. In 1886 it had been the Duren and Jeffers Grocery, a dry goods store that served the residents of Thomasville for decades.

The streets were quieter now, the lunch crowd thinning out and returning to their work. "I'm parked near the Mode Theatre." Essie pointed. "That way."

At that moment, Rob eased Essie's hand into his. In his other hand, he carried the vase of flowers. "My shift is at midnight tonight. Want to walk with me to the Hawkins house. It's just two blocks down Jackson to Dawson Street. We could sit on the porch a while."

Essie heard the longing in his voice. His hand was warm and smooth. His thumb rubbed along the tops of her fingers. Had her hearing been more keen, she would have heard his wildly beating heart. "That's a lovely invitation, but I've..."

Rob stopped in mid-step, his face tormented. "What is it, lassie? You seem so far away." He reached out and touched her cheek.

"Come back, Essie. Be here with me, this moment. Not with Jewell. Not with her daughter. Not with the pain that seems to haunt and devour you." His words were heartfelt, a reaching out that said '*I want more of you.*'

Essie stilled, the realization of Rob's words hard upon her ears. It was true. She had not let go of Jewell or the search for Jewell's child since Jewell's death. There had been no in-between, only a hollow place in her heart. She had not bothered to fill that hole with anything but mournful thoughts, thoughts that would imprison her until she let go.

Rob's hand gently slipped behind her back and pulled her close. His kiss was soft, a tenderness that left her lips, then traced her forehead, her eyebrows, her cheeks. It was then that she not only felt his heart beating, but felt her own, thumping loudly in her chest, taking her breath away. She wanted to pull away but couldn't. Her hand found his face, the roughness of a new beard, and then the softness of his neck.

"Essie. Come to me."

From North Broad Street, the one hundred forty foot bell tower at the First Methodist Church unleashed its carillon of chimes announcing the hour. Three chimes, followed by a hymn proclaiming a sweet hour of prayer.

Essie stepped back, her hand resting on Rob's arm. "Remember Sam? The man you met at the Pryor farm?"

"Aye, I do." A quizzical look crossed Rob's face.

Her brown eyes, the trusting, truthful eyes, lifted and settled on the Irishman's face. "Sam and I have been together for quite a while now."

"Are you engaged?"

"Well, no. But, we…"

"Have you talked of marriage?" Rob folded his arms across his chest in a defiant manner, his chin firm, his eyes bearing down on the farm girl from Madison County.

Essie hesitated. "Marriage? Well, I…"

"So, what yer tellin' me is there's this man called Sam and yer not engaged nor are yer married." Suddenly, the good doctor turned and began walking backwards down the sidewalk, away from Essie, a grin on his handsome face. "Alas, my beautiful lassie. It appears to me that you are footloose and fancy free!"

He turned and skipped down the sidewalk, his hands waving in the air and singing *Thin Lizzy—Don't Believe a Word* at the top of his lungs. *Don't believe me, if I tell you, especially if I tell you that I'm in love with you.* Of course, he was in love with her, as sure as the sun rises across Ireland.

Essie, perplexed, stared after Dr. Grey. She heard his Irish tenor even after he had disappeared around the corner of Jackson street and headed toward the Hawkins house. Standing in the middle of the sidewalk, she held the blue vase of flowers, not moving. *Sam. She must see Sam.*

CHAPTER FIFTY-TWO

It was 3:00 in the afternoon when Essie picked up highway 319 south to highway 93 and the Fair Oaks Plantation. Even though she believed the picture in the *Thomasville Times-Enterprise* was Jewell's daughter, she thought Brigham Britton had seemed uneasy after he looked at the photograph of Jewell. She saw his hands shake a little, a nervousness in his eyes. Then, his mention of his wife, Gertrude. *Come back and talk with Gertrude.*

At the end of the Fair Oaks drive, a woman walked along a garden path, the dog Hero close behind. She leaned over and pruned a few roses. A slim, lovely brunette, Gertrude Britton was a well-educated woman who took her philanthropic duties seriously. When not at Fair Oaks, she and her husband spent their time in Cleveland, their hometown, busy with a myriad of community activities.

Gertrude looked up when she heard Essie's car and waved, but she did not smile. She pulled her sweater together and buttoned it as a cool breeze swept through the pines and down the garden path. Only a few hundred feet away, a cemetery lay tucked in between a stand of maples, the gravestones flat and scarred with time. Only a few could be read.

Essie parked and walked down the path, all the while carrying the photograph of Jewell. She was only a few feet away when the woman spoke. "I've been expecting you." There was a slight smile from a face that seemed pensive. She reached out her hand. "Hello, I'm Gertrude Britton. I understand you're Miss Donnelly."

Essie took the woman's hand and nodded. "Yes, Essie Donnelly from Pinetta, Florida."

"I know of Pinetta," she said. "And of Madison. If my memory of history serves me correctly, Colin P. Kelley, a pilot killed in World War II, is from there."

"Your memory is correct. There is a monument in the Four Freedoms Park in Madison that honors him. He's buried in the Oak Ridge Cemetery."

Gertrude walked a few feet down the path, her hands folded and placed behind her back. Farther down the lane, the grand plantation house was shadowed, the sun easing down behind the longleaf pines to the west. Essie walked beside the plantation's mistress, each step closer to a question she wanted to ask.

"And your knowledge of Pinetta?" she asked, delaying her most important question.

The woman thought a moment. "My husband and our farm manager drove there to buy some Tamworth hogs. It's not a long drive, you know. Just a few miles through Georgia on 84, then across the state line. That was years ago, of course."

Essie nodded and the two women walked quietly on the pine-straw covered path. At last, the woman stopped and turned to Essie. "I understand you have a question for me." Her words were inquisitive, searching.

"Yes. Yes, I do. I have a photograph I'd like you to see. It's of my sister Jewell." Essie licked her lips. "A friend of mine—you know her—Minnie Pryor, tells me she saw a girl at one of the plantations who looks just like my sister. It's possible you may know of her?"

Gertrude Britton eased the photograph away from Essie's hands and studied it for a long moment. "You have a beautiful sister."

"She passed away last summer," said Essie. "She had a baby when she was seventeen years old and the baby was... was given away. I... I didn't know about it at the time. Only... only my mother knew, as well as her best friend." Essie faltered, her throat swelling with emotion. "I'm trying to find her."

Essie unfolded the newspaper article. "Here is a picture I saw in this morning's paper. See the girl in the middle?" Essie tapped the girl's face.

Gertrude smoothed the newspaper and pulled it closer. "Yes, I see."

Long moments passed. A pair of blue jays argued in the tall pines, their squawks loud and menacing. Nearby, squirrels zipped up trees, the bark flying. From the house, chimes rang, melodic and beckoning in the afternoon breeze. Finally, with smooth, manicured hands, Gertrude folded the newspaper and returned it to Essie. "I'm not sure I can help you, Miss Donnelly."

"You don't recognize the girl?"

"No. Not at all."

The mistress of Fair Oaks watched Essie's car follow the lane to the highway, and turn left toward Thomasville. She had not been entirely truthful with Essie Donnelly. She knew the girl in the newspaper article, but felt it was best if Miss Donnelly uncovered the mystery on her own.

CHAPTER FIFTY-THREE

Essie drove slowly, her thoughts mingling together and causing an inner anxiety that she didn't like. She was the kind of woman who never sat on a fence about anything. Decisive, somewhat opinionated, and definitely assertive, she was happiest when her thoughts were clear and everything and everyone was in its place.

Rob Grey had pulled her out of the seemingly contented comfort of her relationship with Sam Washington. How could she let him do that? She would blame herself for allowing him to find his way into her life, to put his arms around her, to kiss her. She would blame that on her vulnerability, a state of mind that left her confused and searching for answers. Again, she thought of Sam. *I must see Sam.*

Dusk had settled on Pebble Hill as she pulled off 319 and steered the Pontiac down the lane to the overflow cottage. There were a few lights on here and there, but no one stirring. Across the way, the big mansion's windows glowed like yellow stardust, while faint sounds of music drifted across the massive lawns and gardens. She parked under a large oak tree at the edge of a small wooded area behind the cottage where a few peacocks strutted past and disappeared into the trees, looking for a place to roost.

The vase of flowers Rob had given her were still fresh and colorful, a reminder of their lunch together, as well as the parting kiss. He had yelled '*Alas, my beautiful lassie. It appears to me that you are footloose and fancy free.*'

Was she footloose and fancy free? Deep in thought, she closed the car door, the vase of flowers in one hand, Jewell's picture in the other. The pain shot up through her arm and shoulder, a blunt strike that caused her to stumble. In the near dark, she lost her bearings, staggered and then was pulled backward by her hair. A hand had yanked her sideways and slammed her into the side of the Pontiac.

She smelled him before she saw him. *Fat Belly!* Essie twisted her body and shoved as hard as she could. Behind her, a gruff voice. "My, my. What are you gonna do now, Annie Oakley? Where's that little biddy .38 of yours?"

He squeezed harder. "You think you can just take my money and then disappear?" He dragged her to the edge of the woods, his hand over her mouth. "Ain't got the posse with you now, do you?"

Essie, still holding the vase of flowers, slammed the vase upward and behind her, finding Fat Belly's head. A sharp groan and a relaxing of his grip allowed her to regain her footing, but Fat Belly's fist found her stomach and she doubled over. Essie had no breath and fell to her knees, a firm hand pushing hard at the back of her neck. She reached out and grabbed his leg. With all her strength she pulled and her teeth found his calf.

A loud cry pierced the air. "You bitch!" The big man leaned over and brought his full strength onto Essie's shoulders, sending her into the dirt. "Where's the money?" he growled.

From behind, as if in flight, a body slammed against Fat Belly. An elbow jabbed hard into the big man's neck and an arm encircled his head, wrenching it to the side. Fat Belly fell to his knees as Sam Washington kicked hard into his face, blood spewing from his nose.

Essie pulled herself up from the ground and grasped the fallen vase. She lifted it high and brought it down toward Fat Belly's head, aiming perfectly until Sam grabbed her arm. "Hold on, my dear. Don't kill him."

Breathing hard, Sam pulled Essie to him. "Essie. Are you okay?"

Essie gasped. "I think so." Leaves and dirt smeared her face and blood streaked across her blouse.

The big man lay on the ground and moaned, his face covered in blood and dirt. "Essie, if you're up to it, run get your daddy's gun while I watch this guy."

Despite her bruised body, Essie stumbled back to the Pontiac and retrieved the .38 from the glove compartment. Her hands shook as she checked the bullets. Fully loaded, she took the gun back to Sam.

Incredulous, Essie asked. "How did you know?"

Still panting, Sam chuckled. "Oh, those brothers of mine. Couldn't keep a secret. Told me everything."

"But, how did you find me?"

Sam placed a foot on Fat Belly's stomach and pressed. "You're not going anywhere. Lie still." He turned to Essie. "Jeanette told me you called Judge Earp's office and told her you were staying at Pebble Hill. I drove up to check on you." He pulled her closer. "I'm glad I did."

Two sheriff's deputies handcuffed *Fat Belly*, whose name was Harland Prescott, arrested him for assault, and took him to the Thomasville jail. Sam and Essie both completed the necessary paperwork and, most likely, would have to appear in court at some point. They were both happy to do so.

Harland Prescott had evidently been stalking Essie, followed her to Pebble Hill and found an opportune time to accost her. Sam Washington had prevented a near tragedy.

It was late evening when Essie and Sam talked quietly in the cottage kitchen. Talked about the vase that almost crushed Harland's head. On the table, the shattered photograph of Jewell lay in pieces. The glass had broken, and remnants of the picture had been pieced together like a puzzle. Sam reached out and placed his hand on top of Essie's. "I've missed you, Essie. When are you coming home?" His blue eyes seemed weary, a tiredness that spilled over into his soft words.

Essie, her auburn hair pulled back from her face, touched a small cut above her left eyebrow. She was pensive and shaken by her skirmish with Harland Prescott. Even two hours after the assault, her body tensed at every movement. Had Sam let her crack the flower vase on Fat Belly's head, she would have felt more triumphant that good had overshadowed evil.

When are you coming home? Sam's question had caused a quieting of her heart. *Home? The farm. DooRay. Jewell's empty chair at the end of the porch. The cemetery where her sister, mother and father lay.*

"Soon," she replied, a tremble in her voice. Her eyes found his, a melancholy glance that told him her heart was tender, her search for Jewell's child had taken her to a fragile place.

Sam's work as a defense attorney for Madison County had shaped him into an analytical individual, his maturity deepening with his substantial exposure to people and the law. At thirty-five years old, he had evolved into a man whose thoughts were clear and decisive. Essie's search for Jewell's child had become a priority for her, pushing Sam into a part of her life that she deemed unimportant. Or, at least, he thought so.

Essie had been compelled to find Jewell's child, a sense of duty, but Sam wondered if her motivations had been truly transparent from the beginning. In his heart, he wondered if the father of Jewell's child had been the primary reason for Essie's tenacious search.

Autrey Browning had been Essie's first romantic relationship, an unforgettable blending of two hearts at an age that forever branded them as first loves. The discovery of Jewell's pregnancy and subsequent birth gave rise to the question of *who* had fathered the child. The discovery that Jewell's dalliance—a fleeting affair with Autrey—had devastated Essie, although the revelation occurred eighteen years later.

Those aware of the pregnancy at the time were Edith, Jewell's mother, Jewell and Bootsey Birthright. And, of course, Autrey Browning. Autrey was threatened and banished from Madison County by Edith Donnelly. The banishment had left Essie bewildered and confused when Autrey simply disappeared.

Sam cleared his throat and chose his words carefully. "Essie, I'd like to know about something?" He had the right to ask this question. His deep love for Essie gave him permission to delve into her thoughts. It would be a gentle question, asked with love and respect.

Essie nodded and looked inquisitively at Sam. Her eyes wide, she leaned back and waited, her face pale.

"Essie, I'm wondering how you feel about Autrey being the father of this child of Jewell's. The father of your niece."

A stillness crept into the room, a nearby table lamp cast dim light into the small kitchen. Shadows fell on Essie's face, a softening of her features as though an impressionist painting. Her eyes, moist and sad, flitted to Sam. She licked her lips. "I understand your question, Sam.

You're wondering if a part of me wants to see Autrey again—through his child."

Essie faltered and fiddled with the remnants of Jewell's photograph for a long while. Finally, with hesitancy, she continued. "I think... I think having two people I have loved deeply as the mother and father of a child is a wondrous thing."

Essie closed her eyes, tears forming in the corners. When she opened them, a smile formed on her lips. Radiant and joyous, it spread wide. "My inspiration for this grand search for my niece is... *love*. My love for Jewell and for Autrey. They are both gone from this earth, but they left something behind. They left me many memories... and a *child*."

From the open window, a whippoorwill called, a melodious sound that promised a peaceful night. Nickering came from the horses in the stables, the sounds deep and rumbling softly across the plantation's gardens.

"And you, Sam Washington, are truly a light in my life. I've taken a little detour from you, but that doesn't mean I won't be back." Essie took a deep breath. "Does that answer your question?

Sam stood from the table and paced the room. In his courtroom voice, he spoke. "Essie, you do realize it's possible this girl's not Jewell's daughter, don't you?"

Essie spent the next hour telling Sam about the plantations she and Minnie had visited. The people they had met. The trip to the courthouse. The picture in the newspaper. The rose parade, the beauty pageant and Minnie's fervent insistence that, indeed, the girl she saw was Jewell's child.

"The parade begins at 10:30 in the morning. She'll be on the float, Sam. Right there in front of my eyes. So close."

Sam and Essie held each other under the many stars that blinked across the Thomas County skies. They walked the garden paths, rubbed the noses of the quarter horses, peeked in on the Jersey cows and ended up in the gazebo at Pansy Poe's teahouse.

"Essie," said Sam, his words barely audible. "I'm not sure about us anymore. You left not only Madison County, but you left me. Come home now—with me."

"I can't, Sam. Please understand." Essie saw Sam's body stiffen and step away from her. His face hardened as though he was standing before a jury and asking for the death penalty.

"I'll not follow you across these miles again, Essie. And I'm not so sure I'll be waiting for you if you ever return to Madison County."

There was so much finality in Sam's words that Essie couldn't speak, a feeling of helplessness washing over her.

In a culmination of a long-brewing anger, the tall, lanky lawyer strode across the lawn to his car without turning around. He never looked her way again. Essie watched as the car's tail lights faded into the night, an overwhelming feeling of loss squeezing her heart.

Chapter Fifty-Four

Near midnight, Minnie returned to the small cottage, her evening filled with stories of Mrs. Poe's fabulous dinner party, a gala event leading up to the City of Roses' grand festivities.

"Oh, Miss Essie. I done worked so hard, but I had me so much fun. All that music, all those fine people laughing and singing." Minnie plopped onto her bed. "You know what I think? I think those white peoples know how to live. They's all so beautiful in their tuxedos and rhinestone dresses. Why those ladies had big ole diamonds all up and down they's fingers. 'bout blinded me when I served them champagne.

"So many famous peoples, my head's swimming. Oh, Miss Essie. I saw this tall, handsome man and I say to my friend 'who is that?'" In her excitement, Minnie gasped for breath. "They called him Mr. Grant. Mr. Grant this and Mr. Grant that. Finally, somebody done say, "Cary, play the piano for us. Then, this woman named Betsy, I think it was his wife, sat down at the piano with him." Minnie sighed dreamily. "They was so beautiful."

Minnie rolled over and glanced at Essie. "You being mighty quiet over there, Miss Essie. Got somethin' on your mind you can tell Minnie about?"

The table by Minnie's bed held a small lamp, a Hobnail milk glass base with a soft blue shade. Its light spread softly across Minnie's face, a wondrous face with large brown, questioning eyes. Her smile was thoughtful as she sat up and waited.

Across the room, Essie sat in a tall, wingback chair, its fabric embroidered with colorful pheasants and quail. She leaned back and closed her eyes. She felt she had not slept in days; her body ached from fatigue and Fat Belly's pummeling. It seemed years instead of weeks that she had been away from Madison County, away from the serenity of the farm. Away from DooRay and his wise perspective of life.

The one-armed black man had taught her many things, things that had changed her life. She found herself missing his sage advice, his humor; but most of all, his high tenor voice as it rang through the moss covered oaks surrounding the farmhouse. *I come to the garden alone, while the dew is still on the roses…*

Before she left Pinetta, his last words to her had been perplexing. She had not forgotten his sad face, his question: *Miss Essie, you gone take that baby away from its new mama?*

"Miss Essie. You asleep?" Minnie leaned forward. Again, she waited for Essie's reply.

"No, I'm awake." Essie opened her eyes and sat up in the chair. Her tired eyes found Minnie. "Minnie, that fellow at the little store near Boston was here tonight."

"Lordy! That mean man in the red truck?" Minnie jumped from her bed and sat near Essie.

"Yes. Him." Essie could hear Minnie's quick breaths. "He attacked me out behind the cottage when I got out of the Pontiac. Had it not been for Sam, I don't know what would've happened."

"Miss Essie! Didn't you have your gun?" Wide-eyed, Minnie licked her lips and shivered.

"No, I didn't have that .38. Wish I had though." Essie closed her eyes again.

Minnie noticed the cut above Essie's eye. "That man cut your face?"

"I think so. Don't know exactly how though." When she opened her eyes, she was smiling. "You should see him, Minnie. Sam gave him a good whupping."

The wide-eyed Minnie cackled. "Where is he now?"

"Jail."

Minnie wrinkled her brow. "Reckon next time he give us some coffee wif out a fuss?"

Essie grinned. "If he knows what's good for him."

Of course, it could have all turned out differently. It was luck the

Pontiac outran the red truck on that lonely highway to Boston. And it was quite convenient that Bill and Mike Washington had agreed to help her confront Fat Belly after he slaughtered Ollie Pryor's sow and piglets. It was, however, her daddy's .38 that convinced the man to make restitution to the poor sharecropper.

"Just want you to know, Minnie. I'm going to the parade tomorrow. It starts at 10:30 in the morning." Essie smiled at her friend. "I'm glad you got to see all those fine people at Mrs. Poe's dinner party."

Minnie yawned. "Uh, huh. But, I am so tired." She crawled into bed and pulled the covers over her head.

Essie slept fitfully and dreamed of Jewell. It was summer and, together, they ran through the cornfields, laughing and singing, their faces flushed pink from the sun. They collapsed in the farm pond and swam in the cool water while nearby their daddy hollered at them and told them to get back to work—there were chicken houses to clean.

Near daylight, Essie drifted into another dream, a dream of Jewell's child, a young woman now, sitting atop a float piled high with roses, waving and smiling. Essie ran after the float trying to catch a glimpse of Jewell's daughter, but just as she reached the float, it pulled forward, just out of reach. Essie ran for miles, panting and waving and calling out, but never quite reaching the float.

In the dream, Sam ran behind her, his hands grabbing for her, pulling her away from the float. She ran faster, leaving Sam behind, his face fading away into the darkness of the dream.

When she finally awoke, her body was soaked with sweat, her hair plastered to her head, tears on her cheeks. *Sam. She had lost Sam.*

At sunrise, the cottage lay in serene morning quiet. Minnie had already gone to the big house and begun her day's work for Miss Pansy. Essie pulled herself up from her bed and looked out the window. It would be a glorious, sunny day—a perfect day for a grand parade. She smelled coffee and reached for a cup and saucer, thankful Minnie had been so thoughtful.

Outside, still in her night clothes, Essie peered east and into a sunrise the color of flamingos. She squinted past the tall longleaf pines, up high, where a covey of quail soared into the tops of the trees.

Today, Jewell. It will be today. I'll see your child. She looks just like you, you know.

CHAPTER FIFTY-FIVE

Essie dressed in a soft yellow, sleeveless dress, a narrow belt clasping the waist together. She slipped on a pair of white straw flats with a small bow across the top. Around her neck, she wore a single string of Jewell's pearls. Inside her small handbag, she carried a camera. Nervous, she quickly patted soft rouge on her cheeks. Her lipstick had hardly any color, but it made her lips moist.

On Highway 319 Essie drove northeast to Thomasville. Only eight miles from the City of Roses, the road was clogged with traffic. Car after car inched along the highway, each one getting closer to a festive visit to the Rose City. A southern tradition since the 1920's, the rose festival hosted visitors from all across Georgia, even Marvin Griffin, Georgia's governor, would lead the parade down Broad Street, among thousands of spectators.

Essie found a parking spot for the Pontiac on East Calhoun Street, near the Hardaway House, and walked a block over to Clay Street where the parade participants were lining up for the grand parade. The noise was deafening. At least a dozen bands made last minute adjustments to their instruments, while nearby, horses pulling wagons yanked on their reins, impatient to begin their illustrious prancing down Broad Street.

A short way down Clay Street, the Thomasville football team chanted "Go Bulldogs"—their excitement evident as they jumped on top of the high school float, their uniforms freshly washed and depicting their red and black school colors. Coach Joe Sumrall yelled above the sounds of trumpets, tubas and French horns. "You guys settle down!"

Player #37, Cawood Arrington, threw a football to #26 Jerry Musslewhite, who missed it, even though he jumped high into the air. Behind him, #17 Rhydon Mays scooped up the ball and threw it back to Cawood. Nothing Coach Sumrall did seemed to control the rowdy football players. Perhaps they were showing off for the cheerleaders, who performed cheers up and down the float behind them, kicking their legs high into the air.

Nearby Georgia Tech's Yellow Jackets marching band eased into formation, the drum corp stepping in place, while their sticks drummed paradiddle; slow at first, then rising, only to fall back down to barely a sound. Director Ben Logan Sisk stood nearby and watched his performers with a keen eye.

Essie slipped past Thomasville High School's girls basketball team float and continued down Clay Street, all the while looking for Dr. Grey. They were to meet at the Fannie Bottoms house. It seemed he, too, was looking for her. From behind came a loud shout. "Essie!!"

Essie turned in time to see Rob Grey steer around the Flowers Bakery float and cross Clay Street. "This way," Essie called, waving him to the corner of Clay and Crawford Street, where Fannie Bottoms' Queen Anne style house stood nestled in the shade of a large oak. When he came closer, she called. "Good morning."

The doctor smiled and yelled above the shrill *Up With the White and Gold* from the Yellow Jackets marching band. "Ah, good morning, Essie." He placed an arm around her shoulder and pulled her gently. "Come, let's get off this footpath."

They left the sidewalk and found a somewhat quiet spot on the far side of the oak tree, whose branches towered above them. Dr. Grey leaned over and seemed to shelter Essie from the noise and pandemonium that surrounded them. "This is unbelievable! I've never seen so many floats and bands and people." He grinned, then noticed the cut above her eyebrow. "A wee cut on your forehead. What happened?"

"Not to worry. A small mishap." There was no need to explain the complications that had developed the night before. The perpetrator was in jail and Essie was out of harm's way.

Dr. Grey frowned and studied the small cut. "Perhaps a suture?"

"Oh, no. No stitch needed." Nervous, Essie tucked a strand of hair behind her ear.

Unconvinced, Dr. Grey nodded, his eyes narrowing. "Say, I won't be able to watch the parade with you. I've been called to an extra shift at the hospital." He glanced at his watch. "I've got just enough time to check in."

"Of course. Sorry you'll miss all the excitement. It should be a lovely day."

Snare drums exploded a half block away and Essie jumped. They both laughed and moved farther behind the trunk of the tree. Dr. Grey, his face ernest, took Essie's hand. "Shall I meet you later? Around 6:00? Maybe at Pebble Hill?"

A squeal of laughter pealed across the sidewalk as a group of young girls skipped toward Broad Street, their hair tied back and held with pink roses. There were at least a dozen and each of them dressed in white. Essie watched silently for a moment before she turned back to Rob. "Dr. Grey, perhaps we can talk another time. You see…"

"Ah, here it comes?" The good doctor grinned and cocked his head to one side. "You have yet to convince me about this other fellow. This… this fellow from… Madison County."

"Well, yes, I…"

Rob placed a finger over Essie's lips. "You don't have to say another word. I truly understand." He sighed deeply. "I've got to run. Hospital needs me."

The tall doctor turned and began jogging toward Archbold. A half block away, he turned and waved. "Take care of that cut!" And he was gone.

Essie leaned against the oak tree. She had known Rob Grey for a short few weeks, yet he had impacted her life in many ways, all positive. In another place, another time, perhaps she could have been open to more than a friendship. She watched until the good doctor was only a speck in the crowd and wiped the tears from her cheeks.

For at least a mile, Clay Street teemed with bands and floats as participants jockeyed into position for the grand parade. It was an orderly chaos despite all the commotion. Mr. Garner, Thomasville's high school principal, and Mr. Harper, principal of the junior high school, had ordered the schools closed for the day. After all, it was *parade day*. It seemed every man, woman and child in Thomas County had turned out to celebrate rose week.

Essie hurried along Clay Street to Broad where the parade route would officially begin. All along Broad Street, people leaned out of second story windows, waving at the throngs below. Above the city, blue skies stretched endlessly, not a cloud in sight. There could be no rain on *this* parade.

At the corner of Broad and Monroe Street, Essie found a spot that gave her a good vantage point. She pulled her camera from her purse. Unsure when the Rose Queen float would pass, she nervously scanned Broad Street, the sounds of the approaching parade filling the air.

Next to her, a woman in a blue dress, waved to someone across Broad. "Yoo, hoo," she called, standing on tiptoe and flapping her arms. "Hey, Peggy! Peggy Barhite! Is your mama here, too?" Across Broad Street, Peggy pointed toward Washington Street. "Oh, I see her! Hey, Lorena!"

The woman in the blue dress, about fifty years old, was attractive, her blond hair beauty-shop styled into a French twist. She, too, held a camera and tapped her foot in time as the Thomasville High School band led the parade with *Dixie.* The crowd quieted as the de facto national anthem of the South was played in an eight measured fiddle solo, its tempo slow. The lone fiddle player, standing still, dropped his chin onto the chinrest and closed his eyes, the stream of *Dixie* rising high above the Rose City. It ended with a gust of sound from the trombone players... *way down yonder in the land of Dixie...*

It seemed the woman in the blue dress knew everyone and they knew her. Tall and slim, she moved with grace. Essie was certain the woman entered fashionable society as a debutante at a grand ball. "Hey, Paul!" The woman greeted Paul Hjort, who owned the local nursery and played a huge role in the rose festivities. His *Double Delight* and *Sunrise Sunset* were prize winning roses. "I'll be over to your tent around 1:00. Can't wait to smell those roses," she said, in her long southern drawl.

Paul held out his hand. "Hello, Annalee. I bet you're here to cheer that daughter of yours."

"Oh, yes. But, it'll be awhile before her float arrives. It's the last one, you know."

Paul nodded. "You've got a long way to go." He glanced up in time to see Fire Chief C. C. Dunlap wave to the crowd. The chief's wire-rimmed glasses were down on his nose, the sun baking his prominent freckles. Paul waved to the chief and the firemen on Engine #1. "Pal" the fire dog wagged his tail and jumped into the lap of Henry Clyde "Sleepy" Kelley. Nearby, Wyatt Revell, Billy Pittman and W. T. McKenzie threw out candy to the kids who lined Broad Street. Three young boys pushed their way to the candy. Zack and Steve Varnedoe beat Dicky Thompson to the prize Tootsie Rolls that lay scattered across the pavement. Miriam Funderburk, a beloved teacher, snatched the boys back into line with a hard shake of her finger.

Paul continued walking down Broad Street, passing Henry Russell and Hershell Snuggs, giving them a slap on the back. He stopped a moment to talk with Alex Butler, one of Thomasville's favorite policemen.

The friendly woman leaned over to Essie. "By the way, I'm Annalee. Don't believe I know you." She smiled warmly, her red lipsticked mouth moving into a big smile.

Essie shook her head. "No, I'm not from here, but I'm certainly enjoying your parade. It's wonderful. My name is Essie."

"Oh, yes. Why, I believe this is the 35th year of this parade. Started in 1922. So glad you're visiting Thomasville."

The woman jumped forward. "Oh, here comes the Georgia State Patrol. Hey, Addison!" She waved heartily. "That's Addison Barnes and next to him are Cecil Plymale and Harry Knight." She squinted. "And I believe that's Troy Hardin on the end. The men were dressed smartly in their Georgia State Patrol uniforms, their hats pulled low over their foreheads.

Annalee chatted on, a camera in her right hand. "My daughter is in the Rose Queen court and will be along soon, I hope."

"Oh?" Essie wondered if her daughter knew the dark haired, green-eyed girl who had befriended Minnie a few summers ago.

"Oh, yes. She's a junior this year at the high school. Oh! Here come the Bulldogs!" Annalee pushed forward, raising her camera. "My daughter wanted me to get pictures of all the school floats. Believe this is the first one."

Annalee snapped a few pictures. "Goodness! I hope this film holds out." She waved wildly as the float paused in front of them. "That's Coaches Putnam and John Duke. See #47? That's Joe Harvard. I think my daughter has a crush on him." She laughed. "I'm sure that will last five minutes or so.

"That's #15 Doug Vick next to Joe and #16 Doyle Vismar. Both great boys. Good students." Annalee leaned forward. "That tall boy #46 is Jimmy Stroud. I believe he's dating LuLu Stillwell. Not sure. See #44? The handsome Hinton Bradford. I know his mama real well. Nice family."

The Cairo, Georgia, band followed Thomasville's Bulldogs, playing *Everything's Coming up Roses.* The screaming trombones pleased the crowd and they yelled for more. The band obliged and began playing *Mexicali Rose.*

The band moved on and was followed by the Flowers Bakery float and the National Guard Armory, with Major Lindsey Watt at the helm. "We love our armory. Hey, Jack! That's Jack Carmen standing by Jerry Searcy. Good folks."

Thomasville firemen Kenneth Asbell, Hershell Harvell, and Bill Hunter rode in a yellow convertible, followed by the bands from Central High School, Colquitt, Lowndes and Tift County.

Annalee continued snapping pictures while Sunnyland Foods and Dairyco floats passed in front of them. The Girl Scouts and Boy Scouts joined the festivities with their decorated floats and enthusiastic boys and girls.

Marvin Griffin, Georgia's governor, stood tall in the City's float. "There's the Governor of Georgia," yelled Annalee.

Essie smiled at the woman's enthusiasm for the parade and its many participants. In just thirty minutes, Essie had been introduced to the football team, the fire department, city employees, and dignitaries from all across the State of Georgia. Annalee was a true southern belle, undeniably charming, and bestowed with a dazzling smile. She had called Essie *darlin'* and *sugar* at least a dozen times.

"Are you here to see anyone special?" asked Annalee. Her large blue eyes scanned the floats as she flashed a sun-splashed smile.

Essie peered down North Broad Street, her heart beating wildly. *Oh, yes. I'm here to see my sister's child. At least, I think it's my sister's child. You see, Minnie Pryor declares a girl in Thomasville looks just like my sister. My sister is no longer living, but she had a baby some eighteen years ago and I didn't know about it until last summer. And, I'm..."* Essie felt her throat tighten, felt the wetness of tears. *So close.* She was so close to seeing the black-haired, green-eyed young woman who had eluded her for so long.

"Here come the cheerleaders!" Annabelle quickly opened her camera and inserted a new roll of film. A chorus of Bulldog cheers rang across Broad Street as Thomasville High's cheerleaders chanted *Hey, Bulldogs! Tighten up that line! Block that Quarterback! Hold tight!*

"Oh, look!" Annalee was on tiptoes again. "Celia Chestnut's had her hair cut. See over there. The tall blond." Annalee pushed farther to the curb, her camera ready. "Hey, Inky!" she called, lifting her camera and snapping a picture. "That's Emily McBride, but everybody calls her Inky."

Annalee whispered to Essie. "I hate to say this, but those cheerleading skirts are just too short." She waved again. "Theresa and Beatrice, look this way!" Annalee held the camera high and caught Judy Jones and Cardin Ackerman in a high jump in the middle of the float.

The girls basketball float followed the cheerleaders, Coach John Norwood at the helm, Lulu Stillwell and Virginia Lamb flanking him. Linda Hiers, the co-captain, and probably the tallest player, jumped from the float to retrieve a dropped basketball, laughing as she climbed back on and raised the ball high into the air as everyone cheered.

A loud cheer rose from the throngs of people lining Broad Street. The Rose Queen float pulled into view. Pink crepe paper covered every square inch of the float as well as the Queen's throne and the seats of the six princesses in her court. Roses of every color filled baskets and vases aligning the thirty foot length of the float. Mixed with ivy, the roses gave the appearance of a spectacular rose garden upon which lovely princesses and their queen sat in regal splendor.

Essie swallowed hard, her mouth dry. Closer and closer, the float moved in a mirage of pink. From the Queen's throne, Nancy McLean waved to the crowd, her rhinestone crown glistening in the morning sun.

Annalee, her arms waving wildly, camera in her hand, was jubilant. "Essie, that's Sandra Larson to the right of the Queen, Nancy McLean. She's our neighbor's daughter. Next to her is Betty Lou Eldridge. Then Deryl Parker and Yvonne Gibson."

Essie strained to see above the heads of the crowd in front of her. She moved to the left, then to the right, her anxiety mounting. Where was the girl she saw in the newspaper article? She pushed forward, bumping into a man with two children. "Sorry," she said, as she moved to the left of a street lamp.

Annalee tugged on Essie's arm and they moved into an empty spot nearer the curb. The float eased to a standstill while the Queen and her Court threw roses to the crowd. At that moment, the girl on the far side of the float turned and looked their way. A dark-haired, green eyed girl, the girl in the newspaper, the girl Minnie saw. *It's her, Jewell. Your daughter.*

The girl recognized someone in the crowd and waved frantically. Above the loud music and the cheering of the crowd, Essie read her lips. *Hi, Mom!*

Essie turned and looked to her right, to the person called *Mom*. It was Annalee.

Dazed, Essie held onto the street lamp, her chest pounding. In front of her, the float continued down Broad Street,taking Jewell's daughter with it. Essie watched the morning breeze lift the dark hair, the sun glisten on the beautiful face. *She was Jewell's daughter.*

CHAPTER FIFTY-SIX

Essie!" Annalee shook Essie's shoulder. "Come with me to the Farmer's Market on Smith Avenue. That's where the parade disbands. I'm supposed to meet my daughter there for pictures. I'd like you to meet her."

Without waiting for an answer, Annalee grabbed Essie's hand and pulled her down Broad Street, the southern belle chatting away. "It's almost a mile, but what a lovely walk. Let's go!"

Essie struggled to keep up with the energetic woman as they crossed Washington Street, then Jefferson. At the corner of Jefferson and Broad, the Hotel Scott, named in honor of a former president of Flowers Food, stood next to the J. C. Penney building. They zipped past Izzo's Pharmacy and crossed Jackson Street, nearing the Mode Theatre where the marquee boasted a new movie: *An Affair to Remember*, the names of Cary Grant and Deborah Kerr in tall letters at the bottom of the sign.

They hurried past Inman's Drugs, then bore left onto Smith Avenue and bounded toward the State Farmer's Market where a hubbub of laughter and shouting accompanied dozens of bands, floats and parade participants, all of whom began scattering their separate ways.

The Rose Queen float eased next to the Atlantic Coastline railroad tracks, near Hansell Street. Annalee and Essie slowed their pace and meandered toward the floats. "Your daughter is lovely," said Essie.

Annalee swatted the air. "Thank you, but I can't take credit. Neither can my husband. We're not her biological parents," she said casually.

They stopped under the shade of an oak tree. "She's been a

wonderful daughter in every way. She knows she's adopted and, since she was twelve, she's wanted to know more about her birth mother and father." Annalee lifted her hands in frustration. "But we have no clue who they are or where they are."

Essie shrank back into the shade of the tree. "What about the adoption agency?"

"Oh, sugar, that was a lost cause from the beginning. We were called one night by the midwife who said she had a baby girl for us. Why, when we got that baby, the only thing that came with her was a diaper and a blanket and a bottle of milk. Not one shred of history! We asked, of course."

Annalee shook her head. "I've still got that baby blanket."

A train inched its way down the track, a short whistle burst to clear the tracks. Essie studied Annalee's face. "Where was she born?"

"Somewhere in Atlanta. Gossip abounded regarding my daughter's birth, but we couldn't verify any of it. The midwife said a woman from Madison County, Florida, had orchestrated the adoption of the baby."

Annalee took a quick breath. "About four years ago, while our daughter was at summer camp, my husband and I drove to Madison County to look around. Had to. Our daughter was so curious and asking so many questions we couldn't answer."

Annalee glanced across the chaos of bands and floats, and spoke quietly. "It was a fruitless trip."

From the Rose Queen float, a voice called out. "Mom! Come take some pictures!"

"Oh, sugar, let's get on over to that float so you can meet my daughter and we'll get some good pictures." Annalee steered Essie toward the rose float, her camera at the ready.

"Oh, darlin', you're so beautiful!" The proud mother's camera went into rapid clicking while her daughter posed and smiled her beauty queen smile.

Essie stood a few feet away. Her body seemed to float, just like in her dreams of Jewell. In her mind, she reached out and touched the black haired girl, looked into the green eyes, listened to her sweet, soft voice.

The girl stood in the middle of the float and looked down. "Mama! Come up here with me and let's get a picture of you with all these roses!"

Annalee motioned to Essie. "Come on up here, Essie. Take our picture and then we'll take one of you. Come on, sugar." Her fingers beckoned Essie. "Come on up!"

Essie followed Annalee onto the float. The fragrance of roses swept the air, their colors vibrant as they twisted among the lush green ivy. "Here's my camera, Essie." Annalee handed Essie her camera and stepped next to her daughter, who had sat on a nearby stool. "Oh, where are my manners, Essie. Please meet my daughter Rose. Rose, this is my friend Essie."

Rose. Jewell, your daughter's name is Rose and she looks just like you. When I heard her speak, I thought it was you. Look at her, Jewell. She smiles like you, she moves like you. She is you!

"Hello," Essie said, a catch in her throat. *It's me, Rose. Your Aunt Essie. My sister Jewell was your mother. We lost you eighteen years agos, but we never forgot you. It's a long story, but maybe one day we can talk.*

In the camera's eye, Essie saw the mother and daughter, their smiles radiant. A family. She moved closer and snapped a picture of the mother and daughter with their cheeks together. The roses in Rose's hair were pink. Her green eyes sparkled.

"Your turn, Essie!" Annalee jumped up and grabbed the camera. "Sit right here beside Rose."

Essie did as she was told and sat down, moving the skirt of Rose's soft yellow dress aside. Rose gently put her arm around Essie's shoulders and leaned in for the picture. The fragrance of the roses swept the air, a billowy scent of sweetness, as Essie fought back tears.

"Gorgeous!" Annalee shouted.

"Here's my camera, Annalee. Will you take a picture of us?"

"Sure, sugar." Annalee moved a lock of Rose's hair off her forehead and stepped back. She took several pictures, each one from a different position. At that moment, a gust of wind lifted thousands of rose petals and showered the float like snowflakes, covering Essie and Rose. They held each other, squealing in laughter, and then jumped into the air, grabbing at the rose petals, their faces lit by the April sun.

As the last petal floated away, Rose brushed off her yellow dress and looked at Essie with her green eyes. "That was magic, wasn't it?"

Essie smiled. "Yes. Yes, it was."

Rose turned to her mother. "I've got to go, Mom. They're taking formal pictures for the newspaper. See you later." Rose waded through the roses to the side of the float. "Love you!" she called, as she stepped from the float and was gone.

Annalee and Essie meandered back down Broad Street, weaving in and out of the crowds that filled the sidewalks and streets.

"I hope we got some good pictures. Rose has a scrapbook that has so many school events and pictures. She'll want these pictures for sure."

They passed the Plaza Restaurant and Annalee waved to another of her many friends. "Say, Essie, you never did tell me where you live."

The two women stopped at the corner of Remington Avenue and watched the passing of the Yellow Jackets from Georgia Tech as they marched to the Farmers Market. "No… no, I didn't. I… I'm from Madison County."

"Madison County?" Annalee stared at Essie and it was at that moment her eyes widened. In one swirling instant, Annalee knew Essie was no ordinary visitor to Thomasville. The connection was so swift that a small gasp escaped the debutant's red lips. "You know my daughter?"

The earth seemed to still, the universe wobbling as if trying to put things in their proper place. Essie heard a ringing in her ears. "I… I only know that she looks very much like my sister." Essie leveled her eyes at Annalee. Of the thousands of people in Thomasville, Essie had met the woman who raised Jewell's child. It was meant to be.

"Your sister?"

"Yes, my sister Jewell. She's no longer living." Essie found herself shaking, a tremulous feeling in her chest. "I… I don't know how this happened."

Annalee stared at Essie for a long moment. "What do you know? You must tell me."

The two women strolled slowly through downtown Thomasville, a long walk through memories that, before now, had never been revealed. They compared the stories they had heard about the girls school in Atlanta, the midwife, the baby. The baby's mother. They both shed tears as if a revenant had surfaced and changed each of their lives.

"Jewell loved the farm and mama's roses. We have this big two-story farmhouse in Madison County with a long front porch that faces east and Jewell would sit in her chair and watch the sunrise every morning. And, there's this goat named Murphy and a rooster called Killer and they…."

CHAPTER FIFTY-SEVEN

It was dusk when Essie drove down highway 319 toward Pebble Hill. The Pontiac hummed along slowly, the radio low and playing *April Love* by Pat Boone. Yes, it had been *April love.* Her journey had ended in April sunshine, in a pile of roses, just like Minnie's dream. Pink, red, yellow, lavender and peach roses had swirled around them, binding them together at last. Annalee promised a visit to the farm, to the front porch, to Jewell's chair, to the place where it all began.

Of course, Annalee would bring Rose and they'd visit the Mt. Horeb cemetery, walk the farm and wander the little town of Pinetta, where the Donnelly's had lived for generations. She'd meet DooRay and Murphy, the one-eared goat. In the evening, they'd sit on the front porch and watch fireflies while the Madison County sun faded in the fields to the west of the farmhouse.

In the morning, Essie would leave Pebble Hill. Perhaps return to the Pryor farm for a short while. She didn't know if Minnie would return with her or not. That was Minnie's decision. Essie wanted to see Orland and Pitch. And, of course, their father Ollie. She would lament to Ollie her firm belief that Dr. Grey and Dr. Meyer could, indeed, repair his son's leg. She'd leave the small town of Boston and its community of warm southern hospitality. Its deep history would stay with her forever.

The sun had set by the time Essie parked in back of the cottage. Again, the peacocks sauntered by on their way to the woods where they would roost for the night. The tiny lights in the tea house glimmered like a starlit sky. Every window in the big house glowed with warm light, sending a message of welcome. Faint music drifted across the rose gardens and into the cool April night.

She smelled his cigar smoke before she saw him. She stilled and her eyes searched the teahouse.

"I'm over here," said Sam. "Waiting for you."

Essie turned and there he was, leaning against a dogwood, half hidden by its low branches. He had come for her. She had left Madison County for an unknown, had traversed miles in a search of peace, for understanding. And she had found them. And, all the while, despite his anger, Sam had waited for her.

"Well, I'm here." Essie walked a few steps toward the dogwood and the lawyer from Madison County. "Been waiting long?"

Sam puffed on his cigar and blew smoke into the air. "Not too long. Of course," he said, "I was prepared to wait forever."

Essie moved into Sam's arms, felt the beating of his heart, the warmth of his body. "I want to go home. To Madison County," she whispered.

The End

ABOUT THE AUTHOR

Author Sue Chamblin Frederick. She is known as a sweet Southern belle, a woman whose eyelashes are longer than her fingers, her lips as red as a Georgia sunset. Yet, behind the feminine façade of a Scarlett-like ingénue lies an absolute and utterly calculating mind—a mind that harbors hints of genius—a genius she uses to write books that will leave you spellbound.

A warning! She's dangerous—when she writes spy thrillers, she's only six degrees from a life filled with unimaginable adventures—journeys that will plunge her readers into a world of breath-taking intrigue. Put a Walther PPK pistol in her hand and she will kill you. Her German is so precise, she'd fool Hitler. *Her amorous prowess?* If you have a secret, she will discover it—one way or the other.

When she writes romance, her readers swoon and beg for mercy as they read her seductive stories about luscious characters. Be sure to have a glass of wine nearby as you snuggle up to her books about love.

The author was born in north Florida in the little town of Live Oak, where the nearby Suwannee River flows the color of warm caramel, in a three-room, tin-roofed house named 'poor.' Her Irish mother and English father's voices can be heard even today as they sweep across the hot tobacco fields of Suwannee County. "Susie, child, you must stop telling all those wild stories."

The author lives with her Yankee husband in the piney woods of north Florida, where she is compelled to write about far-away places and people whose hearts require a voice. Her two daughters live their lives hiding from their mother, whose rampant imagination keeps their lives in constant turmoil with stories of apple-rotten characters and plots that cause the devil to smile.

THE FIRST MADISON COUNTY SERIES BOOK

The Front Porch Sisters

A Novel

By Sue Chamblin Frederick

She had no idea why most everyone thought she was a hard woman. There had been times when she'd look in the mirror searching for a clue of some kind, a sign that said *watch out for this woman, she will kick your ass.* It didn't matter how long she stared at her image; she saw nothing that was slap-you-in-the-face, unmistakable, rock-hard meanness. Perhaps, when she wasn't looking, a sign had been taped to her back that said, 'Beware: Hard Woman.'

Then, one day, she figured it out. It was a simple thing, right there in front of her, sitting on the opposite end of the almost endless front porch. Delicate and pretty. Not one single flaw that she could see. All softness, nothing hard to be found, except maybe the black bible she held in her hands. Her sister Jewell. It was obvious she'd never hold a candle to her. Stand the two sisters side by side and there it was, just as obvious as warts on a nose. And that was their life together: hard and soft, tough and tender.

When stars appear in the night sky high above the fields of Madison County, the starlight seems to fall the brightest along the Withlacoochee River, then across the Bellville road before settling quietly on the rooftop of the Donnelly's grand house and its magnificent front porch.

No one could really remember precisely when it all began: the importance of the porch. It was as though its roots were entrenched before the birth of time; the porch façade of faded white boards seeming to wear an expression that fell somewhere between slumber and the prick of a thorn, reminding one of the memories that had been created there, under its sloping roof and where jasmine twisted wildly around the white columns.

There was no doubt that the porch was the soul of the rambling house, its heartbeat lasting at least until the Rapture or maybe even beyond. The porch heard and knew everything; tears, cussing and maybe even lovemaking in the cypress swing with the creaky chain.

The porch ran east and west, all fifty feet of it shaded by hundred-year-old oak trees that promised cool afternoons during the furnace heat of a Pinetta summer. The distance between the two ends of the porch might as well have been to the moon and back—each end separate from the other and divided by the differences of the two Donnelly sisters.

In its heyday, the long porch, studded with rockers like jewels on a crown and swings built from pond cypress, sagged with the onslaught of Sunday afternoon visitors who drank iced tea and ate Edith Donnelly's famous buttered rum pound cake. The women, frilly church hats flopping on their heads, chatted non-stop about the canning of tomatoes and green beans, while the men leaned on the porch railing and smoked their cigars or chewed tobacco, all the while worried if it would rain on their newly-planted tobacco fields.

But, that was then, and the echoes of those times lingered quietly in the nearby Mt. Horeb cemetery, where folks from as far back as

1700 lay in their final resting place, not far from the dark waters of the Withlacoochee.

"Well, I do believe we've got company." Jewell Donnelly leaned forward in her freshly painted Adirondack chair, a chair surrounded by her daily life, a life broken up into piles of lovely books, dainty teacups and the distinction of being one of Madison County's most beautiful women. "I can't imagine who it is."

From the other end of the porch, nestled in a swing made by her grandfather and still in her faded pajamas, Essie Donnelly glanced up from her book. "Well, hell, Jewell. It's DooRay. Who else do we know with one arm and a goat pulling a cart?"

Jewell frowned. "Mama won't like that cussing, Essie."

"Mama can't hear a thing, Jewell. I told you that—she's resting over at the cemetery. Has been for over fifteen years."

The lane was about a hundred yards long from the house to the Bellville road. Made of rich dirt, some clay and a little sand, it was a straight, grassless path to one of the most elegant homes in the tiny town of Pinetta, Florida. Essie squinted and watched DooRay shamble down the lane, the goat following, pulling an empty cart. DooRay reached the edge of the yard and Essie moved to the railing, looking down at the entourage that had arrived just at the top of noon.

"DooRay, where're you going?" She eyed the goat harnessed to the cart and the rooster that sat on top of the goat's back, squatted like it was laying an egg, its pair of bright red, fleshy wattles dangling as if they were small testicles.

"Hey, Miss Essie. Miss Jewell." DooRay pulled the hat from his head and fanned himself. "I reckon I'm going on over to Clyattville."

"Clyattville? That's over eight miles. Mighty long way with those bare feet. How come you're not riding in your cart?"

DooRay grinned and looked behind him at his goat. "Murphy's mad at me right now. He won't pull me nowhere."

"How can Murphy be mad at you, DooRay?" Essie studied the white goat, the long lashes on the dark eyes silently sweeping every time it blinked.

DooRay hung his head. "Guess you hadn't heard, Miss Essie. Lightening done hit my house yesterday evenin' and burned it up into a pile of black ashes. Murphy got singed a little bit. Wasn't nothing I could do it happened so fast."

"Oh, my, DooRay. I'm so sorry. That why you're going over to Clyattville?"

Murphy stuck out his long tongue and bleated softly. DooRay scratched the top of the goat's head. "I sure am. Looks like DooRay gone live with Uncle Mustard a while."

"Uncle Mustard? Mustard Aikens? Why, I know him." Essie hurried down the brick steps into the yard, her bare feet crunching dried oak leaves. "Biggest thief there ever was. Worked for daddy one summer and stole everything he could get his hands on. Daddy shooed him off the place and told him to never come back. He's a mean rascal, DooRay. I can't believe he's your uncle, and you're gonna live with him."

DooRay scuffed his bare foot through the dirt and nodded. "Gots to do that, Miss Essie."

"Oh, no, you don't, DooRay. The old tack room at the side of the barn is a perfect place for you. There are a few spiders in it, but we'll clean them out. It's dry and got a door and window. There's an outhouse only a few yards away down by the tobacco barns." Essie shook her finger at DooRay. "Now, let me get a broom for you..." She stopped and looked at the one-armed DooRay. Essie's voice softened. "Gosh, DooRay. I'm sorry. I guess you can't really sweep, can you?"

DooRay threw his head back, his laughter bouncing up into the branches of the oak tree above him. "Oh, Miss Essie, DooRay can do just about anything. Why does you think I go barefooted all the time?" The skinny black man lifted his leg, pulling his foot level with his chest. "See this? This here is my missin' arm. This foot can do anything my hand can do. Why I can even put a worm on a hook with these long toes."

Essie grinned at the black man and watched as he returned his foot to the ground. "Say, DooRay. Just how did you lose your arm? You never told me, and I've known you since we were kids."

"Oh, that's a story from a long time ago, Miss Essie. A sad story. You don't need to hear no sad story." DooRay was a black man who was not whole yet deserved dignity no matter how poor or damaged the shell in which he lived. It was evident to anyone who knew him that his dignity had been polished by a lifetime of humility.

Essie's eyes held DooRay's face. It was a kind face, smooth and licorice black, his eyes even darker, eyes with wiry eyelashes that were as thick as sheep's wool. "You're right, DooRay."

Essie walked to the edge of the lane and pointed toward the open field. "It's the biggest barn—the one over there. You'll see the tack room on the north side. You pull anything out of there you need to and put it into the barn. I'll check on you later and bring you some iced tea and a sandwich."

"Yes, mam, Miss Essie." DooRay placed his hat on his head and pulled on Murphy's reins. "Let's go, Murphy. We got us a new home." The rooster squawked and dug its feet into Murphy's back, his wings flapping loudly.

When DooRay was only a few feet away, Essie hollered. "DooRay, that rooster isn't going to get into my flower beds, is he?

"Oh, no. Killer don't bother no flowers."

"Killer? Your rooster's name is Killer?"

"That's right, Miss Essie. He do likes to kill snakes. If they's a snake within a mile a this here place, my Killer will find it."

Essie stared a long time at the rooster, then at the goat, then at DooRay. The cart was empty; everything DooRay owned had burned in the fire.

Made in the USA
Coppell, TX
05 April 2021

53118758R00146